THE MODEL

A WORKPLACE ROMANCE

HARLOW LAYNE

THE MODEL

Join Harlow's mailing list to be the first to know of new releases, free books, sales, and other giveaways!

http://bit.ly/HarlowLayneNL

The moment I heard Ryder's voice I was a goner.

As a photographer, I was used to working with beautiful people, but Ryder Williams was the most perfect male specimen that had ever stood before me. I knew without a doubt it would take no time at all for him to be the next big thing... or for him to steal my heart.

Model and photographer, we shouldn't cross that line, but there was no stopping the passion we felt. Nothing else mattered. Not the age difference. Not that he was a client. Not even our pasts.

After my assistant caught us together, he was gone. I tried to put him out of my head, until fate threw him back into my life and my bed.

Time and time again we're brought together, should I keep fighting or finally accept what my heart wants?

ISBN-13: 978-1-950044-08-5 (Ebook Edition)

ISBN-13: 978-1-950044-23-8 (Paperback Edition)

Edited by: Your Editing Lounge - Editor: Kristen

Cover Design: Harlow Layne

Images from Shutterstock

Manufactured in the United States of America.

This is a work of fiction. Names, characters, places, and incidents either are the products of the author's imagination or are use fictitiously. Any resemblance to actual persons, living or dead, businesses, companies, events, or locales is entirely coincidental.

CHAPTER 1
LEXIE

I texted furiously, my thumbs moving rapidly as I repeatedly fumbled for what I wanted to say. I wanted to tell my ex to stop messaging me or I was going to change my number, only I knew he wouldn't believe me since I'd threatened it before, and he knew I needed my phone number for my livelihood. Otherwise, I'd have changed it six months ago when I caught him having sex with my ex-assistant in my bed. That's right in my own fucking bed.

Me: Stop or I will get a restraining order.
Ben: I'd like to see you try. One cup of coffee that's all I ask.
Me: All I asked was for you to remain faithful and that didn't happen so NO!

"Lexie." After a few moments of me not responding, my new assistant cleared her throat. "Um…I think I've got everything set up the way you wanted it."

Taking in a deep breath that I desperately needed, I closed my eyes and counted to ten. My new assistant, Raine, was sweet and tried to get things right, but bless her heart, nine times out of ten she fucked things up royally. Many days I wondered why I hadn't fired her yet, but then she'd look up at me with her dazzling smile, and I'd forget about what she'd done to make my day a thousand times harder. I'm not the only one who fell under her spell. When shit hit the fan, I asked Raine to make things right because I knew she'd bring out her secret weapon. A weapon she had no idea she had.

"Thank you, Raine." I knew I'd have to change a thing or ten, but that was all right. We still had time as long as I could get off my damn phone.

"And…Ryder Williams is here." Interesting. My client, California Tomorrow, had demanded Ryder Williams for the shoot. They assured me he was the next up and coming male model, and I knew with one look I'd be able to tell if they were right or not.

"Is Lana here yet?" I gritted my teeth on her name. I hated working with Lana, but she was also who the customer wanted, and the customer was always right, even if it caused me a migraine and a trip to the dentist from grinding my teeth.

"Not…yet," Raine squeaked.

Of course, Lana wasn't here yet.

"Call her and see where she is," I barked out as another text came in from my ex.

I let out a frustrated sigh at the patter of Raine's feet as she ran across the room. I was such a bitch, but I'd do something to make up for it later.

Ben: I need back into the apartment. Trust me, I wouldn't be asking if it wasn't a matter of life or death. Your doorman won't let me up.

No shit, Henry wouldn't let him up. If he did, he'd get fired. I'd make sure of it.

"Ms. Keene?" A deep rumbling voice asked from behind me. It was so rough and gravely. Pure sex.

"Call me Lexie," I answered without turning around.

After I sent off a text to my ex, I turned off my phone, so I wouldn't be distracted since I knew he would continue to text me until I gave in. Twirling around on my bare feet to see who the most amazing voice in the world belonged to, I stopped dead in my tracks, almost falling to the floor. It wasn't possible for that voice, a voice I would happily spend the rest of my days listening to, to belong to the god who stood in front of me. Had God felt extra giving that day and graced this Adonis with looks and a voice? He was probably an asshole and had a small dick. He couldn't be that perfect. Because standing in front of me was the most perfect specimen of a man I'd ever seen. He was a few inches taller than six feet, golden skin to match his golden-brown hair that was short on the sides and long on the top. It flopped over one eye, giving him a boyish charm that had my lady bits tingling. The other eye was mesmerizing; it was the bluest of blue. It reminded me of looking into the ocean waters of my favorite beach in Palawan.

Ryder Williams was most definitely going to make it big, and it wouldn't take long. After the magazine we were shooting for today published him, everyone would want him.

"I'm here," Lana drawled out from across the room.

The Adonis and I turned to see Lana glaring over at us. I wasn't sure what her problem was, but she always had an attitude. It was probably because she hadn't had a real meal in the last decade.

"You're late. Again," I gritted out. I swore a layer of enamel was rubbed off as I looked at her. Lana was beautiful. No doubt about it, but she was the ugliest person on the inside I'd met in a long time. Too bad that wasn't translated through pictures.

Lana paid me no attention as her death glare turned to lust. Turning to my left, I saw why. The robe of the man beside me had come undone.

And I came undone right along with it.

WITH HIS ROBE OPEN, LANA AND I COULDN'T STOP OURSELVES from taking him in. His golden skin glistened from the oil; I was sure Raine had told him to cover himself with it. I wanted to throw myself at her feet for giving him to me all shiny and slick. If she had done it herself, I might cut off her hands or break a finger. In that moment, I was jealous. Irrationally so, but I wanted him all to myself. My gaze trailed down his long, lean body. I didn't care how unprofessional it was. He had pecs that I wanted to simultaneously lay my head on and swirl my tongue along the flat disc of his nipple. My gaze trailed down to the ridges of his abs. No, he didn't have a six-pack but an eight pack. One I wanted to run my hands over and lick down the 'V' that led into his white boxer briefs.

The sizable bulge in those briefs made me bite my bottom lip. Okay, so maybe he was only an asshole because his flimsy briefs hid nothing as they tried to contain his anaconda. My brain short-circuited for a moment before I continued down his long muscular legs. Legs I wanted to feel brushing against me from behind as he thrust into me. Even his feet were gorgeous.

Closing my eyes, I wasn't sure how I would work with him when all I could do was ogle him. I wouldn't be surprised if I had drool at the corners of my mouth.

He's an asshole.

He's an asshole.

He's an asshole.

I kept chanting it repeatedly in my head. He had to be. Otherwise, he'd be perfect, and we all knew there was no such thing as a perfect man. But the Adonis standing in front of me was as close as it got, I was certain.

Today it was going to be hard to stay focused on my job.

"Are you who I'm working with today?" I heard Lana chirp from only a few feet away. Her tone had changed. She was ready to hook her claws into the new guy, and I couldn't blame her, but I would since I hated her. Lana would do anything, and I meant anything to further her career. Little did she know it was her own actions held her back her back because word had gotten around; that and her shitty attitude when she was around people she knew she couldn't influence. A Swedish filmmaker had let it be known how unprofessional Lana had been when he was filming a commercial with her and Luke Sandström a couple of years back. When word got out that Lana was trying to hit on Luke while his girlfriend, Alex, was there watching, Lana's reputation went down the drain. Everyone loved Luke and Alex, and even though they never commented on it, other's who'd worked with Lana had spoken out.

I loved it, but unfortunately, some clients (probably those she'd blown or slept with) still wanted to hire her. I wished she'd move to New York so I wouldn't have to work with her as often as I did.

"I believe so. I'm Ryder." Even his name was hot. I wanted to write a letter to his parents, thanking them for creating the man before me.

"Lana," she purred.

I simultaneously rolled my eyes and shifted in my wet panties before I noticed Lana's long manicured finger trail up his arm. I saw red. I wanted to grab her finger and break it, or better yet, cut it off. Both wouldn't work well for the photo shoot, so I tried to tamp down my unexplained rage. It wasn't as if I had a shot at Ryder. If anyone did, it would be Lana with her perfect supermodel body. It pissed me off even more that I'd never have a chance with the most phys-ically perfect man on the planet. I knew I wasn't ugly; I was cute. I looked like a rocker with my long blue hair, nose piercing, and tattoos covering my arms. A cute little rocker chick who never attracted the interest of gods like Ryder.

Internally, I sighed. I didn't need to start feeling like shit about myself before a big photo shoot and have it affect the vibe. Or me. I didn't want to start stumbling down that road when I'd been doing so well.

Ryder pulled away from Lana and took a step toward me as he tied his robe. Moving to stand fully next to me, he bit his bottom lip, and in that moment, I knew exactly how Christian Grey felt when Ana would bite her lip. I wanted to pull it out with my own teeth so I could suck and nibble on his full, kissable bottom lip.

Heaven help me. Not once in my thirty-two years of life had I ever felt the urge to tackle a man to the ground and have my way with him. I worked with beautiful men and women daily, and not once had I had such a visceral reaction like I did with Ryder. I could feel the heat radiating from his body next to mine, causing beads of sweat to pop up all along my skin and my panties to dampen further, adding to my discomfort.

"Lana, we're ready for wardrobe," Raine called from across the room. I couldn't help but give her a smile. Raine knew how much Lana annoyed me. Lana knew there was nothing she could do to further her career with me, so she didn't even try to be civil with me on most days. Luckily, Raine was saving me from turning an already shitty day into me losing my shit before the shoot even started.

I watched as Lana swayed her hips for Ryder, but when I looked back at him, he wasn't watching Lana strut away. He was watching me.

"Lexie," he whispered my name. It had never sounded so good on anyone's lips before. I wanted to hear him say my name like that while we were both naked.

I tried to stay calm and professional as I turned to him. He was still biting that delectable lip, so I attempted to look him in the eyes. Everything about him was a turn on. Maybe I just needed to get laid, or maybe he really was my own personal aphrodisiac. Either way, I planned to get laid tonight and work off some of the tension that had been building in my pants since the moment I saw him.

"This is my first shoot like this." His voice was quiet as he looked off into the distance.

"Are you nervous?" I picked up the camera that was around my neck and aimed it at him.

"What if…" he blushed, and I nearly threw myself at him. It was the hottest thing ever, and I knew from that little blush that he wasn't an asshole. He really was perfect. Fuck me. Really, he could fuck me if he wanted to, but I knew he wouldn't. He was only talking to me because Lana was a bitch, and he probably sensed she would take advantage of him.

"What if, what?" My own voice was quiet, as if we were sharing a secret.

Ryder turned with his back to everyone and stared at me for a moment. "What if I get a hard-on?"

"Then think about your grandmother naked."

Ryder sputtered twice and then let out a booming laugh. He threw his head back, clutching his hands to his chest. I couldn't help but watch the way his throat bobbed with each guttural laugh that came out of him. Why was everything he did so damn sexy?

Righting himself, Ryder wiped a tear from his eye. "That will work."

Lana came out then in a bra and panty set, and I hated thinking of Ryder getting hard because of her. I knew what the customer wanted, and they wanted the shots to be hot. They would be practically fucking in front of me the entire day. If anyone was getting laid tonight, it would be them, and I'd be alone with a migraine after keeping my jaw clenched for hours of watching them.

I got them into place and had Raine help me adjust the lighting before I took my place behind my camera and started shooting.

Shot after shot, Lana acted as if this wasn't a photo shoot, but her personal bedroom where she was trying to seduce the man she was with. At first, Ryder kept looking to me for direction, but after an hour, he found his stride and landed everything I gave him. They looked perfect together, and I knew the client would be happy with the shots. Hell, they'd have a hard time trying to narrow down which ones they wanted to use because they were all amazing. They could use them all and have the entire magazine filled with this shoot. Besides the fact that Lana was all over Ryder and seemed to know I found him extremely attractive, she actually did her job without causing problems. Probably because I didn't hide very well how much I hated her touching him.

Once we finished for the day, I watched as Lana whispered in Ryder's ear. She didn't see his grimace, but whatever he said back to her pissed her off. The Lana I was used to seeing returned. Her head snapped in my direction, and her eyes narrowed before she stomped out of the room.

"What's up her ass?" Raine asked from beside me.

Saving all the photos to my external hard drive to go over later, I shrugged. "No idea. Lana being Lana, I presume. Why don't you go make sure she doesn't cause any damage before she leaves? Once she's gone, you can get out of here, and I'll see you tomorrow."

"Are you sure you don't want me to help clean up?" She motioned toward the bed we had set up. The one Ryder was currently standing in front of.

"I'm sure. I've got nothing better to do, and you did well today. You deserve to go have some fun."

Raine beamed up at me with her damn smile, and I knew even if it took me twice the time to get everything put away and ready for the next day, it was worth it. I had a feeling after today, she wouldn't be messing up as much as she normally did.

Walking over to the bed and Ryder, I stopped when I heard him muttering and squeezing himself through his robe.

Maybe he wasn't as perfect as I thought he was.

Moving closer, I could have sworn I heard him say, "Sexy Lexie," but I had to be hearing things after hours upon hours of my lady bits throbbing and lusting after him. There was no way in hell Ryder would call me sexy.

"Ryder?"

Turning toward my voice, Ryder's robe fell open. His boxer briefs were stretched to their limit as his stiff cock pushed against the fabric.

He really did have an anaconda in there. My hands twitched at my sides, wanting to remove those briefs and touch him.

Ryder licked his full pouty lips. His eyes, which had been the color of my turquoise water had darkened. His pupils dilated.

"I held myself back as long as I could," he growled out.

My stomach sank, knowing this was his reaction to Lana.

"If you're quick, you can probably catch up with her."

It wasn't uncommon for models to hook up with each other, especially after a shoot like the one we had today.

Tilting his head to the side, Ryder furrowed his brows before a slow smile crept onto his handsome face. "It's not Lana I want."

CHAPTER 2

LEXIE

Ryder's hands grabbed my hips and pulled me into his strong, firm body. The smell of pine infiltrated my senses. How did he smell so good after hours of posing and almost fucking Lana? His erection pressed into my stomach, making me groan and forget everything else.

"Did you think I was talking about Lana?" Ryder shook his head with a mischievous smile. "You're so fucking sexy, Lexie. It's been you I've wanted since you turned around."

Had I hit my head? Was I dead? Because this had to be a dream.

"Does this feel like a dream?" Ryder ground himself against the overly heated skin of my stomach.

If it was, it was the best dream ever, and I never wanted to wake up.

"I said that out loud?"

He nodded while his hands skimmed up my sides. My hands had a mind of their own, or maybe I still thought I was dreaming. Either way, I would touch as much of Ryder as I could before I either woke up or he came to his senses.

My fingers traced along the ridges of his eight pack and up to his spectacular pecs. My thumbs caressed over his nipples, and Ryder took in a shaky breath.

"I need to touch you," he groaned as my fingernails scraped down his torso. Each muscle contracted with my touch, giving me a heady feeling. I was doing this to him, not Lana.

Towering over me, Ryder pulled my t-shirt over my head and threw it across the room. Unclasping my bra, he pulled the straps over my shoulders and let it fall to our feet. His hands cupped my aching breasts in a rush. "Gorgeous." His eyes zeroed in on my nipple rings, and a slow smile crept across his face.

Manhandling me, Ryder positioned me with my back to his front. He ground his erection into my ass in a steady rhythm as his hands went back to my breasts massaging and plucking my nipple rings until my body sang. His lips trailed up and down my neck, kissing and sucking.

He didn't even know me, and yet he was worshiping my body.

Wrapping my arm around his neck, I held him to me as I moaned. It felt so good, but I needed more. Letting go, I pulled away. My gaze locked onto the wet spot on the front of his briefs, and I salivated.

"When you look at me like that, I want to throw you down on that bed and fuck you hard. Would you like that, Lexie?" Ryder's voice was pure gravel, and I loved it. I loved everything about him, and for once, I wasn't going to think. I was going to have my wicked way with the Adonis standing in front of me.

"Yes," I was breathless with want. My hands went to his shoulders as I pushed the robe off.

He stopped me before I could hook my fingers in the waistband of those pesky underwear. "Perfect, I'm going to strip you down and devour you."

Kneeling, he slowly unbuttoned my jeans and slid them down my legs. Holding onto his shoulders, I stepped out of them. I liked the look of him on his knees before me. It didn't last long, though. Ryder pushed me down on the bed and grabbed my hips, pulling me to the edge. Slowly, he licked up the inside of my leg with his hot tongue. One of his big hands trailed up my other leg spreading them wide.

Pushing my thong to the side, Ryder growled. "If I'd have known you were bare with all these piercings all day, we never would have finished." Trailing his nose through my folds, his thumbs spread me wide as he ground his cock against the edge of the bed. "You're gorgeous everywhere."

His tongue dipped into my core before flattening and licking up to my clit, giving it a slow, delicious swirl. It didn't take much; I was already primed, and with one pull of my ring with his teeth, my head flew back, and my toes curled as he switched to sucking on my swollen bundle of nerves. Lacing my fingers through his thick hair, I ground my pussy on his face, moaning and crying out his name as he took me higher and higher. One thick finger pumped inside me and was soon met with a second , driving me wild.

His fingers and mouth were magic. I couldn't wait to see what he could do with his cock.

One finger slipped out and circled a place no man had ever gone before. He must have felt me tense because I could feel him smile against my slick folds. Squeezing my ass cheek, he pulled back and bit it. "Not today, but one day I'm going to own your ass."

I agreed because I knew there wouldn't be another day after today. But hell, even if there was, I was sure with one look, he could convince me to do anything.

Dipping back down, he pulled my clit between his lips and sucked hard, bringing me over the edge. My legs clamped down around his head as I shuttered underneath him with my head thrown back in orgasmic bliss. Ryder continued to kiss and lick me until every last ounce of pleasure had been wrung out of me.

Ryder kissed up my body, and by the time he reached my mouth, I was primed and ready to go. His talented tongue swept inside my mouth, giving me the most sensual kiss of my life. I panted into his mouth as my hands made their way down his body. I loved how, with each touch, his muscles flexed, and his hands gripped me harder. I'd have bruises tomorrow, but I didn't care. Tonight was worth it, and I wanted the reminder.

Slipping my hands into his underwear, I cupped his firm ass and moved to pull the offending fabric off. Ryder beat me to the chase, stripping quickly before his mouth was back to kissing me like it was his last night alive.

I was disappointed. I wanted to get up close and personal with that anaconda of his, but he never gave me a chance. One minute he was on top of me, and the next Ryder flipped me over, pushing me up on all fours with his body pressed against mine. His length nudged my ass and then slipped through my wet folds as he kissed up my spine, along my shoulder, and up my neck while his hands were back to massaging my breasts. "You have the most magnificent tits I've ever seen. I could play with them all night."

Pulling his face closer, I licked the seam of his lips. My

tongue slipped through as his larger-than-life cock pushed against my entrance. Thrusting all the way in, I gasped at the intrusion. Ryder stilled for only a moment, letting me get accustomed to him. If I thought for one second he was stuffing those briefs, the thought was quickly replaced with awe as he filled and stretched me more than any man before him.

Slowly he started to move. I could feel my pussy clench around him, not ready, but I was a needy bitch and wanting him to move all the same. "Ryder," I moaned and clamped onto one of his arms as his pace quickened.

He bit down on my earlobe and then swirled his tongue around it to soothe the sting. "Just breathe. It will get easier."

One hand slipped down my taut stomach to find my overly sensitive clit and rubbed languid circles around it. His hips slapped against my ass in a furious rhythm, and all I could do was hang on for dear life. I knew it was going to be the best sex of my life, and I wanted to remember every second of it.

Ryder was all over me. It was a total sensory overload, and I loved every minute of it.

"Yes, that's it," he groaned, his hot breath against the shell of my ear. "Squeeze my cock, my sexy girl."

Ryder pinched my clit with his fingers and slammed into me so hard all my breath left me. Black dots floated in my vision as ecstasy took over. My whole body clamped down in one long orgasmic pulse. Ryder continued to pump into me, but it was slower as if he was trying to break the world record for how long one orgasm could last. It was a record I'd be happy to help him try to break as many times as he wanted.

I may have only met Ryder earlier that day, but one thing I knew about him, he definitely liked to please his women in bed. He was a giver, not a taker, and I was there to receive it all.

Pulling me with him down on the bed, Ryder wrapped me in his arms. "Fuck, we've got to do that again and repeatedly." He sighed and kissed my forehead.

I had to agree. After a minute or thirty, I'd be up for another round. One more orgasm like that, and I'd be a puddle of goo and spending the night at my studio. I took a deep breath and caught the strong smell of pine. Did he sweat pine? He was better than any candle or plug-in.

"Lexie, I know you told me to leave, but I hated the idea of you having to move everything on your own."

Ryder looked down at me at the same moment I looked up at him. This was not good. Grabbing the sheet, he pulled it up over us the second before Raine came into view.

"Oh my God!" she shrieked. "I'm so..."

Ryder sat up, blocking me from her view, making the sheet fall, giving Raine the perfect view of his anaconda.

Raine closed her eyes and ran out of the room.

CHAPTER 3
LEXIE

Slipping on the robe Ryder had worn, I chased after a rather quick Raine. It seemed she could really move if she wanted to get away. I wasn't sure why she was running. Was she embarrassed? Surely she'd seen a penis before. Raine was twenty-four. While we never discussed her sex life, I assumed she had one. Or was she running because she thought I was highly unprofessional for sleeping with an employee?

Ryder wasn't technically an employee, though. California Tomorrow was, and they were paying both Ryder and Lana. Not me.

"Raine, stop," I gasped out as I flew out the door and out onto the sidewalk. She was already at her Toyota Prius, fumbling with her keys. She looked over her shoulder at me and swiped along her cheek. Shit, she was crying.

But why?

"Raine, don't go. I know you're upset, but we need to talk." I stood only a few feet from her, but I didn't want to get too close. She was acting like a scared animal. If I'd walked in on what Raine had, I might have asked if they were up for a threesome. But we weren't even doing anything, so it didn't make sense.

"I just want to go home." Her chin trembled, and I hated myself for whatever had made her upset. And even though she still had a lot to learn about being my assistant, I didn't want to look for a new one. I liked Raine.

"You can in a minute. Sit down with me." I pointed to the curb in front of her car and then sat down, waiting for Raine to join me. I watched her out of the corner of my eye. Raine seemed to hesitate, first looking from me to her car door and back again. Was she going to hop in her car and drive away? In the end, she sat down beside me and looked down at her red Converse.

I wanted to hug her, but I knew she wouldn't be receptive, so I kicked out my legs to realize I was barefoot and only in a robe. What a sight I must have been. I didn't care, though, because I didn't want Raine to quit, or worse, and get into an accident because she was upset.

"Can you tell me what's so upsetting about seeing Ryder and me in bed together?"

"I...I'm so sorry. Please don't fire me." A tear slipped down her cheek.

"I promise you I'm not going to fire you." And here I thought she wanted to quit, thinking I slept with every model that came through my door.

"I didn't mean to walk in on you. I thought... I never expected that. I mean, I understand why..." She stopped herself and picked at her frayed jean shorts.

My forehead scrunched up. "Why what?"

"Ryder is drop-dead gorgeous and look at you."

My hackles rose, and my nostrils flared. Look at you.

Yes, I knew Ryder was out of my league, but so was just about every other woman on the planet. Damn, didn't she know it wasn't smart to call your boss ugly? "What's wrong with me? I'm cute, and Ryder obviously liked what he saw."

Lifting her head, Raine's eyes were wide as they met mine. "Cute? Come on. You know you're gorgeous, Lexie. You have a slamming body and boobs anyone would kill for, and then your hair, piercings, and tattoos give you an edge that drives men wild. It's no wonder Ryder wanted you over Lana. You could very well be a model." I snorted. Yeah, right. "You really could."

"You don't need to kiss my ass, but maybe if I'm alone with a hot guy, you should make yourself known…or better yet, just go home." Not that I thought I'd be hooking up with anyone anytime soon, but it was a good rule.

"Again, I'm sorry. I just didn't think you'd…" Her nose scrunched up as she looked me over. "Oh my god, Lexie, you're only in a robe. Go back inside." Raine looked over at my building. "Maybe you can still…" She flushed, and I had to take pity on her.

"Are you a virgin? It's okay if you are, but I thought you—"

"I'm not." She shook her head vehemently. "But it's not something I'm comfortable talking about or seeing."

"That's cool, I didn't mean to make you feel uncomfortable. I thought we were alone." Not that it would have mattered. I would have let Ryder fuck me in a room full of people. I loved how he took over and fucked me hard.

She nodded and looked back at the building. "I'll let you get back to it." She stood, jingling her keys in her hand. "I'll see you tomorrow."

Holding onto the robe to make sure it didn't open as I stood up, I gave Raine a small hug before pulling back. She really was a good kid and worker. "Have a good night."

"You too." Her cheeks turned beet red before she quickly unlocked her car door and got inside.

Not wasting any time, I walked back to my building. It wasn't much from the outside. In fact, it looked like a place for the homeless to squat, but on the inside, it shined. It was so clean you could eat off the floors, thanks to Raine, and it had multiple rooms laid out for different photo shoots.

I made my way back to where I'd left Ryder only to find the space empty, so I continued looking for him. I wouldn't mind testing the bed out again or any surface for that matter. I'd checked almost the entire first floor with no sign of him. I had the dressing room left, but I was starting to think I wasn't going to find my Adonis anywhere on the premises. I knew he couldn't get upstairs; it was locked, which was a good thing since it was a disaster as I renovated it into an apartment for me. I was giving myself until summer to get it finished because then I'd need to use the roof and pool for shoots. While I didn't have any land, which would have been amazing for pictures, I had lucked out with a pool that hadn't been used in forever. The building was taking all my savings, but it was going to be worth it once it was finished.

I was happy to see the hair and makeup people had cleaned up. Sometimes they left their stations a mess, and it drove me insane. "Ryder," I called out as I walked into the dressing room. Yes, I'd seen him naked, but if he was in here, I wanted to give him privacy if he wanted it. That was something this line of work lacked when you were on set, and I tried my best to give it to my models. He didn't call back, and as I scanned the area, there was no sign of anyone's belongings.

Fuck, I'd missed him. Why had he left without even a word? To say I was disappointed would have been an understatement. Trudging back to the main area, I pulled my clothes back on—since there was no need to be naked any longer—and straightened everything up. I pulled the sheets off the bed and threw them into the laundry before I went into area two to make sure all the lights I needed were in there before I decided to leave.

I grabbed my camera, phone, and purse. I could work on the photos here, of course, but I wanted to get away from the studio. If I didn't, I'd probably put Ryder's robe back on and sit around sniffing his unique pine scent all night or crawl back into the bed and roll around in his scent while I finger-fucked myself. I needed to get away from there and forget about Ryder Williams.

Powering up my phone, a dozen messages from Ben dinged as they came through. One thing was noticeably absent; I had no texts from Ryder. I don't know how I expected him to contact me when he didn't have my number, but I did. Ignoring Ben's messages stating we needed to meet, and he needed in the apartment, I shut down the studio and turned on the alarm before I left.

There was no way I was going to meet up with him. If I did, I'd probably punch him in the junk for bothering me so incessantly. Why did he need to get into an apartment he hadn't been in for six months?

CHAPTER 4
RYDER

4 Months Later

My legs shook as I stood from my squat. French music blared from the speakers of the gym as I worked out. The agency had hooked me up with gym passes in each country I hit, and I was thankful. Today was my day off, and I was grateful for it. I'd been flying for two days straight, and I needed to eat, sleep, and get my workout on. I hated hitting the gym super early in the morning or late at night, but I knew I had to keep my body in shape. If I slipped, so would all the offers coming at me. It was unreal that when I arrived in LA a year ago, I had a hundred dollars to my name, and now my bank account was…okay, I hadn't turned into a millionaire or anything like that, but now I could stop sleeping on my friends' couches and get my own apartment when I had time to settle down enough to look for one.

It was unbelievable that for the last four months, I'd been traveling almost non-stop. Everyone wanted me as the face of their products. It was unreal to see my face in magazines and all over the internet, and it all happened because one company took a chance on me. Once California Tomorrow's magazine hit the stands, my phone never stopped ringing. I had an agent with a prominent modeling agency who was booking me non-stop. I barely had a moment to myself to appreciate how my career had blown up. Now I was in Paris for Men's Fashion Week and going to walk for Giorgio Armani. I didn't care about fashion, but I knew Armani and was astounded at the huge opportunity they were giving me.

Every time I thought about what started my career, I thought about Lexie. How could I not? She was so fucking sexy with the way she held the camera, her breathy voice as she called out positions, and I'd never forget her body with tattoos decorating her skin. The thought of her secret piercings made my dick hard every time I pictured them. Fucking her on the studio bed had been on a constant loop these last few months as I brought myself to release. I knew I'd likely never see her again except in my fantasies, and I was okay with that. I was too busy to even think about having a girlfriend or a steady fuck buddy. I hadn't even been in the same time zone as her since that day.

After showering at the gym, I hit the streets of Paris to be a tourist. I was going to take advantage of my downtime to see the sights, knowing all of this could be taken away in the blink of an eye. When I first started getting jobs, I was intimidated by not being able to speak the languages of the countries I visited but quickly learned it wasn't necessary. All the people I worked with spoke English except one, and they had a translator. Every meal was delivered to my room, making it easy to stay on track with what I needed to eat. I was lucky I found an agency that believed in me as much as they did and made my life easier, for the most part. It was daunting going to jobs when you didn't know where you were going. Luckily, everyone who was in the Armani show was staying at the same hotel. Not that I talked to any of them. It was a competition, and they would happily take me out if they could. It was crazy, but I wasn't going to let it change me.

I spent the day going to the Eiffel Tower, The Louvre, and the Notre-Dame Cathedral. I didn't care that I looked like a silly tourist. I had gotten over that on my first overseas shoot. The only thing I wished was that I had someone to share it all with. When I decided to pursue a career in modeling, I had no idea how lonely it would be. Now that I had the life, I didn't see it changing unless I dated a model and we were booked on the same jobs, which wasn't likely. I knew I couldn't be a model forever, and once my time was up, I'd find that special person who was meant for me. Still, it didn't stop me from wishing I could share it with someone. None of the guys here wanted anything to do with me, and my crappy phone didn't have an international plan, so I couldn't even call my mom to tell her about it.

Heading back to the hotel, my shoulders were slumped with exhaustion and missing my friends and family. Once I got back to my room, I heated my boring dinner of chicken and vegetables and ate out on the balcony, watching everyone pass beneath me.

CAMERAS FLASHED FROM EVERY DIRECTION, BUT I CONTINUED to look straight ahead as I made my way to the end of the runway. Hitting my mark, I counted to four and then turned back the way I came. The moment I disappeared behind the curtain, I couldn't hide the smile that spread across my face. I'd done it. I'd walked my first runway show, and it was for none other than Giorgio Armani. I was flying high as I walked into the area where all the other models were in various stages of undress. Immediately, someone was ushering me back in line for the end of the show. It wasn't like I was going to get lost in the room. There was only one exit; they had the other blocked off. I replayed each step, and each celebrity I saw that was lining the platform in my mind. This high that I was on made up for being lonely, some days barely sleeping, and getting up hours before the sun to get that magical shot.

Someone shoved me from behind, making me spin around and growl.

"Move," he said something that sounded like a curse in French and pointed in front of me. The line I'd been standing in had moved while I'd been daydreaming. I jogged a few steps to catch up. There couldn't be a hole when we walked back out, and I didn't want to be the one who messed up the end of the show. If word got out that I couldn't follow simple instructions, I'd never get another job. Taking a deep breath, I closed my eyes. Ride the high, but don't be a fuck up, man. You've got this.

I hated the rollercoaster of emotions this life put me on. It was another reason I wanted someone to talk to, someone to share all the amazing places I'd seen, but also someone who would understand the lows.

How did it seem, in a city as big as Paris, I was the only person alone?

CHAPTER 5
LEXIE

I sat the fan down on the stair and looked up the narrow staircase. I'd need to invest in another fan because this was going to be the last time I carried this one up two flights of stairs. Maybe I should hire someone to build a little storage area on the roof, so I could house everything for outdoor shoots. It would be smart, but whoever said I was smart when it came to making my life easier?

Wiping the sweat from my forehead, I headed over to my desk to grab my camera. Everything was set up by the pool, and the models were getting oiled up. Raine was in heaven as she helped to slick down Tommy. He was cute, but he knew it and was a cocky asshole. Nova was arguing with her boyfriend on the phone, and I hoped it didn't affect the shoot because it sounded like they were really going at it. She'd slipped into the dressing room for some privacy, but it wasn't working since she kept yelling. I wanted to get away from it, so it didn't affect my mood for the day. I was over men. I thought my ex-boyfriend had listened to me and decided to leave me alone, but yesterday he started calling and texting incessantly again. He was freaking out, insisting that we needed to meet up at the apartment. When I informed him that I'd moved, I thought he was going to explode going by the sounds on the other end on the line. That's when I stopped answering his calls. Only it didn't stop, and he'd been texting me almost hourly since yesterday. I had no idea what his problem was, but I wanted no part in it.

Nova came out of the dressing room in a huff. She was almost six feet tall without heels, and with the five inches stilettos she had on, she still walked like a gazelle. Her long brown hair flowed down her back, and I swear it looked like she had a wind machine on her as it blew out behind her. I loved working with her. She was gorgeous inside and out and fun to work with.

Nova strode to me with her long legs eating up the space between us and stopped with only inches separating us. With the look on her face, I thought she was going to yell at me. Not that she had any reason to, but still, she looked pissed. Either that or she was going to say she couldn't do the shoot. The life of a model wasn't easy on relationships. I understood that and tried to make the lives of the models I worked with as easy as possible. If they needed a break to make a call, I'd let them. I think it was one reason most models liked to work with me. I saw no reason in making the experience difficult for everyone involved. That's not to say that I wasn't a bitch sometimes. It was easy to be the nice photographer when we were working inside, but when a shot depended on the light outside and weather, we all had to suck it up and get it done in the short amount of time we had. We couldn't reset the sun just because we didn't get the shot. At least I had it easier than they did. I could wear whatever I wanted to be comfortable, unlike them. Most of the time, they froze their asses off to get the shots we needed, and I felt sorry for them. Somewhat. They usually made bank for those shoots, and I did everything I could to make them as comfortable as possible.

"I'm sorry you had to hear that." Nova turned, looking toward the front of the building with her mouth turned down. "He doesn't understand that I have to work and has been accusing me of cheating with every man I have a job with lately."

Touching my hand to her arm, I smiled sadly at her. "I'm sorry, I know it can be hard. When was the last time you saw him?"

She tilted her head to the side and hummed. "Probably three weeks ago."

"That's a long time. He probably just misses you." I had a feeling they'd be broken up by the next time I worked with her. He was always a problem, and I knew she could do better than him.

She chewed on the inside of her cheek as she looked toward the front of the building again. I looked around her to see what she was looking at. Was she worried he'd show up because there was nothing else back there except the front door and everyone else was up on the roof waiting for us? "Is it bad that I don't miss him? All we do anymore is fight. Even the sex isn't that great. You'd think with all the making up we do, it would be spectacular."

"Maybe you should take a break?" I shrugged. I didn't want to overstep, but it seemed like she wanted advice. "Or sit him down and talk to him and tell him how you're feeling. I'm not the best at giving relationship advice. My last boyfriend…" I didn't want to think about how I stayed with him for far too long. It wasn't a healthy relationship, and when I found him with another woman, I should have been relieved. Instead, I almost spiraled.

"Men suck." Nova sighed.

She had that right. I seemed to only attract the worst ones. It made me think of Ryder and how perfect he'd seemed. I wished I'd gotten his number but knew he was busy living his best life. I'd been following him, and he'd made it big in the last four months. I was proud of him and that my photos were the ones to break him into the spotlight. Well, my photos and his amazing looks.

Heading toward the stairs, I looked back at her when she didn't follow. "Are you ready to get to work, or do you need a few more minutes?"

"Um…I'm ready. I thought I heard something. There isn't anyone else here, is there?" She stood slightly behind me as if I could protect her. I was scrappy, but I wasn't much of a fighter.

"Just us. Everyone else is upstairs unless someone snuck down here. Why don't you head up there, and I'll look around?"

"Lexie," Nova called when she was at the base of the staircase, "thanks for taking the time to talk to me."

"Anytime." I smiled at her. "I'll be up in a few minutes."

I hadn't heard anything, but I still checked it out since Nova thought she had. My studio wasn't in the best neighborhood, but it had everything I wanted, and I could afford it, so that was all that mattered. That and a good security system. I never would have decided to live here if I didn't feel safe.

Out of the corner of my eye, I thought I saw a shape

move up the staircase but thought nothing of it. It could have been Raine, Tommy, or anyone else from upstairs wondering what the hell was keeping me. Everything on the first floor looked normal. As I started up the stairs, I heard something from the second floor. I'd put a door to my apartment from the stairs so no one could just walk into my space. Plus, that way, I didn't have to make my bed if I didn't want to. I swore I'd locked my door this morning, but maybe Raine had to go in and hadn't locked it back up. Still, that didn't explain why anyone would be in there now. I went up the steps as quietly as I could. There were a few steps that creaked when weight was placed on them, but no one ever came up to my apartment, so I didn't care. That was, until now, and I couldn't remember which ones were the ones that made a noise. One wrong step and whoever was in my apartment would know someone was coming.

I held my breath as I took each step, praying I didn't make any noise. When I reached the landing, I let out an unsteady breath. Someone was definitely in my place, and they weren't trying to be quiet. It sounded like they were throwing shit all over the place. My shit.

I didn't think. Instead, I pushed open the door and let it slam against the wall as I ran inside, looking for the asshole had decided to come into my space. Across the room was a man going through my drawers and throwing everything on the ground.

Stopping a few feet away, I yelled. "What the fuck are you doing?"

When Ben turned around with wide brown eyes that were black and blue and a split lip, I gasped. His brown hair was buzzed, and he looked to have a few scratches on his scalp. His knuckles were scraped and bloody, and he looked like he'd been wearing the same clothes for the last week. They were wrinkled and dirty with a few spots of what I guessed was blood. The last time I saw him, he'd been muscular, but now he was skinny and sickly looking. Ben was a mess of epic proportions.

"What are you doing here, and why in the hell are you trashing my place?"

Turning back around, he went back to throwing everything on the floor. "Where is it, Lexie?" He let out a frustrated sigh as if I had any clue what he was talking about.

Hands on my hips, I fumed. "Where is what?"

"You know what, you fucking bitch. I tried to be nice and wait, but time ran out, and I need it now. If I don't get it…" He swallowed nervously, his eyes imploring me to give him what he wanted.

"Seriously, Ben, I have no idea what you're talking about. I don't have anything of yours. I made sure to pack up all your shit after I kicked you out." I cocked my head to the side, having just realized something. "How did you know I was here?"

Ben threw his hands in the air. "I've been sitting outside your apartment for days and never once saw you leave. Today I went inside, and George told me you moved out a few weeks ago. What gives?"

What gives? Like he had any right to know about my life.

"Not that it's any of your business, but I renovated the second floor into a living space, as you can see, and moved in. Now I don't have to pay rent or deal with traffic on my way to work. It's a win-win. Now, why don't you tell me what you're doing here before I call the cops?"

"You wouldn't dare call the cops on me." He laughed

like the idiot he was. I would most definitely call the police on him.

"I'm not alone here. I have a whole group of people waiting for me, so I suggest you leave."

"I'm not leaving until I get what I came for." He stepped toward me menacingly, and in that instant, I realized Ben wasn't even remotely the nice guy I'd once thought him to be. He would hurt me if he didn't get what he wanted. If only I knew what that was, I'd give it to him.

"What's wrong with you?" I asked, stepping back. There wasn't any place for me to go. I'd made the space into a studio apartment. The bathroom and closet were the only areas with doors and didn't go anywhere. My only hope would be calling the cops except...I patted down my cut off jean shorts to realize I'd left my phone up on the roof. Fuck.

"You're what's wrong with me. I've called and texted you a thousand times, and you ignored me. I told you it was life or death and now..." His fists clenched at his sides. Was he going to hit me?

"Tell me what you're looking for, and I'll help you find it." I was desperate for him to leave and get out of this situation unscathed. At this point, I'd give him whatever he wanted, and I was going to have the doors all locked with the alarm system armed at all times of the day and night. No more surprises.

"Like you don't fucking know. I always knew you were a bitch. What did you do? Did you sell it? Use it?" With each word, his voice escalated as he moved toward me until he was shouting in my face.

What was he talking about? What could I have possibly used or sold? Ben had no money. I'd learned early on that he was a deadbeat and wasn't below having a woman pay his way. I didn't mind at first, but I quickly started to resent him when all he did was sit around the apartment all day playing video games. That was when I should have ended our relationship, but the sex was good, and he knew the right words to keep me coming back for more.

"Lexie?" Tommy called from behind me.

Keeping an eye on Ben out of the corner of my eye, I slowly turned to see Tommy standing in the doorway. He had a frightened-looking Brad behind him. Brad was only a couple of inches taller than my five-foot-four-inches, and he was a skinny little thing, but he could do hair like no other. I appreciated that he'd come down with Tommy.

"I called the police." Tommy's gaze went to Ben, and he tried to look mean but failed miserably. He looked like the stereotypical surfer boy with long, wavy blond hair, blue eyes, and golden skin without an ounce of maliciousness to him. "They'll be here in a few minutes, so I suggest you go."

"I'm not going anywhere until I get what I came for," Ben roared.

Tommy stepped into the room hesitantly but stood tall. "Then get what you came for and get lost."

Ben grabbed my arm and pulled me roughly to his side. I tried to pull my arm out of his grasp, but he only held on harder. Pain shot through my wrist, but I kept quiet. I wouldn't give him the satisfaction to let him know he'd hurt me. "I would, but she's hiding it from me. Either that or she took it."

"Let go of her," Tommy growled and took another two steps forward.

I was impressed. He sounded like he meant business. If

I'd been Ben, I would have let go of me, but he wasn't being smart and only gripped my arm tighter.

Loud knocking came from downstairs, and I heard Raine squeak as she ran to see who it was. Poor thing, she was going to be a mess. I had a feeling today's shoot was going to be postponed for another day.

"That would be the cops." Tommy grinned. He was proud of himself. Hell, I was proud of all of them for coming to my rescue. Only now, I wasn't sure what would happen. Ben pulled me in front of him as he edged toward the window. Did he not believe them? If not, he really was stupid.

"Ben, you need to let me go. Otherwise, you're going to get in more trouble." I wasn't sure why I was trying to help him, except that I didn't want the situation to escalate any more than it had. At least he didn't have a weapon. I had a feeling if he had, Ben would have used it then.

Loud steps sounded on the stairs a moment before two police officers came into view with their guns drawn.

"LAPD," they shouted. "Drop the weapon and let the woman go."

Both Tommy and I gasped. I couldn't believe what was happening. The whole situation seemed unreal. I wasn't sure where Brad had gone, but I was glad he wasn't in the room. He probably would have fainted.

Ben's hold tightened on me, and I wasn't sure what he was going to do next. I definitely wasn't expecting it when he threw me to the side. My hands and knees hit the concrete floor hard. I fell to my side and cradled my right wrist with my left hand as blood poured from a wound. It hurt like a bitch. I must have landed on something, but I had no idea what because it seemed everything I owned covered the floor.

Ben's eyes widened as he hovered over me for only a second before he ran and crashed through one of the windows that lined the left wall. Did he think he was Superman?

Standing up, I staggered over to the window. The two police officers were already there, on their radios. When I looked down at the ground, I expected to see Ben splattered on the grass, but he was gone.

"Holy fucking shit," Tommy said in astonishment by my side, "that was intense."

Intense was putting it mildly.

"Ma'am, maybe you should sit down," one of the officers said.

"Yeah, you're not looking too great there, Lexie," Tommy added. He guided me over to my unmade bed and helped me sit down.

"We have an ambulance coming to check you out," the other officer said.

"What just happened?" I choked out the words as I looked up at Tommy.

He kneeled in front of me with a shaky smile. "Your guess is as good as mine. Who was that guy?"

Taking in an unsteady breath, I looked around the room. Raine, Nova, Brad, and Annalise were all standing by the door with worried expressions on their faces. "That was my ex, Ben. He's—"

For the next hour, I gave my statement to the police and let the EMT's put ten stitches in the gash along the side of my hand. With everyone shaken up, we rescheduled the shoot for a few days later. Tommy was nice enough to board up my window before he left, and Raine ran out to get us lunch. I had a feeling she thought I was going to crack once I was left alone. Yes, I was shaken up, but I was fine. What puzzled me most was what Ben had been looking for in the first place and why he jumped out the window.

Had Ben hidden something of his in my things? And if so, what was it?

CHAPTER 6
RYDER

Walking along the beach in Oahu, I let out a long yawn. I'd been up since three for a four o'clock photo shoot. The early hour was starting to get to me, but it was my first time in Hawaii, and I wanted to experience the beach before all the tourists took over. There were only a few surfers out in the water and scattered across the sand.

The water was beautiful with its various shades of blues starting light at the sand to a deep turquoise the further out you looked. Palm trees swayed in the breeze as my hair tickled across my forehead. The warm water lapped at my ankles. It was perfection.

I'd been walking for a good twenty minutes when I came upon another photo shoot, but what made my steps stutter to a stop was the blue-haired woman behind the camera. How many photographers had blue hair with tattoos decorating their arms? How many were as beautiful as the woman in the distance who hadn't noticed me yet? It had to be Lexie. Even after almost five months, I still thought about her. At first, I replayed our encounter every night before I went to bed. As exhaustion took over and I passed out in my hotel room, her image only appeared in my subconscious every few days now. It wasn't normal for me to be hung up on a woman, but I'd never meet anyone like Lexie Keene.

Now that she was in my sights, I wasn't going to leave until I at least got to talk to her again. I moved up the beach and sat beneath the shade of a few palm trees as I watched her work. It was obvious, even if you'd never worked with her, that Lexie loved her job. Her smile was wide as she spoke to the surrounding people. She animatedly explained what she wanted with verve. Once she hung her camera around her neck as she walked out into the water. She squeaked as a wave hit her at the waist, drenching her short shorts. Immediately she ran back onto the beach and placed her camera on one of the chairs that were set up. Lexie laughed as she skipped back out to the water and maneuvered the woman onto her knees, bending her back until the tips of her hair hit the water. The shot was hot, but I wished they'd change places. I wanted to see Lexie like that. Maybe I could persuade her to do the pose and let me use her camera to get a picture since I still had my old flip phone, and it took shit pictures.

I really needed to upgrade my phone. Maybe I could do that while I was here on the island. That way, I could take pictures of every place I went, post on social media like my agent wanted me to, and keep in contact with my family while I was away.

I sat for another hour, watching Lexie in her element. I desperately wanted to work with her again, and not only because of how our shoot had ended. Although I wouldn't be opposed to sinking deep inside of her and feeling the heat of her tight cunt around my cock again. A groan slipped from my lips at the thought. Damn, I hoped she didn't have a boyfriend now.

When the models came out of the tent with their clothes on, I made my way over. I walked slowly, taking Lexie in as she packed up with her assistant. The muscles in her legs flexed as she moved around the beach with large reflectors in her hands. She threw her head back and laughed at something someone said. Her laugh was breathy and sultry, making my dick twitch in my board shorts.

Her assistant spotted me and stopped short. The last time we saw each other, she had run out of the room when the sheet slipped as I'd tried to cover Lexie, and she saw me in all my naked glory. It didn't bother me, especially now. People were constantly seeing me without clothes on as we quickly changed in small spaces, and I saw them as well. It was normal, but I knew not everyone felt the same.

With her eyes trained on me, I watched her mouth move before Lexie turned in what seemed to be in slow motion. The smile that lit her face when she spotted me made my day. Hell, it made my week, maybe even the month. My feet picked up their pace as I made my over to her and didn't stop until we were toe to toe, and I had my arms wrapped around her in a big hug.

I wasn't normally a hugger, but I figured this was better than me laying a kiss on her in front of everyone. And I was over the moon happy to see her, so I held her in my arms for longer than was probably appropriate.

"I can't believe you're here." My lips brushed her neck,

and I felt her shiver, even in the heat. It seemed I still affected her just as much as she did me.

Pulling back enough to look at me, Lexie beamed up at me and mirrored my same words. "I can't believe you're here." She looked around me for a second. "Are you working?"

"I am, or was, actually. We're done for the day. How about you, are you finished?" The hopeful note in my voice was easy to hear, but hell, who was I kidding? I'd almost tackled her the moment we were within inches of each other. She was still in my arms with her hands resting on my biceps.

"For a few hours, and then we'll be back down here at sunset. I was going to grab some lunch at one of the food trucks if you want to join me and catch up."

Dropping my left arm, I kept my right arm around her waist and started walking. Lexie pulled me to a stop and laughed. "I still have to pack everything up before we go."

"Oh, it's okay. I can get it so you can—" her assistant started.

"I'll help. Three sets of hands are better than one." Plus, that way, I'd get her to myself faster.

Her assistant giggled but kept quiet as we worked. I kept glancing at Lexie every time I passed by her, and every time she had a serene smile on her face. I liked to think I had something to do with it. Once we had all her equipment gathered, we hauled it up to a van. I guess it wouldn't make sense to leave it outside for it to be stolen.

"So, I guess I'll see you around seven?" her assistant, who I thought was named Raine, asked.

"Please make sure everyone knows to eat beforehand. We can't stop just because they're hungry." She rolled her eyes as she looked down at her assistant, who had to be four-foot-ten max. She was a tiny but adorable little thing.

Raine snorted. "I'll make sure to let Brad and Annalise know."

Lexie shook her hand. "If you need anything, give me a call." Her hand wrapped around my arm. "And don't let anyone start drinking."

Raine's eyes widened behind her red frames as she squeaked. "Can you text them and tell them?"

"Since you're letting me run off and have fun with Ryder, I'll be the bad guy and send them a text."

Raine blushed before she turned and started to walk away.

I leaned down, inhaled her coconut scent, and whispered in Lexie's ear. "Is she over seeing my dick?"

"I don't think I'm over seeing it." She bumped her hip into mine and fluttered her eyelashes at me. "I hope I get to see it again."

She most definitely didn't have a boyfriend. "I think that can be arranged." I winked at her. If we weren't out in public, I'd have happily stripped us both right there and then.

"Let's go get something to eat. I've got the perfect place." She placed her hand on my abs and tapped lightly, her other arm wrapping around my waist. I was shocked she was so touchy-feely with me, but I wasn't going to complain. When I was with Lexie, it was like being with my best friend even though we barely knew each other. Something seemed to click between us, or at least that was the way I felt. I was going to relish every moment with her while I could.

Lexie led us down the sidewalk, passing truck after

truck for almost a mile before a lone food truck sat in a parking lot with a long line. As we waited, we talked about what we'd been up to, and I was surprised that she'd kept tabs on me.

"I wanted to call you so many times, but I have this shitty old flip phone without an international plan. Not that I had your number, to begin with." My cheeks flushed.

"I would have given you my number if you hadn't run off before I got back from talking Raine down." She leaned against my side; her head rested on my bicep. "I have a confession. I wanted to talk to you too, but I didn't have your number either."

"You don't have to say that just because I did."

"I wouldn't lie to you. I really wanted to talk to you, so I did the next best thing and watched as your career took off."

Her words made a warmth start deep in my gut and travel to the center of my chest. I pressed her deeper into my side. "That means more to me than you'll ever know."

I let the heat from her body sink deep into mine. Until this moment, I hadn't realized how much I needed real human contact. For someone to genuinely care about me. "Would you like to go with me to get a new phone? I think it's time I upgraded, and that way, we can stay in contact after this." I wasn't sure how long she was going to be here, but I only had two more days. It wasn't enough time, but I'd make the most of it.

Tilting her head up to look up at me, she smiled. "I'd love to be able to talk to you after this, and I'd be happy to go with you to pick out a new phone."

I loved how happy she always seemed and the way she

looked up at me as if she saw the man I was. She didn't only see the physique I worked incredibly hard for or my looks.

"Oh my God," Lexie turned fully toward me, her blue eyes bright, and cupped my cheeks. "How have I just now noticed you have dimples? I didn't think you could be more perfect." The last came out as a grumble.

A silent laugh built up in my chest. "You think I'm perfect?"

"Oh please, like you don't know." She swatted my chest. "But it is good to see you don't have an ego as big as your cock."

I choked on my laughter as all eyes turned toward us.

"What?" She motioned to me like she was Vanna White revealing a new letter. "Like you'd expect anything less with a body and a face like this."

"Is that all I am? A pretty face with a nice body?" I understood the attraction, but I wanted her to like me for more than my face and body.

Stepping up to me, Lexie draped her arms around my neck with a soft smile gracing her pretty pink lips. Leaning up on her tippy toes, her mouth brushed against mine. "You're so much more than your looks."

I groaned, pressing her flush to my body. I wanted nothing more than to be alone with her and to strip her bare. "Maybe we should skip lunch and head to my room." Her stomach growled at that moment, making us both laugh. "Okay, first food and then—"

"We can go back to my bungalow. It's up the road, on the beach, and we'll have plenty of privacy."

"Perfect."

Pulling her back to my front, I wrapped my arms around her as we waited in line. With Lexie, I didn't mind the wait. We talked and got to know each other better. It felt right to have her in my arms, and when we walked hand in hand to her bungalow after picking up a new phone, it was even better.

CHAPTER 7

LEXIE

Stumbling into the little house with Ryder attached to me like an octopus, I was surprised we'd made it inside with all our clothes on. Pushing me up against the door, he grabbed my leg to wrap around his hip. Our mouths crashed together. All teeth, tongues, and passion as we got swept up in each other.

Breaking our kiss, Ryder fell to his knees, pulling at the button of my jean shorts, and quickly had them down to my feet in a matter of seconds. His large hands gripped my hips and opened me wide.

His eyes darkened into stormy pools of lust. "I love this." He flicked his tongue on the ring I had through my hood. "It's so fucking hot. All of your piercings are. I've thought about them so many times over these last several months." He groaned, threw one leg over his shoulder, and dove between my legs.

Ryder sucked and flicked the ring until I collapsed against the wall. Only then did he pull back, with his arms around me to keep me from falling, and brought me down to the floor. The cold tile was a shock to my overheated skin, and my body arched up into his hard frame.

His brows pulled together, and I wanted to kiss the wrinkle away.

"It's just a little cold. Nothing you can't fix in a—"

"Shit, I'm sorry." Sweeping me up as if I weighed little more than a feather, Ryder looked around the little bungalow. It was small but nice. Not that I needed much. Looking right and then left, he spotted the bedroom and the big plush bed. He strode into the room as if he was on a mission, yet he laid me down gently before he desperately pulled off my tank top and bikini.

Crooking my finger for him to join me, Ryder pushed his shorts off and kicked them away before he crawled between my legs. Kissing up my stomach, he licked a path from between my breasts, up to my neck, and behind my ear. "God, you're fucking beautiful."

"So are you." My hands roamed over his smooth skin and over the three blue star tattoos that ran up his side. One's that he hadn't had before.

"You mentioned that in front of a long line of people," he chuckled. His cheeks were pink, and I wasn't sure if it was from embarrassment or the fact that he'd started to rub his length through my folds. It felt amazing, but it was nothing compared to how it would feel once he was inside of me. He flashed me a grin. "Will you still like me when my looks go?"

"I have a feeling I'll like you for a very long time." My reply came out quiet. I wasn't sure if it was wise to confess how much I liked him. "Speaking of age, how old are you?" I groaned as Ryder plunged deep inside of me. The base of his cock rubbed against my clit.

"Twenty," he grunted against my pebbled nipple.

My body stilled with this new knowledge. I wanted to push him off me and run far away, but he swiveled his hips and pleasure shot through me. He sucked me into his mouth and laved me with his tongue before letting go with a pop.

His Caribbean blue eyes met mine. "Where'd you go?"

"You're just a baby."

"Does this feel like I'm a baby?" He punctuated the word 'baby' with a hard thrust of his hips. His hand skated down between my breasts, over my stomach until his thumb found my clit. He rubbed with slow strikes making heat shoot through my body. "Stay with me, sexy Lexie."

"Keep doing that, and I'll follow you around the world, kneeling at your feet."

A cocky grin spread across his gorgeous face. "I like the sound of that."

My hands gripped his trim hips and met his thrust with my own. "Less talking and more moving."

"I don't remember you being so bossy, but I kind of like it." Dipping down, he took my mouth in a blistering kiss that left me breathless. Ryder may have been young, but he was passionate and a good person. Something I'd been missing from my life for a long time.

Swinging my leg up onto his shoulder, Ryder's hands went to my hips, angling me just right before he started to drive into me at a brutal pace. Taking a nipple into his mouth, he bit down, causing pleasure to shoot straight to my core. His tongue swirled around my stiff peak and I let out a breathy moan. Cupping the back of his head, I pressed him further into my chest as I tried to match his wild thrusts. Moving to my other breast, he showed it the same attention, and when he bit down, my core clenched around him.

"Ryder," I moaned his name. The tips of my fingers dug into the flesh of his muscular shoulders.

One hand slipped around to my front and found my over-sensitized bundle of nerves and made slow circles. My back arched off the bed until the hard points of my breasts brushed against his firm chest, and I exploded.

I didn't think it was possible, but Ryder's pace picked up as he chased his own release. My arms wrapped around his back, pulling him closer until his face was buried in my neck. Pumping one last time, Ryder stilled inside of me as he let out the most exotic moan I'd ever heard in my life. I was instantly addicted and wanted to pleasure him any way I could so that I could hear that sound from him again and again.

Kissing my pulse point, Ryder rested his forehead to the side of my face. His heavy pants swept over my blissed-out face. Lifting up only to fall down on the bed, Ryder took me with him. I was half sprawled out on top of him with his arms wrapped around me as if he was afraid to let me go. I could feel his length against my leg that was still half hard. Closing my eyes, I took in his pine scent. I'd forgotten how good he smelled. It was stronger now that he was a sweaty mess.

Ryder ran his fingers through my messy blue hair as I traced the ridges in his abs absentmindedly. "What made you decide to color your hair blue?"

While we had been apart, I'd forgotten how amazing his voice was. It was all deep and gravely. Like sex on a stick, and I wanted to listen to it forever.

"I colored it pink one year for breast cancer awareness

month, and I liked it, so I kept trying different colors until I found the one I liked best. Blue has won for the last five years. What made you get these stars?" I ran my finger over the three blue stars that hadn't been there several months ago.

"I've always thought about getting a tattoo, and some of the guys were going to get tattoos when we were in Spain, so I went with them. It was the third country I'd been to in as many months, and I was already booked up for most of the year. I knew then that I was going to make it as a model or at least for the time being."

Lifting my head to rest my chin on his chest, I found Ryder already looking down at me. I expected him to look happy, but instead, he looked unsure. Reaching up, I cupped his scruffy cheek. "You had to have known you'd make it before then. I could have told you that when you were at my studio before I took one shot." If you'd stuck around, I wanted to add. "Everyone's going to want you for their campaigns. Soon you'll probably be doing commercials, and then you'll be the face of colognes and underwear if you're not already booked for them."

He blinked down at me with his lips turned down. "You don't have to say those things so I'll continue to sleep with you."

I couldn't help but laugh. Rolling to my side, I settled my head on the pillow next to his and brought his hand to my chest and held it there. "Listen, you know you're a good-looking guy, there's no denying that. You literally can't be ugly and be a model." Ryder's chest shook with silent laughter. The way his eyes lit up with humor was what truly made Ryder gorgeous. "Okay, there are some out there that have a certain look to them, but they're limited. You're not. And while yes, your looks help obviously to get you in the door, it's your personality that's going to be why you continue to book with them. You're a good man, Ryder, and so easy to work with. You may not know it, but word gets around on who's easy and difficult to work with. We know all the scandals before anyone else does."

His eyes brightened with every word that came out of my mouth. How did he not believe in himself?

"Look at how you helped us pack up today. You didn't need to do that, but you did because you're a good guy."

Kissing my forehead, he smiled mischievously. "I did it so I could get you into bed faster."

"There's nothing wrong with being a good guy." My fingers traced over his forehead, eyebrows, and cheeks before finally swiping across his pink lips.

"Haven't you heard nice guys finish last?"

"I have, but I know the truth, and in this industry, that's not the case."

He shot back with, "Women like bad boys."

"Until they've been burned one too many times by them. All we want is a man who is good to us and will treat us like a princess."

"Really?" he asked with doubt laced heavily in that one word.

"Okay, we like the bad boy to come out to fuck us," I amended.

"That's what I thought." His face grew serious. "Have you been burned one too many times?"

"Something like that. Right now, I'm looking for a nice guy." I kissed his mouth that had thinned into a firm line with his question until it turned into a smile.

Ryder pulled me close until my wet heat straddled one of his legs. His voice turned husky. "You've got a nice guy right in front of you."

"Lucky for me."

Warm liquid seeped down my leg, and it was only then that I realized I'd once again had sex with Ryder without a condom. I wasn't normally this reckless, but there was something about him that made me forget myself and the rest of the world once he started to touch me.

"Ryder?" I asked hesitantly. This wasn't going to be fun.

"Hmmm," he hummed, and the hand resting on my shoulder twitched.

"I love having sex with you."

"Are you ready to go again?" I could hear the smile in his voice. Too bad I was going to ruin the mood. Pulling out of his hold, I sat up next to him and pulled the sheet to cover me up. The smile that was on his face vanished as soon as my boobs were out of sight and was replaced with troubled eyes. "What's wrong?"

"I like you a lot." I laced my fingers through his.

He sat up against the headboard and answered back in an unsure tone. "Good, because I like you a lot too."

"I'm not a reckless person." Tears pooled in my eyes. Why was this so hard? I didn't think it would be a deal-breaker for him to wear a condom or to talk about his sex life.

"Hey, whatever it is, you can tell me." He bit down on his bottom lip, his blue eyes sad. "Is it because you have a boyfriend?"

"Nothing like that. I haven't had a boyfriend in almost a year, and I'm not a cheater. If I'm with someone, I'm with them, and if I wanted to fuck someone else, then I'd end the relationship before ever acting on it."

"Okay," he swallowed slowly. "You're making me nervous. Whatever it is, just say it, and I promise to not get upset."

Here goes nothing. Taking a deep breath, I let it out and blurted. "Have you been tested recently?"

Instead of being shocked or mad, awareness lit his face. "Fuck, I'm sorry. I can't control myself around you. You intoxicate me and…I didn't use a condom." The last five words came out in a rush.

"No, you didn't. It was the last thing on my mind, and I'm as much at fault as you are—"

"I'm clean," he sat up and pulled me onto his lap. "I promise. I haven't been with anyone since I was with you and I was tested before." I found it hard to believe Ryder hadn't had sex since we'd been together five months ago. How hadn't anyone thrown themselves at him, and why hadn't he taken them up on their offer if they had? My thoughts must have shown on my face. "I have no reason to lie."

"Sure you do, if you want to keep having sex with me while you're here."

His faced hardened. "I'm not a liar. Remember, I'm a nice guy. We don't do that."

"Okay," I said softly as I scooted closer to him. "I believe you, and while I'm glad you haven't had sex with anyone else, it's crazy that you haven't."

"Have you?" His jaw ticked, and I loved that it bothered him to think of me with another man.

"No, and I was tested about six months before we met, after I found my boyfriend in bed with my assistant."

"Is he why you said you'd never cheat?"

"He's one of the reasons. It's not in my nature, to begin with, and after being cheated on by multiple boyfriends, I know how it feels. I don't ever want to be responsible for making anyone feel that way."

"I can imagine. I've never been cheated on. I had the same girlfriend all through high school, but we broke up when she went off to college. Kelly couldn't handle the long distance."

"It's not for everyone. It takes commitment and faith. Something a lot of people seem to be lacking these days." I knew Ryder would have made it work with his ex if she'd wanted to stay with him. "Do you miss her, your ex?"

He shook his head. "Not her, per se. I miss hearing a friendly voice on the other end of the phone or seeing someone I know besides the guys I'm traveling with. I'm the new guy, so they make me feel like the odd man out. They don't want to hang out or have anything to do with me." He shrugged sadly.

Wrapping my arms around him, I hugged Ryder as tightly as I could. I didn't even know the guys he was with, but I hated them for making him feel less than.

"One thing I never thought modeling would be is lonely, but it is. Depressingly so, especially when you can't talk to your friends and family because you have an old shitty phone that doesn't have an international calling plan on it."

"Is that why you wanted to get a new one?"

He nodded against my chest. "That and so I can take decent pictures of my travels. I'm not a photographer like you, but I like to take pictures."

"Well, it shouldn't be a problem now with your new iPhone. What's going to be your first picture?"

Pulling me onto his lap, Ryder grabbed his phone and held it out in front of us. "The first picture I want is of us together."

It was a good thing we'd made a detour on our way to my bungalow to get Ryder a new phone.

We both smiled for the camera as he took photo after photo. They may not have been with my camera, but they were perfect. Ryder kissed my cheek, nuzzled my neck, and licked a path up until he nibbled on my ear all while taking pictures of us in various positions until he dropped his phone down onto the bed to be forgotten. For the next half hour, there was no talking. The only sounds were our moans and the slapping of skin until we had to head back down to the beach.

CHAPTER 8

RYDER

We walked hand in hand along the beach back to the location Lexie had been shooting at earlier. Her tiny hand felt right in mine, and I was already dreading when our time together would end.

"I didn't ask before, but what happened to your hand?" I noticed a bright pink scar on the side that looked new.

Lexie let out a frustrated breath. "My ex showed up at my place. I'm still not sure why he was there or what was wrong with him. I think he was on drugs because his behavior was erratic and had been for a while. We were fighting, and luckily, I had my whole team there on the roof. One of the models came looking for me, and someone else called the police."

"The police? It was serious then."

She rubbed her thumb across the mark absentmindedly. "He grabbed me, and when the cops showed up, he shoved me away. I fell, and my hand landed on something. He had thrown almost all of my belongings on the floor, so I didn't see what caused it, and I still don't know what it was. Raine and Tommy cleaned up the mess before I had a chance to see. I got stitches, and they gave me antibiotics as a precaution. That's why even though we're both clean, we need to use condoms. I'm not sure how effective my pill is right now since I've only been off the antibiotics for a few days."

I blinked down at her in shock. Not once during her story did she stop walking. I wasn't sure if it was because she didn't want to talk about it or if she was over it. Either way, it didn't sit well with me. It didn't bother me to use a condom. In fact, up until I met Lexie, I'd always used a condom every time I'd had sex. Even with my high school girlfriend when we'd been together for years. There was something about Lexie that short-circuited my brain but in a good way. While it was amazing to feel her bare, I'd be buying the biggest box of condoms on the island as soon as possible.

"Have you seen this ex of yours since?"

"That's the crazy part," she laughed without humor. "After throwing me down, he jumped out the window and ran off. The cops still haven't found him."

I stopped dead in my tracks, causing Lexie to jerk to a stop. "Are you in danger?"

"My alarm is set constantly, and I had it upgraded. I don't want anyone walking in without me knowing, so I have a buzzer on the door with a camera so I can see who's out there."

I wasn't sure if that was enough, but what did I know?

Lexie ran her toes through the sand while she looked straight ahead, and we started walking down the beach again. Now, though, with this new knowledge, it didn't look as beautiful as it had before. "Is your studio okay now? Did he break anything?"

"I renovated the second floor and moved up there. He didn't touch the studio luckily, and just threw everything on the floor looking for something."

"What was he looking for?" If he didn't find it, he was sure to come back, and that had me worried.

"That I don't know. Ben seemed to think I knew what it was, but I don't. Raine and I didn't find anything when we looked."

"Please be careful, Lexie. If he didn't find what he was looking for, he'll be back, and he seems desperate after what you've told me."

"I will. I promise. You don't need to worry about me." She smiled sadly up at me. I had a feeling she didn't like talking about it, so I dropped it.

It didn't matter what she told me; I was going to continue to worry until I knew she was safe, and her ex-boyfriend was behind bars.

I spied Raine up ahead, trying to put up the tent, but with her small stature, she was having a hell of a time getting it up. Lexie must have thought the same when she spoke. "What are you going to do now?"

"First, I'm going to help you guys set up, and then I'm going to find a store and buy a giant box of condoms. I might set up an Instagram account, take some pictures. I don't know." I shrugged, not really knowing what I was going to do except help her.

She turned around before we hit her group. Her hands rested on my chest as she smiled up at me. I loved how happy of a person she always seemed to be, even with an ex causing her problems. The diamond stud in her nose winked in the sunlight. "It should only take three hours max. What time is your shoot in the morning?"

I frowned at the thought of having to be separated from her. "I've got to be there at five."

"Is it down the beach again?"

"It is. Where are you going with this?" My brows pinched together.

One of her hands slipped down and around my waist. "I'm going to be along this beach for the next four days, and if you are too…" She shrugged, looking unsure of herself. "I thought maybe you'd like to stay with me while you're here, but if you want to stay at your hotel, that's fine too."

Wrapping her in my arms, I dipped my head down until our noses were touching. I could feel her warm breath skate along my lips as I spoke. "I'd love nothing more than to stay with you for my short time here, my sexy Lexie."

"Ugh, I can't get over those dimples." She hopped in place, breaking our bubble. "We can go get your stuff after the shoot, or you can do it during. Whatever you want." With each word, her smile bloomed further.

"We'll go get it together. I want to sit here and watch you in your element."

Pulling back, she took me in. Her eyes gleamed in the light. "Maybe we'll have our own little photo shoot while we're here."

How did everything she say make me so damn happy? Was it because I'd been alone these last few months, or was it simply Lexie's effect on me? "I like the sound of that. Can I take some pictures of you too?"

"I think that can be arranged." Grabbing my hand, she started to drag me toward the growing group of people down the beach. "I guess I should go help before I put us off schedule."

I trailed behind with her pulling me along, watching her

ass sway in her short shorts. The material cupped her ass and defined it to perfection. When we were only a few feet away, Raine caught sight of us, and I swore I could see her blush from there. The rest of the group soon saw us, too, and started to whisper as they sneaked glances our way. I hoped it didn't bother Lexie that they were obviously talking about us.

"Let me help you with that." I pushed up on the center of the first canopy and continued down the line. There were three that connected with curtains that hung down for walls. It was actually quite genius since it gave them plenty of room to walk and stand beneath as they changed. Once the large canopy was up, I helped Lexie and Raine bring down the garment racks, lights, and reflectors. All the while, the group of women stared at us and whispered to themselves. I couldn't hear what they were saying, but I noticed Lexie gave them an annoyed look.

Pulling Lexie behind the tent, I pulled her into my arms and kissed her. It was brief since I didn't want to distract her too much. "Anything else you need help with before I head to the store?"

"No, but thank you for all your help. You know you didn't have to do that. Go get those condoms, and I'll see you in a little bit." With her fingers in my hair, Lexie guided my head down so she could nibble on my bottom lip before letting go and slowly walking backward until she was out of sight.

On a mission, I headed up the path to the parking lot, unsure of where I was going. I didn't want to pay for a ride, so I walked with hurried steps down the sidewalk until I came across a local convenience store. It was a tiny little thing, but I was in luck and found condoms. They didn't have any big boxes. Only the ones with three to a pack, so I bought four boxes. I had two days with Lexie, and I planned to be buried inside of her as much as possible. The woman behind the counter blinked up at me in surprise as I dumped them on the counter and pulled out my wallet. The guy behind me nudged me in the side with a knowing smile.

I took my time making my way back to where Lexie was set up. I pulled out my phone and took a few pictures of the palm trees and the water. It was beautiful here, and I was thankful my job had brought me to Hawaii and in Lexie's path once again. When I saw everyone in the distance, I slowed down and watched as Lexie situated the bottoms of one of the girl's swimsuit and guided her into place. Raine stood to the side with a reflector in her hands that completely dwarfed her. Another model came out of the tent to a man and a woman who worked on her hair and makeup. The whole setup worked in harmony. They were a well-oiled machine who'd done this hundreds of times before. My shoot hadn't gone as smoothly. The photographer couldn't make up his mind on how he wanted me to pose or what I should wear. I hoped tomorrow would go something like what I saw in front of me.

There were a few chairs set up on the side of the canopy. I spotted one with a large camera battery in it. I assumed it was Lexie's, so I picked it up and sat it in my lap. Pulling up the camera app on my phone, I took a few shots of Lexie as she worked until she turned around and saw me. I didn't think she minded, but if I didn't stop, I probably would have filled my entire phone with only pictures of her working.

After an hour, Lexie called a break so everyone could

change, and she could look at the pictures she'd taken. Plopping down in the seat beside me, she took her battery from my lap and replaced it with the one in her camera.

"Learning anything?"

"That I want to work with you more in the future. My shoot this morning was nothing like yours. You know what you want."

"I've been doing this for a long time." She shrugged like it was no big deal.

Leaning over, I watched as she flipped through image after image. I was in awe of how she captured the lighting and water while still making the women the sole focus and looking beautiful without the help of Photoshop. I couldn't wait to see what the finished product would be.

Turning off her camera, she leaned over and rested her head on my shoulder. "The girls are salivating over you."

"Did you tell them they don't have a chance in hell because I'm your sex slave?"

Her body shook with laughter. "No, but if I see them look at you one more time, I might. You wouldn't mind?"

Why would I mind? I wanted to own her body, mind, and soul. And for her to do the same to me.

"I'd be flattered."

Her head popped up from my shoulder. "I wish I could sit here and watch the sunset with you, but then I wouldn't get my shots. Maybe tomorrow night."

"It's a date." I'd make sure we got to see at least one side by side.

She stood and brushed away some sand that clung to her leg, probably because it knew how cool and awesome she was. Turning to walk away, I leaned forward and wrapped my arms around her leg and pulled her onto my lap. She looked stunned for a moment before cupping my cheeks in her hands and laying the mother of all kisses on me. This wasn't a kiss for out in public. When her lower body started to move against me, I had to hold her still, or everyone was going to get a show.

Smacking her ass, I devoured her body with my eyes. "Get to work so we can have more fun."

The girls on the beach tittered behind their hands as if they'd never seen two people kiss before. Maybe not quite like that. Lexie had tried to consume me, but I loved every minute of it.

While they got into position, I pulled my phone back out to download Instagram. My agent had been on my ass since day one to get an account and start posting, but my previous phone couldn't do anything fancy. I was lucky it still worked for phone calls. Texting was a bitch on it, so I was pretty limited. After putting in my email, I tried using my name Ryder Williams, but it was already taken. Everything I thought of was used by someone else. It was supposed to be something easy for my fans to be able to find me, but I had no clue what to pick if I couldn't use my name.

"Ryder," Lexie called from down by the water. She motioned for me to come down to her. Setting her battery pack back down in her chair, I walked down to the shore where everyone was watching me. Luckily, I was used to it now. "What's got you all stressed?"

"What do you mean?"

Lowering her voice, she stepped over to me. "I could tell from all the way down here something wasn't going right. What's wrong?"

"I'm supposed to pick a name that's easy for fans to follow me, but everything I try is already taken."

"Let me see."

"You don't need to help me. You're working." She held her hand out with an expectant look on her face. I handed over my phone. While her fingers flew over the keyboard, everyone started to move in toward us with curious eyes.

"Take off your shirt and stand in the water until you're about waist deep."

"You don't need to do this." I tried to take my phone back from her, but she sidestepped me and held it behind her back. "You're busy."

"That may be so, but if you hurry, I can quickly get your picture. With the lighting, it will be perfect."

Stripping off my shirt, I did as she requested. When I turned around, Lexie was a few feet behind me, holding up my phone in the air. I should have bought the waterproof case they tried to sell me, but I didn't think I'd need it.

"I'm not going to drop it, and if for some reason I did, I'd buy you a new one, so don't worry."

"Who says I'm worried?" I chuckled nervously, totally giving myself away.

Lexie laughed, shaking her head. "Just give me your best pose."

Placing my hand on my hip, I looked back at the shore and let the world drop away. The group of models was no longer staring at us, and Raine wasn't looking at us with wide eyes. The only person who was with me was Lexie, and she gave me subtle little things to do as she took my picture.

"I think I got it." She turned my phone toward me as I moved closer to her. "What do you think?"

"I think I need you to take all my pictures to make me look good."

She splashed water at me as she started back to shore. "You don't need me to make you look good, but text me the picture, and I'll run it through a couple of apps to make it great. Then you can post it."

"What's your handle?" one of the girls asked. She was beautiful with crazy long legs, but her voice was so high-pitched, it was like nails on a chalkboard.

The hair guy chuckled and patted me on the shoulder. "You don't have to answer."

"Sure, he does. He needs followers." Another girl sidled up next to me, trying to look at my phone.

"Girls leave him alone. You can look up Ryder later if you want. We need to get back to work," Lexie called out in a voice that let them all know she wasn't messing around. Was she jealous? I liked the idea of her being jealous of other women wanting me.

"How the hell does she know him?" one of the other girls whispered to the one with the high-pitched voice.

"I don't know, but she's one lucky bitch."

"Thanks for taking my picture and setting up my account." I dipped down and gave her a wet kiss promising more later.

Her gaze raked down my body, and she licked her lips. "I plan to take lots of pictures of you in the next couple of days. Ones you won't be able to post on Instagram."

"Holy fucking shit," someone murmured.

CHAPTER 9
RYDER

Watching the sun slowly slip down the horizon and the sky light up in beautiful shades of pinks and oranges with the turquoise waters as the backdrop, I pulled Lexie closer to me. Her head rested on my shoulder, where she'd been content for the last thirty or so minutes.

"I wish you didn't have to go tomorrow. This has been fun," she said wistfully out of nowhere.

More than fun. Every moment I spent with her, the more I fell for her. While that normally wouldn't be a bad thing, I wasn't sure when I'd see her again. I was booked until the end of the year when I then planned to take some time off to spend with my family for the holidays.

"We still have time to make it memorable. What do you say we go for a dip in the ocean?"

"Let's do it." She jumped up and quickly pulled off the t-shirt she'd been wearing to reveal her toned and inked body that had me drooling for the last two days. I guess we were skinny dipping as well. Not that I'd complain.

Slipping my shorts off, I threw them to the side and

chased after Lexie. She giggled as the water hit her tanned legs, and she turned back to look at me. I loved seeing her smile. It was infectious and made me wish I could see it every day. Grabbing her around the waist, I ran us deeper into the water until I knew she couldn't touch and would have to wrap herself around me. Lexie didn't disappoint. Her arms and legs circled me. Her hot center brushed my length, causing us both to gasp before she dipped down and slid her tongue across my parted lips.

"Have you ever had sex in the ocean before?" Her lips swept against mine as her hand wrapped around my cock and started to stroke.

"I have a feeling I'm about to." I bit down on her lip and pulled it into my mouth. As Lexie placed me at her entrance, I nipped down her neck. My tongue laved along her collarbone and swirled around one of her already hard peaks. The moment I slipped inside, she threw her head back and moaned. I could feel the vibrations all the way to the base of my cock. Wrapping one arm around her lower back, my other hand fisted in her hair to angle her just the way I wanted her. Heat rushed through every muscle of my being, and lust took hold of me. In a tone I'd never heard from me before, I commanded her, "Ride me."

Squeezing me with her legs, Lexie moved in a tantalizing rhythm as she swiveled her hips on the downstroke. Our lips brushed against each other as we panted and moaned out our pleasure. I cupped her full and perky breast in my hand, pinching and pulling on her nipple ring. With each tug, I felt her core clench around me, driving us closer and closer to euphoria. When heat shot down my spine, and my balls started to tingle, I pulled out, only to stroke my cock a few times before I shot my load into the water.

Lexie moaned as if she had another orgasm by herself. Looking up, I found her eyes trained on the hand still wrapped around my erection. "I love watching you touch yourself. There's nothing hotter than a man taking care of himself." If she only knew how often I jacked off at the thought of slamming into her tight pussy.

Pulling her back against my chest, I guided her mouth to mine. Our kiss was slow, hot, and wet as our tongues caressed each other. I rested my forehead to hers. "I think I love having sex in the water."

Lexie hummed, turning her head so that she could watch the rest of the sunset. It was beautiful but not nearly as stunning as she was. "Maybe someday we'll meet on another beach and go skinny dipping."

"It's a date." Kissing her temple, I turned us so we could watch the final rays of the sun slip beneath the horizon. "Speaking of dates, would you like to go out to dinner with me tonight? We can get cleaned up and find someplace dark and cozy to eat and have a couple of drinks."

"I think I'd be stupid to turn down a date with you."

Twenty minutes later, we were seated at a dimly lit table in the sand. There were only a few tables out on the beach that provided privacy. Both of us had drinks in our hands and smiles on our faces. "Did it bother you when all the women were trying to talk to me?" I asked after taking a large sip of my beer. I was indulging in my last night in Hawaii and having a beautiful woman on my arm. I couldn't afford to put junk in my body, but one beer wouldn't kill me.

Placing her margarita back on the table, Lexie's mouth turned down. "It is what it is."

Cocking my head to the side, I reached out and pulled her chair closer to mine. "What does that mean?"

"It means I know my place in the world, and I know I don't compare to those models." Picking up her drink, she drained half of it in one swallow.

"Can't you see they don't compare to you?"

"I'm not looking for compliments, Ryder." She sighed and signaled the waiter for another drink. "I don't have legs that go on for miles, and I've got more curves in my hips than they do in their entire bodies. I'm a mess. Look at me, I rarely do my hair and makeup."

"That's what I like about you. You're not fake. What you see is what you get."

Lexie snorted. "I'm just saying I'd understand why you'd talk to them. You have more in common with them."

"First of all, I wouldn't disrespect you by doing that. Remember, I'm a nice guy. And second, you're who I'm into. Not them." How could she not see that I only had eyes for her?

"Don't you want a woman your own age?"

My forehead pinched together. "I don't care that you're a few years older than me."

"A few years? Ryder, how old do you think I am?"

"Um…I don't know. Twenty-four or five?" One shoulder lifted. I had no idea how old she was. I did remember her kind of freaking out when I told her my age. She'd called me a baby.

"I'm more than a few years older than you by a lot." She eyed me as if she thought I was going to jump up and leave her there over the fact that she was older than me.

"How much is a lot?" Not that I cared. Maybe if someone had set us up on a blind date and told me her age first, but now I was enamored with her.

"I'm twelve years older than you. That puts me right in cougar territory. Oh God," she covered her face with her hands and laughed. "I never thought I'd say those words about myself."

"You're thirty-two?" Disbelief was evident in my tone. There was no way Lexie was thirty-two.

"A bit of a shock, huh?"

Shaking my head, I answered her honestly. "Age is just a number. I'm serious, I've never met anyone like you. You can't deny our chemistry, and that's all that matters to me." Our chemistry was insane. I'd never felt this way about anyone before. During the last few months, I'd had women throw themselves at me, and not once had I felt an ounce of the chemistry I felt with her. That was why I hadn't taken any of them up on their offers for a night of fun.

"I don't deny the way my body sings when you're near. Never once, with all the men I've encountered, have I felt this way." I didn't like hearing her talk about other men, just like I knew she wouldn't have liked it if I gave more than a passing glance at the models she worked with in the last couple of days. A dark shade of pink crept up her sun-kissed cheeks as she gulped down her margarita. "I thought Bella, Amber, or Drucilla would be more your type."

"Not to feed you compliments since you don't want them, but you're beautiful. Everything about you, so don't put yourself down. Those girls have nothing on you."

"If this restaurant wasn't so busy right now, I'd get under the table and blow you, but it will just have to wait until we're back at my place."

"Check," I called, motioning for our server.

"Ryder," she giggled, nudging me with her elbow. "We haven't even eaten yet."

"That's fine. I'd rather feast on you."

A slow grin grew into a mischievous one. "If you could only feel how wet I am for you."

"That's it, we're leaving." Standing up, I pulled out my wallet and threw down some money on the table before I dragged Lexie out of the restaurant. It was a good thing we hadn't traveled far from her bungalow because I wasn't sure if I could have waited any longer. The urgency that pulsed through my blood had me pulling her around to the back of her place and onto the lounger we'd left in the sand.

Pushing her down on the seat, I unbuttoned my shorts and let them slip down my hips. Kicking them out onto the beach, I stepped between her legs. My hands went into her hair and pulled her head back.

She eyed my straining erection and licked her plump lips. "Do you always go commando?"

"I wear enough underwear for shoots. Now open your mouth wide and suck me hard."

Lexie didn't hesitate, her hot tongue licked my blunt head and sucked it like a lollipop before taking all of me that she could. When I hit the back of her throat, she pulled back and looked up at me with watery eyes. She opened up her throat and took me down with hollowed cheeks as she sucked me off. Her tongue ran along the underside with each upstroke and swirled around my head before bobbing back down over and over again.

"Are you going to be a good girl and swallow, or do you want me to come all over your tits?"

Her answer was to suck me harder and for her hand to

go to my balls and start to massage them. My grip on her hair tightened as I held her in place and let loose a string of curses as I came down her throat.

Withdrawing, I wiped her mouth with my tip. Kneeling in front of her, my knees dug into the cool sand as I slowly pulled her sundress over her head. My tongue licked up the light pink triangle of fabric covering her pussy, causing Lexie to buck up off the chair and throw her head back.

"Now it's my turn for dinner."

LEXIE

"Are you sure you have time to take me to the airport? I could have taken an Uber."

"If I didn't want to take you, I wouldn't. This way, I can see more of the island in our hot rental van." I laughed because there was nothing hot about the van. It was utilitarian and got the job done, and that's all I cared about. "Unless you don't want anyone seeing you get out of it because I can understand that."

He laughed softly. "If you saw my car, you'd know I don't care. This beaut is a luxury."

"Wow, your car must be a total piece of shit then."

"Pretty much. Once things die down and I get back home, I plan to buy a new car and look for an apartment in LA."

"Where's home?" I chewed on the inside of my cheek. I

hadn't realized he didn't live in LA or that I knew so little about him.

"Washington State, up by Olympia. My family lives in a small town. It's gorgeous there, and I miss it something terrible." I felt his gaze look me up and down. "What's that look for?"

"I thought you lived in LA or New York. How does that work if you're up in Washington?"

"Oh," he chuckled. "I was staying on my friends' couches like a bum wherever a job took me. Now that I have some money saved up, I want to find a place of my own."

"When are you going to be back?" I tried to hide how curious I was to hopefully see him again.

"My last job is at the end of November. I'm taking December off to spend with my family, and then I'm back to work."

"Do you ever turn down any jobs?" He was going to get run down from all the travel he was doing.

"Not if I can help it. I'm establishing myself. You know how that is, right?" Taking one hand off the wheel, I placed it on his bouncing leg.

"While I understand, I'm worried that you'll get sick from being run down and traveling all the time."

"I take good care of myself. I make sure I get plenty of sleep, eat what I'm supposed to eat, workout, and take my vitamins. Next year, I'm hoping I won't have to work as much, but also, I don't want to couch surf for the rest of my life."

"You have nothing to worry about. How can you, when you're booked solid for the rest of the year and have some already for next year?"

"I'm sure you're just as busy," he retorted.

I didn't mean to upset him. "While I'm busy, I don't travel all that much. I do a majority of my work in my studio, and that's the way I like it. Travel is too stressful, and half the time, the models show up hungover because they think it's a vacation." He was silent, looking out the window as I drove, and I didn't like it. He had been so easygoing and sweet the last couple of days. Was this what he was really like? "Ryder," I sighed out his name, "I didn't mean to upset you. I understand why you're working so hard, and I commend you. Your drive is admirable. If only everyone in the industry were like you, it would make my job easier. I'm only worried about you." My hand tightened on his knee. "I like you. A lot. And I'd hate to see you get burned out and lose everything you've worked so hard for."

"Sorry, it's a touchy subject for me. My family doesn't have a lot of money, and my parents are always one payment away from losing their house ever since my mom was diagnosed with breast cancer."

"Oh my God, Ryder, is she okay?"

"Oh, yeah, she's in remission, but the medical bills took their savings, and I'd love to be able to help if I could. That's why I work so hard and save every penny I can."

"That's very commendable of you, but you won't be able to help if you get sick."

"I know," he huffed.

"Listen to me. I'm wise in my old age," I snickered. "I've been in the modeling world for a long time now, and if you miss a job or two because you're sick, word will get out. It's all about what people are saying about you. You can't afford to miss out —"

"I wouldn't miss."

"They don't want you on set sick as a dog either. I'm only telling you all this because I care, and I want to see you succeed. If there's anything I can ever do to help you, don't hesitate to pick up the phone and ask."

"Thank you. You've given me a lot to think about." The ring of sincerity in his voice let me know he wasn't upset by what I'd said.

"If you take the right jobs and the ones that pay the most, then you won't have to be on the go so much. Plus, you'll get to spend more time with your family." I hoped he took my advice. It wasn't uncommon for someone to be hot one season and gone the next, and I didn't want that to happen to Ryder.

Leaning over, Ryder kissed my cheek. "Thank you, Lexie. I promise I was listening to everything you said and took it in. I'll be smart, and it's nice to have someone on my side who understands how fickle this world can be."

Lacing his fingers through the hand I had resting on his knee, we drove the rest of the way to the airport in comfortable silence. Luckily, it was early enough that there wasn't much traffic or many dropping off in the unloading zone. My stomach twisted in knots when I realized I was going to miss Ryder. He was right. We had undeniable chemistry, but that didn't matter when he was half a world away most of the time.

Hopping out of the van, I watched as Ryder pulled his large duffel out of the back and placed it on the sidewalk. "Come here." He held his arms open wide, and I didn't hesitate to snuggle into his chest and let him wrap me in a warm hug. "While I didn't expect to see you here, it was the best surprise. Thank you for everything." His large hand cupped the back of my head as he kissed the top.

Tears stung the backs of my eyes, but I fought them back. I cried easily, and I didn't want him to take it as something it wasn't.

"This isn't goodbye, it's an I'll see you later." He frowned at the thought and pulled me tighter against him. "We just don't know we'll see each other, but I promise to keep in contact with you. And hopefully, we'll work together again."

"I have no doubt we'll work together again, and I'll talk to you soon." I smiled weakly at him. We had said before we'd stay in contact, but I knew he'd be busy, and in crazy time zones, so I expected nothing.

"I'll message you when I land in Moscow." He looked down at his phone, shaking his head. "I have no idea what time that will be since it's a long-ass flight."

"Don't stress about it. I know you'll be tired when you get there, so…"

"I said I'd message you, and I will. I always do what I say. Remember, I'm a good guy, and I'm doing it for purely selfish reasons since I have no friends on the road."

"Use me if you want." I slapped my hand against his hard chest. My voice was barely more than a whisper as I got out two simple words. "Goodbye, Ryder."

His smile was barely more than a twitch of his lips as his Caribbean blue eyes gazed into my own and darkened. I thought he was going to kiss me breathless by the look he was giving me, but instead, he kissed the corner of my mouth. His lips lingered there as he pressed his eyes closed and held me tight before he pulled back and grabbed his bag.

"Goodbye, Lexie."

I stood rooted to the sidewalk as I watched him walk away. We'd only gotten to know each other for a few days, so it shouldn't have been so difficult to say goodbye. Instead, it felt as if he'd taken a small part of me with him.

CHAPTER 10
LEXIE

2 Weeks Later

True to his word, Ryder texted me at two when he landed in Moscow. Since then, he'd called or texted about every other day when he got up. I wasn't sure how he did it because there was no way in hell I could wake up day after day at three or four in the morning to go workout. Let alone with the time zones. I didn't even work out per se; I hiked the trails around LA three to four times a week, and they kept me in shape and toned, and that was good enough for me. I didn't want to be stuck in a gym when I could enjoy the outdoors. I couldn't imagine how much time Ryder spent in the gym to look the way he did.

Raine had figured out it was Ryder who called every afternoon at four, so she tried to help me out so I could take his brief calls. Today, though, we were doing business stuff, and I'd been at my desk for hours emailing, scheduling, and ordering supplies. When my phone started to ring, and I saw Ryder's name pop up at two, I was worried something was wrong. Why the hell was he awake at one in the morning?

I stood from my desk and answered the phone as I started pacing. "What's wrong?"

Ryder's soft chuckle filled my ear. "What makes you think something is wrong?"

Making my way up to the roof for some air and sunshine, I stopped at my apartment door. It was cracked open, but I thought nothing of it. I had Raine grab my iPad earlier from upstairs, and she probably hadn't closed the door all the way. Closing the door, I slowly made my way up the stairs.

"It's one in the morning in Russia, and you're a good little boy who makes sure he gets all of his sleep."

"My shoot was over early, and we went out to celebrate. I thought I'd call you before I went to bed since I plan on sleeping in before I do some sightseeing tomorrow. What are you doing?"

"Working. Always working. I have a client who wants me to find the models for a big campaign they're doing. They want me to plan everything."

"Is that normal?"

"I've never had to do this much, but they've given me some of the details so I can pick a location. They want me to be creative with it and find the perfect models for it. First thing, I'm trying to find the perfect place and date that's in the time frame they've given me."

"Sounds like a lot of work, but it could be great for you."

"They are paying me an insane amount of money, which

I like. But I've only just started, and I know I don't want to organize this much ever again. It's so much work." I sat down on the edge of the pool and put my feet in the water.

"You'll do great at it; I know you will. I can let you go if you're too busy…" Ryder paused. I knew he didn't want to get off the phone, so I saved him.

"No, I needed the break."

"Lexie, I'm sorry to interrupt, but I noticed your door was open, and wanted to let you know." Raine looked unhappy to interrupt my time with Ryder.

Cocking my head to the side, I scrunched my nose at her. "Are you sure? It was open when I came up and I closed it. Let me go look. Maybe I need to send someone out to fix the door because I don't like the idea of it creeping open."

"Is everything okay?" Ryder asked from the other end of the line.

"My apartment door keeps opening today." I sighed with annoyance. "I thought it was Raine who left it open, but I guess not."

Ryder yawned, and it made me smile. He was like an old man and could barely stay up past eleven o'clock unless he was working or busying doing something else. "Maybe I should let you go so you can investigate." And so he could go to sleep, but I didn't say anything. "It will probably be a few days before I call again. I'll be headed to Rio on Thursday."

Another long flight. "I'm sorry we couldn't talk longer, but you should probably get to bed before you fall asleep on the phone. Maybe we'll talk this weekend once you get settled." I headed back downstairs to my apartment.

"I'll call, Lexie. I always call."

He did, but I couldn't trust how long that would last. It hadn't been that long since we saw each other.

"Good night, Ryder. Safe travels."

"Night," he replied before he hung up.

Placing my phone in the back pocket of my jean shorts, I opened the door to my apartment, my gaze immediately going to the window that had been replaced from when Ben jumped out of it. The cops hadn't found him yet, but I wasn't sure how hard they were looking. I had a feeling he wasn't a high priority. Raine had convinced me to get a restraining order against Ben, but since no one had been able to find him, they hadn't served him the paperwork, and a court date had never been set.

Walking cautiously around my apartment, I saw nothing out of place. I searched the places someone could hide, and they were all clear. Thinking about Ben stressed me out. I went back downstairs to find Raine sitting at my computer, typing.

"What do you say we get out of here and have a late lunch? I've been craving Mexican, and we can talk shop and brainstorm while we eat."

Raine's eyes lit up. I knew I'd won her over when I said Mexican food. She loved a good burrito, and I knew just the place for us to gorge on chips and salsa while getting our margarita on. "Let's go. I'll grab your iPad to take notes."

An hour later, we were sitting in our favorite Mexican restaurant, both of us with a margarita in hand. Raine had the iPad notes app open and ready. "Where do you think this shoot should be? Mathers wants it glamorous."

"I'm thinking Vegas. I need to find the right hotel or hotels and see if they'll be willing to work with us. We'll probably be working in the middle of the night when it's not as busy, so that means some long nights."

"I think if they hear that it will be for Skön and all the publicity they'll get—"

"They don't need any more publicity." I laughed and stuffed a chip in my mouth.

"It can't hurt to mention it." She was right, it couldn't hurt, but I doubted it would help. "Did you see that they want to be there for the shoot?"

"I did; that's why everything has to be perfect. They're paying the big bucks and giving me creative control. If I mess this up…"

Raine placed her hand on my arm. "You've got this. I know we don't have a long time to figure this out, but all your ideas so far have been perfect for Skön." After taking a healthy swallow, she continued. "I may have looked up who we're working with." Raine's eyes widened. "Have you seen him?"

"Mr. Jacobs?" I shook my head. "Is he ugly and fat?" I didn't care what he looked like as long as they paid. With the money they were willing to fork out, I wouldn't need to work for a few years.

"More like the exact opposite. He could be a model and…" She sucked her lips into her mouth.

"What?" I laughed at her. I had no idea what she wanted to say, but the look on her face, had me wanting to crack up.

"He's married to an older woman. That's his boss." She whispered the last part as if she was afraid, they'd hear her. I wanted to laugh at her, but I had no idea where she was going with this line of thought.

"Why does that matter?"

"I thought it was interesting and since you and Ryder—"

"There is no me and Ryder," I interrupted her. "Ever since we got back from Hawaii, you keep insinuating something, but I promise you there's nothing there. He's off becoming the next male supermodel, and I'm here where I want to be."

Raine nibbled on a chip as she stared across the table at me. "Why do you keep talking to him if there's nothing there?"

She had me there.

"I'm not saying I don't like Ryder because I do, but we're in two very different places in our lives. He's young and gorgeous, and I don't want to turn into some crazy jealous girlfriend because of all the beautiful women he'll be surrounded by, while I only get to see him a couple of times a year. He's a good guy, but eventually, he'll cheat."

"You don't know that. Not all men are cheaters."

All the ones who'd been in my life had been. "He has needs that should to be met."

"Didn't you say that he hadn't had sex with anyone else since the last time you saw him?" She threw my words from a couple of weeks ago back at me. "If you could have seen the way he looked at you when we were in Hawaii when you weren't looking." She rested her chin on her clasped hands and sighed dreamily. "I want a man to look at me that way."

"You will, but you have to put yourself out there to meet him." Raine was such a cutie, I wasn't sure how she didn't have a boyfriend or a long line of them waiting for her.

"Don't turn this on me. We're talking about you." She giggled into her drink.

"You wanted to talk about me. I was fine talking about the job and eating my weight in chips and salsa."

"Okay, just let me say one thing, and then I'll drop it." I motioned for her to go ahead. It wasn't like it would change my mind. "Don't rule Ryder out because he's young and traveling all the time because you might never find someone else that you have that kind of explosive chemistry with or that looks at you like you're the only person in the world."

Everything she said made sense, but I was going to take each day as it came. I wouldn't say no to Ryder if he wanted to be in a relationship even though I knew it wouldn't be easy, but I wasn't holding my breath either.

"Just eat your burrito and be quiet."

She aimed the smile that made everyone adore her at me, and I was instantly less annoyed. "You know I'm right."

Instead of answering her, I finished off my margarita and looked at pictures of hotels in Vegas to try and find the right one.

After finishing off her burrito, Raine started to shift in her seat nervously. "I'm sorry for upsetting you, but I don't want you to miss out on a great guy."

Finally looking at her, I patted her hand. "I know you didn't mean anything by it, but there's no use in thinking about feelings and hormones when I don't know if I'll ever see him again."

"He likes you. Of course, you'll see him again."

Raine really was naïve if she thought that. Ryder could easily find his soulmate when he got to Rio or his next location. "Let's focus on what Mathers wants because if we pull this off, you'll be getting a big bonus."

Her mouth popped open and hung in an 'O.' "Thank you, Lexie. That would be wonderful. Then I wouldn't have to have three roommates who annoy me to no end. I could probably have only one."

Maybe I needed to give her a raise. I couldn't imagine living with three other people, especially ones that got on Raine's nerves since she was one of the sweetest people I'd ever met. Nothing seemed to bother her, and yet these people did.

Eating the last bite of my fajitas, I patted my stomach. "I think we should get out of here before I have too much to drink and have to leave my car to take an Uber."

"I agree. I'll just wait until I get home to make my own." She sat up straighter in her chair. "That is if you don't need me."

"No, I'm good. I'll probably be on the internet searching for venues all night."

I paid the check, and Raine and I went our separate ways. She wanted to use the restroom before she had to drive home while I just wanted to get home. Maybe I'd swim a few laps in my pool before I got back to work.

Walking out to my car, I deleted all the emails that were trash and had started to read a new one from Mathers. They had given me a list of models they would like to see, but ultimately if I found better ones, to hire them. At least I knew what they were looking for. In the end, it would make my job easier.

As I was reaching for my car door, I was pushed to the side and pinned against the window by a hard body. "You're going to give me my shit, or I'm going to fucking end you," a familiar voice said above my head.

"Ben?" I tried in earnest to turn away until I felt something sharp at my throat. How had I been so wrong about him? Never in all our time together had he ever been violent. He was more of a lazy bum than anything else. "Why are you doing this? I don't know what you're talking about. I've been through all my things and didn't find anything."

"Don't play stupid. I told you this was life or death. Now, I'm giving you twenty-four hours, and then I'm coming for you."

"What are you looking for?" Maybe if I knew, I could get him out of my life once and for all, because after this I was never going to let him anywhere near me.

The knife he had to my throat dug in and I felt wetness start running down my neck and into my shirt. "I know you have my drugs, you stupid bitch."

"Lexie?" Raine shrieked. I could hear her feet on the concrete as she ran toward us. "Someone call 911."

I wanted to turn to her, but I couldn't without the knife going in deeper.

"Fuck, you always mess everything up." He pressed the knife harder, cutting a line down my throat before his rank breath was in my face. "Twenty-four hours for you to get me my stuff."

The next thing I knew, I was falling to the ground as Ben ran in the other direction, and Raine was kneeling beside me.

"Oh my god, you're bleeding." Tears streamed down her face. "Don't worry, the police should be here soon."

I couldn't feel anything, even though there was blood on the front of my shirt, my hands, and my knees. My head had hit the side of my car as I sat there waiting for something to happen with Ben.

I wasn't sure how long we sat there until an ambulance and the police showed up. It was all a blur as I sat stunned and tried to answer their questions. They told me I was probably in shock and wanted me to go to the hospital to make sure I was okay. All I could do was nod.

I thought I heard a phone ring, but there was too much going on around me. Looking to my right, I saw Raine talking on my phone, but I had no idea who she'd be talking to at a time like this. When she was done, Raine came over and stood by my side, her face streaked with tears.

"How are you doing?" She barely got the words out, she was so upset.

"Fine, but they say I'm in shock. They're going to take me to the hospital to check me out just in case."

"Do you want me to come with you?

"I don't know." I shook my head. This all felt like a dream. I'd never been assaulted before, and now Ben had attacked me twice. This time he'd been waiting for me to come out of the restaurant. "Can you drive my car so you can take me home?"

"Of course, anything you need."

"Thank you, Raine." I rested my head against her arm. I was starting to get tired. "You're a good friend. I don't know what I'd do without you."

"You might not think that after I tell you who I was on the phone with."

Lifting my head, Raine's body was held tight as she looked down at me. "Just spit it out because I have no clue who it would be. My family is dead, and you're my only friend."

Her eyes got glassy behind her glasses. "Please don't be

mad, but it was Ryder. He was calling you back, and I told him what happened." She bit her bottom lip. "You really should call him back. He seemed really upset when he heard you were hurt."

Holding my hand out, I tried to keep my voice calm. It wouldn't do any good for her to know how pissed off I was at her for speaking to Ryder. "Give me my phone, and I'll call him while I'm at the hospital since I'll probably be there a while." I spit the last part out.

Handing my phone over, she looked everywhere but at me. "Please don't be mad. What was I supposed to say?"

I guess I hadn't hidden my anger very well. "You shouldn't have answered my phone, no matter who it was."

Raine's hands went to her hips. "Why, so you could never tell him?"

"He's all the way across the globe. What would telling him do but make him worry?" Closing my eyes, I took a deep breath and let it out. "Let's just drop it. What's done is done, and I don't have the energy to argue with you."

"I'll see you at the hospital." Turning around, she walked over and got in my car without a backward glance. I wasn't going to feel bad for being mad at her for meddling in my life.

"Lexie," Ryder answered the phone worriedly. "Are you okay? Raine said—"

"She overreacted," I interrupted. "They brought me to the hospital to make sure I'm okay, which I am."

"The hospital? She didn't mention you were going to the

hospital. That sounds serious." I hated that he was worried about me for no reason.

"It's not. I only have one superficial cut, and they've already fixed me up. Now I'm just waiting to be discharged so Raine can drive me home." Only I didn't want to go home now. I was afraid Ben would show up tomorrow, demanding some mystical drugs.

"Your voice tells me something different. Talk to me, Lexie. You can tell me anything." Even all the way across the world, he could tell something wasn't right.

"I'm scared to go home." Tears filled my eyes, and my chin started to quiver. "He…Ben said he'd be back in twenty-four hours, and he wanted his drugs. But I…"

"Take a slow, deep breath." His deep voice soothed me. "He can't get you right now. Do you think he has drugs in your apartment?" he asked calmly.

"If you had asked me a month ago, I would have said no, but now I don't know. When we were together, he didn't do drugs, so I don't know why there would be drugs in my stuff."

"Okay, I don't know the law, but maybe you can have the cops come with a drug dog to see if it can sniff out any drugs if he hid some in your things."

"That could work. Maybe they can stake out my place and catch him. Only…"

"Only what?" He tried to pry the rest out of me.

I was usually a strong person, but Ben's attack had shaken me up more than I wanted to admit. "I don't want to be there. I don't want to be anywhere near here right now. Maybe I need to go back to Hawaii. It was nice when we were there. Or go to—"

"Come to Rio and stay with me. You can be on a plane

tomorrow morning, and we can spend the week together. That would be nice, wouldn't it?"

He couldn't be serious. I didn't want to run away from my problems—but I also didn't want to hurt anymore…or die.

"Pack a suitcase full of bikinis and condoms."

"Have you already used all the condoms you bought in Oahu?" I wasn't sure I wanted to see him if he had been having sex with other people in the last couple of weeks.

"I'm not even going to dignify that with a response. If we're together more than a couple of days, we'll need more."

"What if I'm on my period the whole time?"

I wanted to laugh at the grunt that filled the phone and then the short pause. "It will be the perfect time to get into your ass."

It was my turn to choke. I wasn't sure if I was ever letting Ryder back there. He'd probably do irreversible damage.

"Or…" He chuckled, and I loved the way it sounded. I liked how, for a minute, he made me forget about Ben and him attacking me. "We can do other things. I like hanging out with you. Plus, there's always oral."

"There is that," I agreed.

"I'll be at the Windsor. It's probably not as nice as what you're used to, but—"

"Do you have to stay there?" If I was going to go on a vacation or run away from my ex, I wanted to stay somewhere nice. There was no doubt in my mind the hotel he was staying at would be fine, but I wanted luxury.

"Does that mean you'll come?"

Did it?

"Only if we don't have to stay at whatever hotel they have set up for you." I was itching to start searching for a place. Was I really going to run off to Rio with Ryder for the week?

"I…I don't think they'll shuttle me to the locations if I'm not staying at the hotel, but I don't think it's mandatory I stay there. I am an adult."

"Fine, I'll rent a car too. We'd need one, anyway. What time does your flight leave?"

"At five-thirty, I…let me look. I get in at six forty that night. It's a long flight, but if I have you waiting for me there—"

"Cool your jets, big boy. Your enthusiasm is infectious, so when I get home, I'll look into flight times. Why don't you text me your flight info, and I'll do the same once I have some information to give you?"

"You're really going to come?" he asked in awe. "Is it bad that I'm kind of happy you were attacked so I can see you again?"

Laughing, I answered. "Yes, it absolutely is."

"I'm sorry, Lexie. I really am. I'm just happy to spend more time with you. You know I'm not happy you're hurt, right?"

"I know," I reassured him. "Don't worry about it. I should probably let you go so you can get some sleep. Enjoy your last day in Moscow, and I'll see you in a couple of days."

"Now that I know you're okay, I am about ready to fall on my face, I'm so tired." He laughed like a drunk person down the line, making me smile. "Good night, Lexie. I'll see you soon."

"Thanks for making me feel better. I appreciate it more than you know."

"Hey, Lexie," he called as I was about ready to hang up, "if you need anything, call me. I'm here for you."

He was, until he wasn't.

CHAPTER 11

RYDER

RIO

2 Days Later

For the last forty-eight hours, I'd been a mixture of worried and elated. Lexie's situation with her ex was troubling, to say the least, and I couldn't do anything to help her. I hated how much I missed while I was gone, but I knew if I wanted to be able to help my parents, I needed to make money by taking pretty much every job that was offered to me. Lexie's advice about getting sick and burned out ran through the back of my mind. I knew she was right, and after this year, I would slow down and analyze each offer, but until then, I had to keep pushing and fulfill the obligations I already had.

Stepping out of baggage claim, I couldn't hide the grin that I'd been pushing down for the last two hours of my flight. While I'd be busy for some of the time, I was excited Lexie had agreed to spend the week with me. It was lonely being a tourist in a city where you couldn't speak the language, and what better way to enjoy the sights than with a beautiful woman at my side. In actuality, I was surprised she took me up on my offer.

Looking around, I searched for Lexie. She wouldn't be hard to spot with her turquoise hair and inked skin. Maybe this time I would ask her if her tattoos had any meaning. They were beautiful watercolors that fit her perfectly. She had been my inspiration for finally getting inked for the first time. It also wasn't a coincidence that the stars I got along my side were the color of her hair.

When I finally spotted her, Lexie's head was down, and her hair was a curtain hiding her beautiful face, with her arms wrapped around herself. She moved to the side as someone passed by her, and I could see her eyes shifting from side to side as if she was afraid that at any given moment, someone in the airport might assault her. In the past, she was always so self-confident, but in that moment, she was broken. While I knew the attack on her was going to affect her after hearing her voice, I had no idea it would crack her tough exterior.

I made sure to walk up to her as slowly as possible so that she would see me coming. Scaring her first thing wouldn't do her any good. Adjusting my duffle on my shoulder, I wasn't sure how to address her. I shouldn't have been nervous, though. The second I was within reaching distance, her head lifted, and her bright blue eyes twinkled up at me.

That was when I saw the long red mark on her neck, the evidence of the knife wound her ex had given her. There was a butterfly bandage on one part, probably where he'd dug the blade in, and the rest had glue covering it. Her wound was worse than I'd imagined. Worse than she had led me to believe over the phone, but I should have known it was bad after how upset Raine had been when she told me about it. Maybe she was self-conscious about it, and that's why she'd been looking down, but I didn't think that was it. I thought my first hunch was correct, and she was afraid. I wasn't going to let her know that it bothered me to see her beautiful skin marred and how I hated I hadn't been there to protect her. It would heal, and so would she.

Pulling her into an all-consuming hug, I kissed the top of her head. "Hey, beautiful."

"Hey, dimples," she answered back, her arms holding me a little tighter as she rested her head against my chest. I couldn't help but laugh. "What are you laughing about?"

"I think you're the only one who likes my dimples. When I was young, I used to get made fun of for having them."

"Well, those guys were assholes, and I can say with the utmost certainty that I am not the only one who loves your dimples. I'm surprised there isn't a fan page for them yet," she said, her voice muffled with her face buried between my pecs.

Pulling back, I smiled down at her knowing good and well that my damn dimples would pop out. "You're just saying that to stroke my ego."

"I'm really not, but I do love them. I'd claim them as mine if I could." The tip of her finger stroked my right dimple. "And don't tell me you're not showing these to anyone but me."

"It would be a lie if I said I wasn't." Someone shoved me

from behind, and it was like a snap of the fingers, and we weren't alone anymore. Whenever I was around Lexie, the world seemed to fall away, and it was only us. "What do you say we get out of here?"

"Ugh, yes, please. I hate airports." She eyed my duffle. "Is that all your stuff?"

"Yeah, I don't need much." I threw my arm around her shoulders. "How many bags did you bring?"

Her arm wrapped around my waist as we left. "A big suitcase and an overnighter for my carry-on."

"How many bikinis did you bring?" A low laugh came out as I joked with her. I didn't think she'd actually bring only swimsuits and condoms, although I wouldn't have minded.

"Probably like fourteen, give or take. I own an insane amount that I don't use often enough."

"Well, we'll have to change that and make sure you wear each one you brought. Where'd you park?" I asked as we stepped off the curb.

"Ryder, man. Over here," one of the models called. I looked over to see him standing by a van waving us over.

With my arm still around Lexie, we walked over to Parker and a van full of bodies and equipment. "What are you doing, man? Your ride's here." I liked Parker. I'd done a couple of shoots with him before. Where he had looks, unfortunately, he had no brains.

"I'm going with Lexie, but I'll see you in the morning."

"But your ride." His brows pulled down as if he was trying to solve an impossible math problem.

"I know. We've got a car. I cleared it with Tom, so don't worry."

"Who are you?" he asked in his best seductive tone directed at Lexie.

I could feel Lexie's body shake against mine as she held back her laughter. She obviously wasn't falling for his charm.

Lana stopped by Parker's side and looked Lexie and me up and down with a sneer. "That's Lexie Keene, Parker. I can't believe you don't know who she is. She's one of the top fashion photographers." With the compliment, you would have thought the words coming out of Lana's mouth would have sounded nice, but they came out in an irritated bitchy tone. I wondered if Lana knew how much Lexie didn't like her. I had a feeling she did.

Parker's eyes widened as his mouth fell open. Not that it was hard to shock him, but it was always comical. "You're Lexie Keene?" He held his hand out to shake hers and proceeded to shake it the whole time he spoke. "I've been dying to work with you. How can I make that happen? Wait, are you the photographer for the Romadi shoot?"

Lana rolled her eyes as she left her bags on the sidewalk and got inside the van.

"I'm only here on vacation, but I'm sure I'll see you around." Turning to look at me, she asked in a quiet voice. "Are you ready to go? You must be hungry."

I was starved. I hadn't eaten anything in hours. I wasn't about to put the airline's food into my body, so I was on the verge of ravenous. "Starved."

"Where are you going? Maybe we can all go to dinner together." Parker inviting himself was annoying. I didn't want to hurt his feelings because he was nice to me, and I liked to hang out when we were working together, but there was no way we were having dinner with him, Lana, or anyone else.

"Oh, I didn't know Ryder would be flying with others, so I only made the reservation for the two of us. Maybe next time." Lexie rested her hand on my waist and pinched my side.

"We didn't fly together. I've been here for like two hours waiting for Lana to get here."

Stupid. That was the only word that could describe him for waiting in an airport for two hours. Although I would have waited for Lexie if I'd arrived sooner. Maybe they were hooking up.

Lexie turned to me fully, her mouth pinched. "Did you fly with Lana?"

"Not from Moscow, I think she got on in Amsterdam," I shrugged the shoulder without my bag on it. "I didn't see her on the flight."

She turned to the van and narrowed her eyes at Lana, who was peering through the window at us.

"Okay." I started to pull Lexie away. I didn't really understand her disdain for Lana, and while she was normally professional, I had a feeling she might lose her shit on Lana if she provoked her in even the slightest way. "I'll see you tomorrow morning." Parker made some confused noise as we walked off. When we were out of earshot, I asked, "You want to tell me what that was about?"

"The way she uses everyone within a ten-mile radius drives me nuts. Parker was sitting there for two hours waiting for her." She shook her head, her mouth in a thin line. "I have no doubt it was her idea. She's known to try to sleep her way to the top, and since she can't have sex with me, she doesn't hide how shitty of a person she is around me."

I remembered when I first met them both in Lexie's studio, and Lexie thought I wanted to have sex with Lana. I knew that if I had fallen prey to Lana, I wouldn't have my blue-haired girl by my side now, and I'd never been more thankful.

"Do you really have reservations somewhere?" She'd only been in Rio since early this morning.

She stopped us by an old Jeep. "No, but there was no way in hell I was going to eat dinner with them. I'd rather stab my eyeballs out than eat with Lana."

I chuckled to myself. "Is this your rental car?"

"Yep, get in because I really am hungry. I fell asleep when I checked in and haven't eaten all day. I figured we can eat at the hotel tonight unless there's someplace you want to go."

"That's fine. I'm sure they can make me some chicken and vegetables."

She groaned. "That's got to be hella boring."

"It does get old sometimes, but I splurge every once in a while. I plan on eating whatever I want in December when I take time off." I couldn't wait to eat my mom's zucchini muffins and her sesame noodles. "Are you regretting coming now that you know Lana's here?"

"She may not be my favorite person, but I'll live. At least I don't have to work with her." She started up the Jeep and pulled out of the parking space.

"Were you surprised that she said you're one of the best photographers?" I certainly was.

"I don't think I've ever heard anyone say something so nice and have it come out of their mouth like an insult."

"I thought the same thing." I had to laugh at that. Reaching over, I grabbed her hand and placed it on my thigh. "I'm glad you're here." Giving her hand a squeeze, I asked. "Tell me, are you okay?" I was worried about her after what Raine told me on the phone and seeing her neck.

"It's nice to be away. There's no way Ben's going to find me here, and I get to sit on the beach, relax, and look at your pretty…" Her gaze raked over me from head to toe. Her eyes darkening with each inch she took in. "All of you is gorgeous. Inside and out."

If she kept looking at me the way she was, I was going to jump her the second we got out of the Jeep. The problem was, I didn't think she'd try to stop me. It would be my luck to get arrested for indecent exposure or worse my first night here. Needing to change the subject, I asked, "Have you talked to Raine to find out if anything's happened?"

She shook her head, and her voice took on an uneven tone. "No, after she dropped me off at the airport, she was heading out of town. I don't want her to get hurt in case Ben followed her home one night and finds out where she lives." Looking over at me, she frowned. "This all still seems like a dream until I see myself in the mirror, or I accidentally touch my neck." Her hand rose as if she was going to touch the cut but thought better of it.

Pulling up to the hotel, I could smell the saltwater in the air as I took everything in. It was dark so I couldn't tell much, but I knew the hotel was much nicer than the place the agency had booked.

Hopping out of the car, Lexie handed her keys to the valet and came around to my side. Slipping her hand through my arm, she pointed to my bag. "Can you have that taken up to my room? We're going to go eat in the restaurant and don't want to lug it around."

"Of course, Ms. Keene. I'll happily place it in your room." The short, stocky valet slipped my bag from my shoulder and placed it over his own.

"Perfect." She handed over a tip and pulled us inside the hotel in the direction of the restaurant. "Under normal circumstances, I would order room service, but I know we both need food, and I also know the second we step foot inside our room, our clothes are going to come off, and all thoughts of food will be forgotten."

"Do you take me for someone who's easy to get into bed?"

The hostess gave us the side-eye, and both Lexie and I clutched onto each other as we burst out laughing.

"Are you telling me differently? Is it normally hard for women to seduce you into their beds?"

The topic made me uncomfortable, but I didn't want Lexie to think I was a manwhore. I knew the stigma that came along with looking the way I looked, but I was the furthest thing from it. The way we hooked up the first time probably didn't help her opinion of me either. There was something about the woman on my arm that made my primal needs take over. I was inexplicably drawn to her.

After the hostess showed us to our table that looked out onto the dark ocean waters, I cleared my throat, ready to confess when a young waiter came to take our drink order.

"Is the water here safe to drink?" I whispered across the table to Lexie.

She turned to the waiter and asked. "Is your water filtered?"

He blushed as he answered in a heavy accent, "Yes, minha senhora, it is."

Our waiter only had eyes for Lexie, and I didn't blame him. There was no one like her, and that made her all the more alluring.

"Two waters then, please."

"Do you want to hear the specials for tonight?"

"Oh, no, that's okay. Ryder here will be eating grilled chicken with whatever veggies you have. No butter." She looked at the menu for only a moment before she continued. "I'll have a bacon cheeseburger, medium well, with the truffle fries. Wait, do I want onion rings instead? Which is better?"

"The fries, minha senhora, there are the best in the city."

Lexie gave him a disbelieving look. "We'll see about that. I'll have the fries with my burger. Did I get your order right?"

"Yeah, not that there's much to get wrong. I'm feeling a little risky tonight, so can you make it grilled teriyaki chicken?"

The waiter glanced at me and then back to Lexie. "We can make whatever you want."

"Perfect, make it teriyaki then."

"Very good, senhor." He wrote something down on the ticket and then gave us a little bow before scurrying off.

"Is it going to bother you that I'm eating yummy delicious food in front of you while you eat your boring chicken?" She bit her bottom lip to hide her smile.

"Will I probably want a bite? Yes, but I can control myself when it comes to food." I leaned forward and lowered my voice. "When it comes to you, I seem to have a harder time holding myself back."

Placing her hand on top of mine, her eyes flashed a dark shade of blue. "Good, because it's one of the things I like most about you."

After our waters were placed on the table, I cleared my throat and tried again with what I wanted to clarify. "Before, when you asked about women seducing me into their beds..." I looked down at her hand on top of mine and went for it. It wasn't like she'd tell me to fuck off after learning the truth. "I want you to know there haven't been many women. I'm not a manwhore, I promise you."

"Is that what you think my opinion is of you?" She laced our fingers together with her mouth set in a thin line.

"In all honesty, I don't know. What I do know is that's what people expect of me." I'd traveled a great deal with my job and had women hit on me in almost every city. What they didn't expect was for me to turn them down.

"That's not what I expect, and while I love your passion, I don't really want to hear about all the women you've shared it with. I'm sure you can understand."

"I do understand. I hate the thought of you with other men, but I know it's happened. You weren't a virgin when we met."

"And for that, I'm glad. You and your big dick are not friends to the virgins of the world."

Of course, that was the moment the waiter brought our food out to us. Quickly placing our dishes in front of us, he asked if we needed anything else and hightailed it away from our table.

"You're going to give our waiter a heart attack if you don't stop." I tried to say it seriously, but my laughter won out.

"Oh please, he's had to of heard worse."

"I'm sure he'll be hanging around to see what else he can hear."

"Oh, he'll come back all right, just to hear more." She shook with laughter.

"Probably to see more of you. He's so got a crush on you. Not that I blame him."

Her eyes lit up. "Do you think I'm teenage boy spank bank material?"

"I think you're any male's spank bank material," I told her truthfully.

Lexie leaned back in her seat, cheeseburger forgotten. "Have you pleasured yourself to the thoughts of me?" Her brows lifted to her hairline.

"Almost every day that we've been apart."

Her mouth inched up at the sides until she flashed her white smile and clasped her hands together. "Tell me more. What do you think about?"

"Do you not think about someone when you get yourself off?" I'd love to hear all about her sexual fantasies.

"We're not talking about me right now. I want to hear all about you and what you're picturing." Picking up her cheeseburger, Lexie took a big bite out of it and moaned loudly. It rivaled the sounds she made when I was pleasuring her and made my dick swell. "This is so fucking good." Holding it out to me, she asked. "Do you want a bite?"

Rolling my eyes at her, I cut a piece of chicken and placed it in my mouth. It wasn't horrible, but it didn't cause me to moan. "How do you expect me to keep looking like this if I eat cheeseburgers all day?"

"Sucks to be you. Now back to you getting yourself off thinking about me." She slicked a fry through ketchup and plopped it in her mouth. Thank god she didn't moan this time.

"I think about you sucking my cock our last day together, our first time, and the way you rode me in the water; those are my go to's. What about you?"

"Oh, I play a slide show of all our times together, and sometimes I make up things that I hope to do in the future with you."

"Anal," I supplied.

Tilting her head to the side, she looked at me like I was insane. "Crazily enough, that hasn't been one of them."

"While I love talking about this, I'd rather not sit here with my dick about ready to break my zipper. How did we even get on this topic?"

"The waiter. Let's talk about something not sexy like stinky feet."

"That does it," I laughed as I shifted in my seat to get comfortable. I decided it was probably better to spit out what I wanted to say so there wouldn't be any more interruptions or talk that led to me getting hard. "I've only been with three women."

Lexie was mid-chew when I dropped my bombshell on her. She sat her cheeseburger on her plate and patted her mouth with her napkin without ever taking her eyes off me.

"Okay…that was unexpected."

"Why?" The one word came out harder than intended.

"Are you just naturally gifted in all areas?" My brows pinched together, and she must have seen the question on my lips because she answered me with her next words. "To put it bluntly, you fuck like you've been doing it all your life. Like you've been with at least a hundred women."

I didn't understand.

"You know how to pleasure a woman, or I should say, me. Easily. It doesn't seem hard for you in the least. It's like you know exactly what my body wants, and the raw passion you exude—"

"I don't know what to say. I've only ever been that way with you," I cut her off. "Yes, I pleasured the women I've been with, but it's different with you. When I'm with you, something deep inside of me takes over, and I go with my instincts."

Lexie sat quietly for a few moments. I wasn't sure if I'd stunned her into silence or not, so I continued to eat my food. I glanced up at her a few times, and when she picked up a fry and ate it, I thought she wasn't going to say anything until she placed her hands on the table like she was bracing herself.

"I'm not going to say how many men I've been with unless you really want to know, but I can tell you this…" My smile dropped. I definitely didn't like thinking of her with other men, so it was probably wise not to know the number. "While I've had good sex, the sex with you is amazing. It's beyond amazing. It's the best I've ever had. I don't think there are words to describe it."

"It's our undeniable chemistry. I can feel it all the way over here."

Picking up a fry, she rubbed it over her lips like it was a tube of lip gloss or the tip of my cock. "I agree, but I'd like to feel something else up close and personal." Her gaze flicked to my mouth and then lower before coming back up again to meet my eyes. "What do you say? Are you ready to blow this popsicle stand?"

"I'm ready for you to blow me."

CHAPTER 12
LEXIE

Stepping off the elevator, Ryder wrapped his hand around mine and pulled me down the hallway. His large stride making it difficult to keep up with my short legs.

"It might help if you knew which room we're staying in." Ryder's steps faltered in the middle of the hallway as pink crept up his stubble. "We're in room 1120."

He looked around the hallway for a moment before he took off again, dragging me with him. Slipping the keycard out of my purse, I jammed it in the card reader and waited for it to light up green. Stepping inside, I thought Ryder was going to throw me down on the bed, but instead, he looked at the room in awe.

Making his way to the sliding glass doors that led out onto the balcony, he looked over his shoulder at me. "I can guarantee you this is way nicer than where I was going to stay."

"My main requirement was a room with an ocean view. If you haven't figured it out yet, I love to fall asleep listening to the waves."

Opening the balcony door, salty air rushed into the room. "Why don't you live on a beach back in California?"

"Because I couldn't afford any buildings to run my studio. When I bought my place, I knew I'd eventually renovate the second floor into an apartment for me to live in. I have to say it's been nice not having my drive take almost forty minutes every day."

"Makes sense. Maybe someday you can live on the beach." Ryder leaned over the rail. There wasn't much to see in the darkness, but you could hear the waves crashing, and it was music to my ears.

"That's the dream." I walked out onto the balcony and rested my arms on the railing beside his and breathed in the air.

One arm wrapped around my waist and pulled me in front of him, my back to his front. Caging me in with his hands on the railing on either side of me, his hot breath tickled my ear. "I'm glad you came."

Reaching around, I pulled him closer until his body was plastered to mine. "Me too. All my worries disappeared the moment I got off the plane."

Feverish kisses trailed down my neck as his hands moved from the railing to slide underneath my t-shirt until his palms cupped my breasts. "I missed you in my arms, my sexy Lexie."

I loved his nickname for me. It still astonished me he thought I was sexy, but I believed him when he said it. Raine was right about the way Ryder looked at me. There was no hiding how into me he was.

Turning around in his arms, my fingers immediately went to the hem of his shirt and pulled it over his head. My hands skimmed down the soft skin over hard muscle until I reached the waistband of his jeans. Flicking the button, I reached down to be met with his impressive length. The first time I'd gone down on him, I was surprised I was able to take him all the way in. Now my mouth watered at the thought of pleasuring him.

Ryder guided me around a table and into a chair before he did the fastest strip show known to man. Standing before me, his cock bobbed as if anticipating my waiting mouth. Wrapping my hand around his length, I stroked the velvet over steel that twitched in my hand. Still, I had no idea how he went without sex for so long. When Ryder was around me, he was like a horny teenager.

Leaning forward, I licked the tip and swirled my tongue around. Ryder sucked in a sharp breath and fisted my hair in his hands. He was done taking this slowly and took over. I let him fuck my mouth. His thrusts were deep, hitting the back of my throat time and time again. His grip on my hair tightened as I felt him swell in my mouth.

"Your mouth is heaven." He let out a deep moan that soaked my panties. It was so damn sexy. Pulling out with a pop, he demanded. "Take off your shirt, I want to paint your perfect tits with my cum."

In a matter of seconds, I had my t-shirt off and my bra on the ground as I watched his hand stroke up and down his length. His grip was brutal when he squeezed the tip and let out another panty-melting moan.

My hands went to his tapered hips and grabbed his superb ass as I licked his tip. With his hand still in my hair, Ryder pulled my head back as stream after stream of his cum coated my chest and neck. His gaze was transfixed as he watched his hands rub the thick warm cream into my skin.

Ryder studied me for a moment as if he was trying to decide on something. He nodded once to himself before he claimed, "Now you're mine."

My brows rose. This was new and confusing, but I decided to play along with him. "What do I have to do to make you mine?"

A slow seductive smirk came over his face, and when that dimple popped out, I almost melted in that very spot. "You want to mark me?"

That did sound fun. Although I wasn't sure where I could mark him that it wouldn't be seen. I guess I'd have to get creative.

Running my hands up his muscular thighs, I brushed over his semi-erect cock and up his ridged abs. "I do like the sound of that. I'll have to be extra creative on how and where." Leaning forward, I nipped at his chin, causing those dimples to flash at me again.

"I could get a tattoo?"

The corner of his mouth tipped up while my eyes nearly bugged out of my head. My mouth repeatedly opened and closed without anything coming out. I didn't know what to say or how to respond. Did he mean a tattoo in general, and I would be there when he got it, or did he mean my name or something that symbolized me?

"Don't implode over it." His eyes glittered with amusement. "It's something I've been thinking about for a while now. I was thinking of a camera on the inside of my bicep. For me, you've always been the one who started my career, and now we have this." His long arms pulled me up and into his warm chest. "I don't know where this is going, but I don't want to ever forget you or where I started."

Without realizing it, my hand cupped his face. The way

he looked down at me, so open and honest, wasn't something I was used to. The blue of his eyes was like a crystal ball, begging me to never look away. I couldn't believe Ryder wanted to remember me for the rest of his life. I wasn't sure how I felt about that. "That's a big commitment. You should never get ink that you're not one hundred percent sure you want forever. Plus, you've got to think it's going to be photographed over and over again. What are you going to tell others when they ask you about it?"

"That it's a representation of my life that I like. How else would you suggest I show it?"

"I don't know," I answered softly as my thumb caressed his cheekbone. One moment it was sexy times, and the next Ryder was talking about marking his body for life to remember me. I was flattered, truly, but I was afraid he'd come to regret it down the line. At least he wasn't talking about getting my name inked on him.

My finger traced the inside of his bicep as I imagined a camera there. When I looked up to meet his eyes, his pupils flared, and his lips parted. "I like the idea of being with you forever."

"Good." His voice was deep and husky as he said that one word. "Why don't we go get dirty again in the shower before we get clean?"

"Mmm," I hummed. "I like the way you think."

Leaving our clothes out on the balcony, we stepped into the cool room. Goosebumps erupted across my skin as I rushed into the bathroom and quickly turned on the water. Ryder was right behind me, pinning me against the cold glass wall of the large shower. His tongue licked a trail from my shoulder up to my ear. His teeth nipped at my earlobe before his hot tongue eased away the sting. The way he made my body feel was unlike any other. I wasn't sure how I was going to let him work while we were here. I wanted to feel him with me the entire time. As his body pressed into mine, warming me up, his husky voice sent shivers down my spine. "Thank you for coming and letting me stay with you."

Opening the door to the shower, I stepped into the spray bringing Ryder along with me. I could only stand there as I watched water darken his hair, and droplets trail down his defined chest. He was a masterpiece, and for the next week, he was all mine.

Spotting a ledge in the shower, I pushed Ryder over to it with a plan in mind. He quirked a brow but didn't argue as I manhandled him into the corner. Stepping onto the ledge, I tugged Ryder until we were skin to skin. Now that I was on the step, we were better suited for a little shower sex.

"I can't do a condom in here." His hard length slid through my folds and hit the center of my pleasure, causing me to jerk and the tips of my breasts to tease against his firm chest.

"You can pull out or if you don't feel—"

Ryder's mouth crashed against mine as if he'd been dying to kiss me. As fast as he'd come, he pulled back with a devilish smile. Leaning in, his warm tongue swept slowly across the seam of my lips. His breath ghosted across my face. Tipping my head back, I opened for him, allowing him access to what we both desperately wanted. Plunging his tongue in at the exact moment, he impaled me with his cock, we both moaned. I'd missed feeling him inside of me, stretching me, filling me to the brim. He pulled my bottom lip between his teeth, and my sex spasmed around him.

With each precise thrust, the base of his cock hit my

bundle of nerves and my ring. It was the best decision I'd ever made getting that rod through my clit. The pleasure it brought me was unlike anything I'd ever felt up until that moment.

"What you do to me," Ryder growled before he took my nipple into his mouth and sucked hard. The sting and the pleasure brought me over the edge. My pussy clenched around his thick rod as I threw my head back in bliss. It was true what they said; I saw fireworks go off behind my eyelids as he kept hitting me over and over again, drawing out my pleasure.

Pulling out, Ryder trapped his cock between us and let it slide over my wet body until he shot his load across my stomach. His eyes were dark with lust as he stared down at me. No one had ever looked at me the way he did, and with each time, I wanted more from him. More than I should have after only knowing him a short time.

Stepping away and helping me down off the ledge, Ryder pulled a warm towel off the rack and wrapped it around his tapered waist. The sight of it hanging low on his hips and his 'V' so prominently displayed had me ready to go again. Taking another towel, he set about drying me off inch by inch until not a drop of water was left on my body. He took his work seriously, making me fall even harder for him. When he was done, he asked me to bend down so he could wrap my hair up in the towel to dry. "Let's go to bed. I've got to be up bright and early tomorrow."

Silently we moved into the bedroom side by side. I slipped under the plush comforter while he pulled a charger out of his bag and plugged it into the socket on the nightstand beside mine. Ryder walked over to the sliding glass doors and cracked it open enough that we could hear the crashing of the waves.

My stomach fluttered at his thoughtfulness and knowing he'd been listening to me earlier.

Walking around to the other side of the bed, he slipped in beside me. His lean frame cradled mine as he reached over me to turn off the light, and then settled back behind me and pulled the covers up to our shoulders. With our legs tangled together and his arm draped over my waist, I pulled his hand up to rest between my breasts so I could hold on to it as I fell asleep. My eyes, which were already heavy from being sated, fluttered closed with a smile on my lips as Ryder nuzzled the skin of my neck before placing a soft kiss there.

CHAPTER 13
LEXIE

"ARE YOU SURE YOU DON'T MIND ME TAKING THE JEEP?" Ryder brushed a stray strand of hair from my face as he sat on the side of the bed.

I looked to the sliding glass doors and was met with darkness. "It's not even light out yet. I'm happy staying here and sleeping. If you're not back by the time I'm up, I'll head down to the beach and read a book."

Leaning down, he cradled my cheek in the palm of his hand. Brushing his full lips across mine, Ryder's minty breath ghosted across my face. "Go back to sleep, and I'll see you later."

I watched him pick up his cellphone and the keys off the nightstand and quietly walked out of the room. Once I heard the hotel door click closed, my eyes fell shut and didn't open until the sun reflected off the crystal blue waters, lighting my room.

Turning over, I was shocked to find Ryder lying on the bed next to me with one of my romance novels in his hands.

Setting the book down on the other side of him, Ryder turned on his side, wrapped his arm around me, and pulled me flush against him.

"Good morning, sleepyhead." He kissed the side of my head. "I thought for sure you'd be sitting on the beach with a tropical drink in your hand by the time I was on break. Imagine my surprise to find you curled up under the covers."

Snuggling into his chest, I yawned. "Why didn't you go back to sleep?"

"And pass up reading a romance novel?" His light chuckle sent shivers through my whole body. "Is that what women want from men?"

"What book were you reading?" I had brought quite a few with me, and they ranged from sweet to dark romance. He picked up the book and showed me the cover of a bully romance. "We definitely don't want our men like that, but we do like to read about them. I would never tolerate a man treating me the way he does. I like good guys." Now, I amended silently.

He let out a puff of laughter. "I was worried that's how you expected men to treat you."

I couldn't help but laugh. Did men really think we wanted our lives to play out like they did in books? "I don't expect my life to be like a romance novel. Good or bad."

"Good to know."

"What time to do you have to be back?"

Looking at his phone, Ryder's lips turned down. When his beautiful blue eyes landed on me, they were almost sad. "An hour and a half, so that means I have to head back in an hour. We broke to eat lunch. I was actually surprised they gave us so long, but I guess they did have to move everything to a new location."

I wanted to ask about Lana, but I didn't want to ruin our time with talk about her. "Have you eaten lunch yet?"

"Nah, I was waiting to see if you'd wake up."

"What were you going to do if I didn't wake up before you left?"

He shrugged with me in his arms. "Something quick. It's not like I can eat a whole lot either way."

Heaven forbid the man eat a hamburger.

"Where is your shoot?" Please say the beach. I repeated over and over again.

"This afternoon, it's at a waterfall. They told us it's a bit of a hike to get to it. Why?"

"Do you think there's a place I can camp out and chill, or should I just head down to the beach and wait for you to get back?"

"I can't say, but hanging out at a waterfall could be cool." His arms tightened around me. I had a feeling Ryder wanted me to go with him. The only problem was, I knew Lana would be there.

Wiggling enough so I could look him in the eyes, I brushed away a piece of hair that was covering one. "How about I get ready real quick, put some things together, and then we can get something to eat on the way there? I don't want to be the reason you're late."

He flashed me his dimples, and all in the world faded away. "I think they'll understand when they see you."

"I'm not going to make you late. Just let me throw on a bikini and a pair of shorts. I'll be quick. I promise."

Ryder's hold on me didn't loosen. Instead, it did the

opposite. His Caribbean blue eyes slowly took in my face. I was probably a mess since I'd slept so long, but with the way he was looking at me, he didn't seem to care. Ryder made me feel beautiful every time he cast his gaze on me.

When he finally got his fill, he crushed his mouth to mine in a searing kiss. Just as quickly, he pulled away and got off the bed. "Hurry up." His voice was even more rugged than normal. "If we don't leave soon, I'll be the one making us late." I was confused as to what he was talking about until he adjusted himself in his shorts. Only then did I notice the sizable bulge he was sporting. His nostrils flared when he saw me taking him in. "Please get dressed, Lexie. You're killing me here."

Looking down, I saw that the blankets had fallen to my waist. My nipples strained from the cool air of the room.

Hopping out of bed, I raced over to my suitcase to grab what I needed and then into the bathroom. When I stepped out after getting ready, Ryder was waiting for me.

"I thought I'd pack a bag for you. I put your book from the bedside table, a towel, a couple of bottles of water, your camera with an extra battery, and sunscreen. Do you need anything else?"

Where had Ryder been all my life? Seriously, could he get any better?

"Thank you, I was worried I'd forget something."

Slipping on a pair of tennis shoes and my sunglasses, we were finally ready to go. Only I had no idea where we were going.

Almost an hour later, Ryder wrinkled his nose at the food as I tried another bite. I had no idea what I'd ordered, but it was gross. Wrapping it back up in its wrapper, I put it back in the bag. "I can't take another bite, or I'm going to puke."

He laughed at me. "I don't know why you ordered it."

"Because I like to try the food wherever I go." I tried to explain before I chugged half the water bottle to get the taste out of my mouth.

"You're lucky you need to keep your boyish figure otherwise..." I wanted to be sick just thinking about what I'd eaten. Only I didn't speak Portuguese, so I had no idea what I'd ordered. The picture looked good, so I thought it would taste like it looked. I was wrong.

"I'd be throwing up in the bushes. No, I'll happily stick to baked or grilled chicken. We should probably start trying to make our way there. When I looked at the email, they said it would take about twenty-five minutes to get there."

It was lucky I'd brought tennis shoes because I couldn't imagine what the hike would have been like in flip-flops. I wasn't one for footwear, and if I had to wear something, it was usually flip-flips, but I'd had a feeling I'd need them.

Ryder carried my bag as we followed along the trail. His hand was in mine like it was the most natural thing in the world. I loved how he didn't shy away from affection.

By the time we made it to the waterfall, we were both a sweaty mess. I was glad I'd thrown my hair up on top of my head. Otherwise, it would have been sticking to the back of my neck, making me feel even grosser than I already did.

The waterfall was one of the most beautiful places I'd ever seen. It was a little oasis with steep rock walls and palm trees surrounding pretty blue-green water. It was the perfect place for a photo shoot, and I couldn't wait for everyone to leave so I could enjoy it with Ryder. I itched to pull out my camera and start taking pictures.

"There he is," Lana called out, ruining the moment. She acted annoyed, as if she'd been waiting hours for him when we were right on time.

All heads turned to us, and their eyes widened.

"What is she doing here?" Lana pouted. I internally rolled my eyes and smiled at the fact that she didn't like that I was there.

Letting go of my hand, Ryder wrapped his arm around my waist. "I asked her to come. Do you have a problem with that?" That time I had to try extremely hard not to smile. Instead, to show him how much I liked what he'd said, I laid my head on his arm. His bicep flexed in response.

Lana's dark eyes narrowed my way, but everyone else seemed happy to see me. In fact, a man with a camera around his neck scrambled over to us with a wide smile on his face. I assumed he was the photographer, but in all honesty, I didn't recognize anyone except Parker and Lana, who was furiously whispering to him while giving us evil side-looks.

Whatever, the feeling was mutual. I was pretty sure she had tried to get her hands on Ryder, and in all likelihood, he'd shot her down.

The gangly photographer beamed as he held out his hand. "It's an honor to meet you, Ms. Keene. I'm Rob Thurman. I've admired your work for years and to have you here..."

He bounced on his heels and seemed at a loss for words, so I decided to try and save him. I shook his hand and smiled. "It's nice to meet you. I hope you don't mind if I hang out. I've never been to the waterfalls here and wanted to check them out with Ryder."

"Of course. You're welcome whenever you want."

Lana scoffed behind him but didn't say a word when Rob turned around with wide eyes.

"Good to see you again, Lexie," Parker called from Lana's side.

"Right, make yourself comfortable, and if there's anything you need, Sheila will get it for you." A willowy looking girl by a tree trunk waved. Turning to Ryder, he asked. "Are you ready to get to work?"

"Direct me to where you want me." Handing over my bag, he squeezed my hip with his other hand. Dipping down, he brushed his lips against mine. When he stood tall again, Ryder had a slight blush to his cheeks.

Grabbing his arm as he moved away, he looked at me with confusion. "If it makes you uncomfortable to kiss me in public—"

My words were cut off with a blistering kiss. Ryder's fingers threaded through my hair, breaking it from its messy bun as he dipped me back like an old Hollywood film. Just as quickly, we were upright, and his soft words were spoken for only me to hear. "Make no mistake, I have no problem kissing you in public. It takes all my restraint not to fuck you in front of others."

With those words, he left me a tingling mess. My fingers traced my swollen lips as I watched him talk to Rob. He nodded once before he was handed a pair of navy swim trunks that would have all the ladies drooling and stepped behind a screen. I stood in my spot as I watched him change. Each muscle flexed as he stripped down, and when his bare ass came into view, he looked over his shoulder and winked. He knew I was watching.

Pulling my gaze away, I moved back out of the way so I could set up a place to watch. Laying a towel down on a rock that overlooked the pool of water, I slipped my shoes off, pulled my t-shirt over my head, and slid my shorts down my thighs. As I fixed my sunglasses back on my face, I noticed Ryder watching me with heated interest. He shook his head and turned back to Parker, who was talking a mile a minute.

Before sitting down to soak up the sun, I pulled my camera out of my bag and started shooting the beautiful scenery. I wasn't sure if they'd be back, and I didn't want to miss getting my shot. I was already trying to figure out a way to have my own shoot here in the future.

As they started to get into place, I put my camera away and sat down to watch the show. Rob had no idea what he wanted, it was obvious. The shoot started and stopped half a dozen times before they broke apart. I had no idea who the customer was or the vision for the shoot, but I wanted the best for Ryder, and if I could help him, I would.

Taking a sip of my water, I stood, taking my camera with me as I walked down to where Rob was looking back and forth from his camera to the water and back again.

Stopping a few inches from him, I looked over his shoulder and asked as politely as I could. "Trouble?" I didn't want to bruise his ego or make him think he wasn't doing a good job even though from what I saw, he was doing a terrible job.

His shoulders deflated. "Nothing is working out the way I envisioned." He'd barely started, so I wasn't sure what had gone wrong. The only thing I saw was it looked like an amateur taking photos. His camera wasn't the best, but it was capable of doing the job.

"What's your vision?"

I saw Ryder watching me out of the corner of my eye with a frown marring his usually warm features.

"A push and pull between lovers. Two men and a woman. I want to show the tension, the yearning." He indicated Ryder, Parker, and Lana. "I can get the tension since no one likes Lana," he chuckled as he looked over his shoulder at her. "It's the yearning I'm having trouble with. I thought this location would bring it out."

"What if you show the woman, Lana yearning for both men?" There was more of a possibility of that happening than the other.

Rob tilted his head as he took in what I'd said. He looked over at the threesome and nodded his head. "That could work."

"Is the client here? Do you need approval first?" Some customers were very rigid about what they wanted. Hell, I didn't even know what this shoot was for, but I didn't see his original vision coming to life. They were models, not actors. Yes, you have to be able to take direction and be able to deliver a look, but you couldn't hide the disdain Parker and Ryder had for Lana. It shined brighter than anything else when they looked at her.

"Over there." He flapped a hand in the direction of a man standing by himself with his arms crossed over his chest. He was easily overlooked, wearing a non-descript t-shirt and shorts in a sea of barely dressed models. He could have been an assistant with a sweeping glance. "Let me go talk to him, but I don't think it will be a problem since they wanted it with two guys and a girl." He waved off my concern.

Moving in beside me, Ryder watched as I took a couple of pictures of the water for the new angle. "What's going on?"

Tilting my head toward him, I spoke quietly. "He doesn't know what he's doing. From where I was sitting, I could tell." I shook my head. "I don't understand why people keep hiring Lana. She only makes shoots more diffi-cult. He wants you to look at her with adoration and love, and I told him it wasn't going to happen."

Ryder moved until his back was to the crowd so they couldn't hear. "She was horrible to Parker this morning, making him feel like a worthless piece of shit. He can barely stop glaring at her between shots, and I…" He clamped his mouth shut, and his eyes got wide.

I let out a breath of frustration. "Let me guess. She's been relentlessly hitting on you."

He quirked a perfectly shaped brow. "How did you know?"

"Because that's who Lana is. She wants to fuck you and be your girlfriend to further her career. I'm sure she's noticed how popular you've become since your last shoot with her."

Ryder's forehead pinched together. He stared at me for a moment and then looked over his shoulder toward Lana. The moment she saw he was looking at her, she smiled and batted her eyelashes at him. Did she really think that would work?

"She's delusional. I wouldn't have anything to do with her if she wasn't put right in front of me. What can I do to get her to leave me alone?"

"You'd have to be an asshole, and we both know that's not you." One shoulder lifted in an attempt to say, 'what can you do?' "I suggest trying your best to ignore her."

The usual light in his eyes dimmed as he hung his head. "I hope I don't get any more jobs with her."

I did too because if I knew she was going to be there, I wasn't sure I would be making any more trips to see Ryder.

Feeling bad, I stepped into Ryder and wrapped my arms around him to give him a hug. "Me too." An idea popped into my head. "Hey, do you want to have a little fun while you wait?"

He gave me a half-assed shrug but said sure.

"Good, because this place is beautiful, and I want to capture some pictures of you here. I want you to go out until you can't touch the bottom, and then I want you to start coming back toward me out of the water slowly. Can you do that?"

"Anything for you." He dipped down again and brushed a sweet kiss to my lips.

He strode out into the crystal-clear water in only his tiny navy trunks. Looking over his shoulder, he called out. "Are you ready?"

I gave him a thumbs-up as I looked at the LED screen, my finger on the button, ready to take his picture. I could feel that we had everyone's attention, but I didn't care. By the time they were done, the lighting would be all wrong for what I wanted. These were for me and me alone. They'd be my spank bank material if they came out the way I thought they would.

Ryder disappeared into the water for only a moment, and when he reappeared, it was like a dream or a sexy commercial. He moved in slow motion; his eyes locked on me as my finger held down the shutter button. If we didn't have an audience, I would have dropped my camera to the ground and jumped him. Water trickled down his torso, and my eyes were riveted on each drop as they moved down his body.

Snapping out of it, I ordered. "Push your hair out of your face."

I saw a twinkle in his eye, but other than that, Ryder seemed unfazed as he did as I told him. The crowd moved in closer to watch, their shoot forgotten, and for a split second, I felt bad, until Ryder's eyes heated and he bit his lower lip. My ovaries let out a sigh, and my sex clenched in need. Dear God, he was otherworldly; he was so gorgeous and perfect.

"Come to me. Large strides," I commanded. I squatted down to get him from a new angle. I wished I had another camera to get him in at least one other direction.

Ryder walked to me like he was on the catwalk. My body rose, the closer he got to me. His stare was directed at me until he was right in front of me. Taking my camera, a smile danced on his lips, and when those dimples popped out, I was done for. One big hand reached out and grasped my waist, pulling until every inch of skin from my waist up came into contact with his. Dipping down, his soft lips found mine in the single best kiss of my life. It was the perfect mixture of soft and hard, passion and need with a dose of possession. It ended far too soon, and when Ryder's lips left mine, I let out a soft cry. I wanted to pull him back to me, but when someone cleared their throat, the world that had disappeared suddenly came rushing back.

"That was fucking hot," Parker whispered none too quietly.

A round of chuckles filled the air, further breaking the spell. Ryder and I pulled apart with his hand still on my hip. He handed me back my camera like the last few minutes hadn't occurred.

"I'm sorry if that took too long, but I wanted to get Ryder in the water when the lighting was just right."

"You have nothing to be sorry for, young lady. It was perfect. In fact, I'd love to use the shots you took and what Rob got of the two of you for Romadi."

I blinked back at the man Rob had said was the client. "I'm sorry. You are?"

"Carlos Antonio." We shook hands as I stood there in a daze. "That was the most natural and insane chemistry I've ever witnessed, and we managed to get it all. I'd love to discuss buying your photos and paying you for—"

"You want to use us?" I blurted out, interrupting him.

"If you could have seen your..." Parker bit on his fist, making everyone laugh.

"I think I need to see these pictures before...it was a personal moment."

"In front of a dozen people." Lana rolled her dark evil eyes.

"Can we negotiate a price on your photos? Rob told me you're a famous photographer."

"I'm not really famous," I argued.

Rob scoffed. "She's being modest."

It didn't matter what I was; I took those photos for myself, and I didn't want to share with the world. "I'm not a model and —"

Ryder stepped in, trying to help. "Why don't you show her the pictures you took?" he looked to Rob. "You don't have to have all the pictures, do you?"

Carlos' brows furrowed for only a moment before he was smiling. "I guess that could work. A few great pictures are better than hundreds of subpar ones." My eyes almost popped out of my head at his dig at Rob. Carlos had hired him for some reason. "If you agree, then I think we can be done."

Rob turned toward Carlos in a frenzy. "With the entire shoot?"

"I think we got what we need if Lexie's willing to give us what we want."

I didn't like the position they were putting me in. Did I say no, knowing the pictures of Ryder wouldn't be as good and that he'd have to continue working with Lana? Or did I suck it up?

"Let me talk to Lexie for a few moments, and then we can figure this all out." Ryder didn't give them a chance to object. He pulled me over to my stuff on the rock and sat me down with my back to everyone. He sat in front of me with a soft look on his face. "What are you thinking? I can tell you're not too happy about this."

"I wish I would have waited until we were alone, but the lighting was perfect, and I got excited."

Scooting closer until our knees were touching, he wrapped his hand around mine. "You don't want to sell them your pictures." It wasn't a question.

"Those were taken for my private collection, and I'd hate to give any up." I hadn't even looked at them, but I knew without a doubt there wasn't one I wanted to part with, and I knew Carlos would want the best of them all. "I want this to be a successful job for you, and I know my pictures can make that happen."

"I have no doubt, but if you don't want to do it, I understand. How do you feel about them wanting to use pictures you'll be in?"

A bitter laugh escaped before I could stop it. "It's no secret I'm not a model. I don't want to hear the criticism of what others will think about my body or how we look together." Tears stung my eyes, making me grit my teeth.

Taking my camera, Ryder turned it on and started looking through the pictures I'd taken. After a moment, he moved to sit beside me and angled the screen so we could both see. "These are phenomenal, Lexie." He said my name with wonder, making my tears dry on my cheeks, and my lips tip up.

Leaning my head on his shoulder, I watched as he went through picture after picture. "You did all the hard work, I just captured it."

"It was a team effort." Wrapping his arm around me, Ryder pulled me against his side. "I told you, you should always be the one taking my picture."

"You know where I am."

"I know. Why don't we go see the pictures Rob took? There's no reason to stew over it until you see the evidence."

"I guess you're right. If I'm lucky, Rob's pictures won't be any good."

Standing up, Ryder held his hand out to help me stand. "You're going to look amazing in them. I know it and fuck what others say. Your body is perfect. I love that your body isn't model thin." Placing his hands on my hips, he leaned down and bit my earlobe. "Let's do this."

I could feel Lana's glare the moment I stood up but chose to ignore it. At least this time, I understood the reason for her attitude. I wasn't sure if she or Parker would be paid if they weren't in any of the photos. Plus, she knew what being in more photos with Ryder would do to her career.

Rob was looking a little glum as we walked over while Carlos couldn't stop smiling. It made no sense, but I didn't have time to think about it. The second we were within reaching distance, Rob handed over his camera. He already had the first picture up and ready for us.

While I didn't love looking at myself, I had to admit the shots were hot. Rob had taken amazing pictures of us, and our passion shone through as I flipped through each one. The only thing I knew was I didn't want to give up any of them, but I was going to for Ryder.

"Why don't you send me your pictures, and I'll go through them tonight and decide which ones I'm willing to give up out of the bunch. Deal?"

"You can't decide now?"

I cleared my throat. "Unfortunately not. Can you send me a link to look over them a little better if I give you my email address?"

Carlos let out a frustrated sigh. "We'll make it happen." Turning toward the crew, he clapped his hands together. "Alright, pack up. I'll let you know if I need anything else."

While they packed up, I went back over to my rock. I wanted to enjoy this magical place a little more. Once everyone was gone, I had plans for my young hottie.

After everything was packed up, Ryder slowly walked over, eyes shining. "You didn't want to help pack up?" The twitch of his lips had me wanting to lunge for him and bring him down on top of me, but I refrained. It wouldn't be long before we'd be alone. "What's going on in that pretty little head of yours?" He bit his bottom lip as if he knew exactly what it did to me. "You look like you're up to something."

"Oh, it won't be me who's up." My eyebrows rose at his heated stare. "I thought we could enjoy the water once everyone leaves." Patting the area at my side, I asked, "Why don't you have a seat?"

"Do you have a thing for me and the water?" He cocked one eyebrow in question.

He had no idea. Especially after earlier today. I was still all hot and bothered by reliving it through the pictures I took.

Rob and Parker made their way over to where we were sitting on the rock. They stopped a foot away and looked up at us. "We're getting ready to head out."

"We're going to hang back and go for a swim before we leave." Ryder's palm resting on my knee gave me a little squeeze.

"Okay." Rob drew out the word. "I look forward to hearing from you later tonight."

As if he had to remind me. I gave him a tight-lipped smile, afraid that if I opened my mouth, I'd tell him I'd changed my mind.

"Relax," Ryder whispered in my ear.

Only then did I realize that my body had tensed up.

Parker hung back when Rob returned to the group as they started to leave. A big cheesy smile grew on his face. "Do you need a third?" He wagged his eyebrows comically.

Not knowing Parker, I didn't know if he was serious or not, but it didn't matter. Threesomes were not my thing, and even if they were, I wasn't sharing Ryder with anyone. Male or female.

Ryder threw his head back and laughed. "Get lost, Parker."

Stepping away, Parker looked over his shoulder. "You two are no fun."

No fun for him, but I couldn't wait to be alone with Ryder.

CHAPTER 14
LEXIE

RYDER'S NIMBLE FINGERS UNTIED THE TOP STRINGS OF MY BIKINI top. Leaning forward, he flicked his skilled tongue across my already hardened nipple. I let out a breathy sigh from being wound up for so long. I was surprised I had lasted until now. My control had slightly slipped as I watched Ryder emerge from the water. I'd pushed it down for as long as possible and now I was ready to strip Ryder down and have my wicked way with him.

One long finger slipped inside my bikini bottoms and glided through my slick folds. "I love how wet you always are for me." He groaned deep in his throat. "It makes my dick so hard."

My lips trailed from his neck and over his collarbone before moving down. My fingers fell to the waistband of his board shorts and slipped my hands over his firm ass cheeks before I pushed his shorts down until they fell to his feet. My tongue swirled around his nipple once before I nipped it with my teeth.

He groaned, putting his hand on the back of my head

and held me there. "You're trouble. The best kind of trouble, my sexy Lexie."

Ryder plucked the strings on the sides of my bottoms, letting them fall away. His fingers dug into my soft flesh as he picked me up. My legs immediately wrapped around his waist. One of my hands slipped into the longer tresses at the top of his head and pulled it to the side. My mouth found the column of his neck and sucked, licked, and kissed my way up. His piney scent infiltrated my nose. How did he still smell so good?

I nipped his ear. "I love the way you smell. The way you taste."

Warm water hit my most sensitive places. I hadn't even realized Ryder had started to move toward the water, I'd been so consumed by him. My lips found his, and as if he'd been waiting on me, Ryder took my mouth into a searing kiss. Our kiss deepened the further into the water we went. The water hit my shoulder blades, and we were both panting for breath.

One hand fisted in my hair and pulled my head back. His other palm skated from my neck down to my breastbone, pushing until I was lying back in the water. One hand on my hip and the other cupping my breasts. I'm tethered to Ryder only by his touch.

"Your hair matches the water." He flashed his dimples at me. "It's…you're beautiful all the time, but like this, you're ethereal."

I wanted to say something. Do something. The look on his face, the way his eyes glowed down at me, I knew he meant every word he said. Before I could collect myself enough, the pad of Ryder's thumb pressed down hard on my bundle of nerves and started to circle in rough strokes.

My body bucked up out of the water. My inner thighs trembled with need.

My hands clutched his forearms as Ryder brought me to completion. My body jerked in the warm water with my eyes trained on his. Ryder's eyes matched the water perfectly, and with the way the sun reflected back into them, he glowed like a devilish angel. Once the tremors finally settled, I closed my eyes and let the water and Ryder hold me. It was a warm cocoon of safety that I never wanted to leave.

This would forever be my happy place.

"Come here, pretty girl." Ryder scooped me up out of the water and cradled me to his chest. It was as if he knew I was a boneless mess. As I lay my head on his shoulder, he rubbed one hand up and down my back. He swayed us back and forth in the water, bringing me down from one of my highest highs.

"You're good at that," I spoke against his shoulder.

He kissed the top of my head and rested his chin there. "At what? Bringing you to orgasm or soothing you?"

"Both." My lips brushed his shoulder. "Why are you so perfect?"

His arms tightened around me. "My sexy Lexie, are you falling for me?" His voice was now a choked whisper.

Turning my head, my lips scraped against his neck. "Maybe. It wouldn't be hard." Sitting up, I looked at him. His face was soft and dreamy. "How does that make you feel?"

Ryder's gazed searched mine. "So fucking good." He chewed on his bottom lip with a moment of hesitation. "You know, there's nothing wrong with falling for each other."

Except we'd be apart from each other the vast majority of the time.

Instead of answering him with words, I cupped his face in the palms of my hands. Leaning in, I sucked on his bottom lip. I let my arm fall away from around his broad back. My hand skimmed down his side and reached down between us to brush against the velvety steel of his shaft. I loved the satiny feel of his skin against my fingertips.

Ryder sucked in a shaky breath as his hips bucked into my hand. "I need to be inside of you right now." I stroked him up and down, squeezing his tip. "I'll…I'll pull out."

Rising up, I placed the tip of his cock at my entrance and slowly sank down. God, I loved his cock and the way it filled and stretched me. We moved in a synchronized erotic dance. Our movements were fluid in the warm water. The more we moved, the closer we got to the waterfall.

Water crashed over me as wave after wave of pleasure shot through me. The way each drop of water hit my aching breasts heightened every feeling. My nails dug into Ryder's back as he pumped faster and harder, dragging out the rapture that was filling my body. Tilting my head up, I let the water wash over me. The moment Ryder pulled out of me, I cried out aching to have him back inside of me.

Ryder's lips brushed against the shell of my ear as he let out a low laugh. "I promise when we get back to the room, I'll fuck you all night long."

Looking down at him, I laughed. "You know all the right things to say."

"It's no hardship making…" After a long pause, he continued. "What do you say we get out of here?"

"You don't want to enjoy the waterfall a little more?"

He nipped my chin. "We don't have enough time for all

the things I want to do to you, but if I had to choose, I would be deep inside of you, to release inside of you, while you milk my cock. There's no better feeling."

Resting my forehead to his, I wrapped my arms around his neck. One of his hands slipped under my ass as he held me to him. "Then let's go back to our hotel."

Soon, Ryder had us out of the water and headed back to the jeep. Every few minutes, he looked back at me with a smile on his face and his eyes bright.

Each second I spent with him, I fell a little bit more for him.

CHAPTER 15
RYDER

Lexie's long blue waves were tied up in a messy bun atop her head as she sat with her sunglasses perched on her nose and a book in her lap staring out at the ocean. I almost felt bad as I continued to stare at her. She photographed some of the most beautiful people in the world and yet didn't see it in herself. She was a knockout without even trying. I saw it and wanted nothing more than to bask in her beauty day after day. The only problem was we were flying out tomorrow and had no idea when we'd see each other again.

I wanted to make plans during the holidays, but that was several months away, so instead, I kept quiet and enjoyed our time together. I wanted to ask her to be my girlfriend but wasn't sure she'd say yes. I'd rather keep it as it was than for it to end in a ball of flames.

"Are you sure it will be safe to go home?"

"I can only go by what Raine's told me. Am I one hundred percent sure? No, I'm not, but I can't hide out in Rio for the rest of my life, no matter how wonderful it is here with you. It would be nice if the police found Ben, but he never showed up at my place." She tapped her fingers on her leg. "Maybe he watched the police show up and search for his drugs, or maybe he's given up. Raine's been watching the security cameras, and nothing has shown up."

"Maybe, but he's dangerous, and I only want you to be safe. I wish I could be closer, but I can't, and it kills me to think he could hurt you again."

"It scares me too, but I have work to do, and I'm not going to let him fuck with my career. You have to understand." Her eyes begged me to acknowledge her plea.

"I do, but that doesn't mean I have to like it. Security cameras only show what's happening or has happened. They can't protect you, and that's all I want."

Slipping off her lounger, Lexie rose above me and straddled me. Her hands went to my chest as mine went to her hips. "I love that you're worried. I really do, but let's not ruin our last day together."

My thumb caressed the soft skin of her hipbone. "It's hard to be happy when I'm worried about you." And our imminent goodbye.

"Would it make you feel better if I hired a bodyguard until Ben is caught?" She rubbed her bikini-clad pussy along my length.

"It would make me feel better, and what would make me feel even better is if I could push those tiny bottoms to the side and slip inside you."

"What's stopping you?" My grip on her tightened.

I shook with silent laughter until my tip hit her entrance, and I groaned. "I'm not into exhibitionism."

Cupping my face in the palm of her tiny hands, her thumbs swept over my cheeks and lips. "Neither am I, dimples, but when I'm around you, the world seems to fall away. I wouldn't even realize we had an audience until it was too late. Why don't we go upstairs and get cleaned up? We can take advantage of that big tub."

Liking the sound of spending more time in any type of water with her, I licked my bottom lip. Lexie's eyes followed my tongue and fought against my hold as she tried to grind against me. If she hadn't been on my lap, I would have jumped up and thrown her over my shoulder.

My dick in her sweet, wet pussy was pure bliss, and I wanted nothing more than to spend the rest of the night in her.

Sliding her off my lap, I stood wrapping her hand in mine and pulled her along the sandy beach. My toes dug into the warm sand as she giggled behind me. One of her soft hands rested between my shoulder blades as she kissed along my back.

I tried to adjust myself, so everyone didn't see how hard Lexie made me when she was pressed up against me. "My sexy Lexie, you're causing me to give quite the show. Behave."

"Then you better walk faster because I'm not sure how long I can keep my hands to myself." Her hands slipped down and around my waist with her fingers resting just above my waistband.

Clasping her hands in mine, I brought her flush against me. I hadn't thought when I stopped her, and now I realized I'd made the wrong move. When Lexie was near, my body had a mind of its own.

We stumbled into the hotel elevator, drunk on each other. I pressed the button for the eleventh floor and then pulled her back into my chest. I stared back at us in the mirrored walls. Even though we were an unconventional pair, I could see us together in the future. As I swayed us to the music piping through the speakers with her petite frame fitting perfectly against my body, I closed my eyes and tried to memorize what her body felt like against mine. I would miss falling asleep and waking up next to her, and after this last week, I knew I'd be even lonelier than before.

"Let me see your phone." Lexie broke me out of my trance. I held out my phone to her. Holding it up in front of us, she ordered. "Say orgasm." We both laughed as she took our picture. It was perfect and so us. We'd never looked happier.

"I'm going to make that my lock screen so I can look it all the time while we're apart," I whispered in her ear. I felt her body relax a little at my words, making me hold her tighter.

"I can't believe I gave up my pictures." It took her hours to pick which ones she could part with. I didn't think she normally would have had such a dilemma. She was attached to those photos from the moment she'd taken them.

"Only a few and not the best of them." I kissed the skin beneath her ear. "I can't thank you enough for doing that for me."

"You've thanked me enough to last a lifetime. I told you I'd do anything within my power to help you."

"And you did." I still couldn't get over how much they'd paid her for two photos and then given her all but one of the pictures that Carlos took. I'd been wondering about it and finally got up the nerve to ask her. "Do you usually make that much money on the pictures you take?"

"That was pretty standard." The elevator doors opened

to our floor, and this time it was Lexie who was guiding us. "I've gotten more and less."

How did she work as much as she did and make that much and not live in a mansion on the beach like she wanted?

"I see that look on your face. Living in LA is expensive and the taxes…" She shook her head as she slipped the keycard in the door. "I'm saving my money for the right time, the right property."

Opening the door, she went straight to the bathroom and turned on the water to the tub. It was big enough for at least three people and would take a few minutes to fill. I leaned against the counter as Lexie looked at all the bottles the hotel provided.

"You don't have to explain it to me. I've been living on friends' couches while I saved enough to afford my own place. I don't even have my own car in LA. Most of my possessions are in Washington at my parents' house."

"Got it." She lifted one bottle to her nose. Spinning around, she poured the contents under the fall of water, and the smell of lavender and vanilla filled the air.

Pulling off my trunks, I sat my phone by the tub in case I was inspired to take more pictures while we were in the water. So far, I only had a few pictures of my travels. The vast majority of the images were of Lexie and our time together.

Letting her top fall to the floor, she asked as she stepped into the nearly full tub, "Have you ever thought of becoming a photographer?"

"No, I don't have the eye that you do." I stepped in behind her. My legs went to the outside of hers as I leaned back and rested my head on the back of the tub.

"You have more than you know. It takes practice. While I do think you'll have a long career, you can't always be a model." She leaned back against my chest, bringing my arms around her. "It's something to think about."

"Will you teach me?"

"Someday."

"If I can make even half as much as you did on—"

"Remember when I talked to you about being picky about the jobs you take? That's what I do. I don't take low-paying jobs unless it's for a good cause or a friend."

That made sense. "You choose wisely and know what you're worth."

Turning her head, she kissed my chest. "You're young, but one day you'll know your value."

"You're already making me see." I thought my agent knew the way to make me successful, but after meeting Lexie, I soon learned the opposite. Yes, Angie knew how to get me a lot of jobs to get her commission. When I confronted her about being more choosey and take the ones for the right money, she told me I didn't know what I was talking about. Lexie was right, if I continued on the way I had, I'd become run down and hate my life. It wasn't easy to be secluded from your friends and loved ones for so much time. I was glad I'd taken steps to slow down, and that I had the woman in my arms to consult with about my path.

Turning around, Lexie straddled my hips like she'd done out on the beach. This time I welcomed the rocking of her hips against mine. "Are you okay?" She let her finger-tips trace along my collarbone and around each dip and groove of my torso.

"I am. I was just thinking of what you said, and my

agent. When my contract is up at the end of the year, I might look for a new one. She didn't like the idea of me taking fewer jobs."

"I can help you find the right one when you're ready." Leaning forward, Lexie licked the seam of my lips. Her warm breath caressed my skin. "I know many. All you have to do is ask."

Sitting up, I captured her mouth with my own. My hand dipped between her legs, and I ran my fingers through her folds. Two fingers slipped inside as my thumb found her pearl. She was so sensitive with her ring; it took no time at all to bring her close to orgasm. Her walls clenched around my fingers while her moans filled my mouth.

"Ryder," she called out my name on a contented sigh.

I stood, Lexie wrapping her legs around my waist. While the water was nice, this time, I didn't want to pull out. I wanted to feel each pulse of her pussy around my cock while I pleasured her, and I couldn't do that in the water.

"You want me to fuck you outside where anyone may see? Let me take you from behind on the balcony." We stopped at the door of the balcony and could hear the waves crashing. The sun had almost set, and the stars had started to twinkle in the twilight. It would be hard for anyone to see us up here.

With one hand on the handle, Lexie turned me around to face her. "Ryder, sweetie," she pulled my face to look at hers, "I have no need for that. I may forget our surroundings, but I can't say I don't like the idea of looking out onto the ocean while you fill me. I don't want you to do anything you don't want to."

Ripping the condom wrapper open, I sheathed my

aching length and pulled Lexie's back to my front, giving her my answer. "Are you ready for me, sexy girl?"

She ground her ass on my cock, and I wanted nothing more than to explore her tight hole, but as I rubbed my tip between her cheeks, she tensed up. Leaning forward until her top half was bent over the railing, I kissed up her spine. "Relax, sweet girl. I won't go there until you're ready."

Lexie looked over her shoulder at me and bit her bottom lip. "What if I'm never ready? Seriously, I'm not sure how you think that thing of yours is going to fit."

I understood why she was so apprehensive. I wouldn't want anyone sticking anything up my ass either, but I knew it would be pleasurable for her if she could relax enough and give herself over to it.

"I could just put in the tip." I bit back a laugh at the incredulous look she gave me.

"Why don't you just stick your big cock in my pussy and fuck me already?" She shoved her hips back into me.

"Your wish is my command." With my hand around my engorged length, I plunged into her hot depth. I loved the way her pussy clenched around me as I filled her. I moaned against the nape of her neck and pulled her tighter against me.

Pumping into her from behind, my hands cupped her supple breasts. My mouth explored the skin of her neck, licking, sucking, and nipping as Lexie panted, her white-knuckled grip on the railing.

Lexie moaned and squeezed my cock as she circled her hips. "Oh my god, Ryder, keep doing that." I wanted her to keep doing that thing with her hips. I continued my kisses up her neck. Wrapping my hand around her jaw, I angled her head and brought her mouth to mine.

Fuck, I was going to miss this. Miss her.

Bucking into me with her head thrown back against my shoulder, Lexie's walls started to clench around me. With every pulse, I felt my balls tingle a little more. Wrapping my hand around her throat, I pulled her up until she was flush against my chest. Her chest heaved as she panted in the now dark of night. With my other hand, my index finger found her nub and circled. Every time I came into contact with one of her piercings, I nearly came on contact. I never thought I'd find them hot, but the moment I saw them on Lexie, it drove me wild.

"Milk my cock, sexy girl." I stilled, deep inside of her, and let myself go.

Feeling Lexie's body go soft, I let go of her neck and wrapped my arm around her waist. Pulling her inside the room, I walked her over to the bed and laid her down. Covering her up with the blanket, I kissed her on the forehead before I disposed of the condom and climbed in behind her.

Wrapping her in my arms, I kissed the top of her head.

"Where'd you go?" she asked sleepily.

"To get rid of the condom."

Turning in my arms, Lexie snuggled into my chest. After a few minutes, she tangled her fingers into my hair. "I can't believe we're leaving tomorrow. I have so many jobs to do when I get home, and all I want to do is sit on a beach with you."

That did sound perfect.

"I'm going to miss this," Lexie slurred. Instead of sounding sleepy, she sounded almost drunk. That's what good sex will do to you.

Looking down at her, I ran my fingers through her long, wavy hair. "What are you going to miss about this?"

Yes, I was fishing.

"Smelling your piney scent. I love it so much. I'm going to go on Amazon and buy something that smells just like you."

Not knowing what she was talking about, I tried to hold back my laughter but ended up shaking us both with it. "If you like the way I smell so much, you can take one of my shirts home with you."

Her head popped up. Her smile was blinding. "Really?"

I had no idea she enjoyed it that much. "Sure thing. Is there anything else you'll miss?"

"Seeing your dimples every day." Reaching up, she traced along one cheek. "Being in your arms, listening to you talk."

My brows furrowed. "Even though we'll be apart, we'll still talk as often as we can." Was she done with me once we separated? "You're not done with me, are you?"

"I don't think I'll ever be done, but it's different hearing your voice in person than on the phone. It's still…good, but not the same. I don't know how to describe it." She took in a deep breath and let it out. I felt it fan over my confused face. "I don't think I ever told you what I thought about you when we first met."

"No, you didn't. What did you think?"

"The first thing was your voice, and it immediately got my panties wet." I liked the sound of that. Sitting up against the headboard, I dragged Lexie on top of me and let her sit back against my knees. I tried to keep my eyes on hers instead of drifting down to her perky breasts and lower, but I failed quite a few times. Lexie didn't seem to mind and continued on. "I loved the sound of your voice, and while I knew you'd be good-looking since you're a model, I wasn't prepared for what I turned around and saw. Ryder, you're perfection. Your body and face," she let out a dreamy sigh. "Even your hair. So I thought this man can't be that perfect. He must be an asshole and have a small dick because it wouldn't be fair for you to be the total package. At every turn, you proved me wrong. You, Ryder Williams, are the total package. Inside and out. And I'm just lucky enough to be on this ride with you. I'm in awe you'd want to be with me when you could literally have any woman in the world. Hands down."

I had no idea Lexie felt that way about me. None whatsoever.

"Sometimes, I feel like I'm objectifying you with the way I can't keep my eyes off you and the way you turn me on without even trying, but then you do something so amazingly sweet and caring..." Leaning forward, she cupped my cheeks. I didn't even notice her breasts as I listened to all the amazing words Lexie had to say about me. Her beautiful words were only going to make our separation harder, but I didn't care. I ate up every syllable that fell from her mouth. In that moment, I knew I was falling in love with her. "I know that even if you were ugly, I'd look at you the same way because you are so undeniably beautiful inside."

I wanted to marry this girl.

Eliminating the distance between us, I crushed my mouth to hers. I knew our lips would be swollen and bruised in the morning, but I didn't care. Each touch, each caress was like a sip of elixir that I never knew I needed. She was the balm to my lonely soul, and I never wanted to be apart from her. I wanted the world to know that my lips had been attached to hers for the entire night.

Laying her down on the bed, I hovered over her. When our eyes locked, she smiled softly at me. Slowly her hand came up to rest on my cheek. "Does that mean you liked what I said?"

"I more than liked every word that came out of your pretty little mouth," I nipped at her bottom lip before sucking it into my mouth.

"Show me." She demanded breathlessly from underneath me, so I did as I was ordered. For the rest of the night, I tasted every inch of her beautiful body, kissed her until our breaths were ragged, and brought her to climax more times than I could count. It was the perfect way to end our time together.

When we headed to the airport the next morning, our eyes bleary from getting no sleep, we had contented smiles on our faces until we pulled apart and it was time to say goodbye.

I left a little piece of my heart in Rio that day.

CHAPTER 16
LEXIE

1 Month Later

Crossing through my schedule, I marked out the hotel I'd just booked. Raine walked in with her giant cup of Starbucks and sank into the chair in front of my desk.

"Rough night?" I asked as I looked at her over my monitor.

My usual perky Raine was nowhere to be seen. Her clothes were rumpled, her hair was in disarray, and she had bags under her eyes. "You could say that. My roommate's boyfriend broke up with her, and Sierra was up all night crying, so I was scrolling through different social media sites and…" She looked down at her lap and then up at me with tears in her eyes.

What had Raine so upset?

"What, honey? You can tell me whatever's upsetting you."

She took in a shaky breath before she opened and closed her mouth a few times. "I don't think so; you're not going to like it."

"Was someone talking trash about me?" I didn't really care if they were. It wasn't going to hurt my feelings.

Raine shook her head vehemently. If no one was trash-talking me, then what was it?

"Am I supposed to guess?" When she shook her head again, I started to get annoyed. It was too early to be playing games. For the last few days, I hadn't been able to get into contact with Ryder. Last I knew, he was in New York, getting ready to head to Australia. We had planned to talk after he was settled and got some sleep, but with the time difference, it was hard to find a time for us to talk. After not hearing from him for three days after he arrived, I didn't know what to think.

To top it all off, Ben had been calling me non-stop since I got home from Rio. I'd blocked his number on my iPhone, but he could still leave voicemails and took advantage, leaving at least one an hour. Every day he filled my voice-mail with his endless rants. They were nasty, ugly, and hateful voicemails talking about all the horrible things he was going to do to me if he ever got the chance. I'd had my security system upgraded again while I was away, but it still didn't make me feel one hundred percent safe. I was afraid to leave my house, but I was lucky to have Raine and to live in a big city where literally everything could be brought to your door.

With all that going on, I wasn't sure if I could handle any more. Turning her phone so I could look at it, I nearly lost my breakfast. On Raine's screen was Ryder with Lana in his lap. Lana was holding the phone out while she kissed his cheek. Ryder looked happy with one arm around her waist. They appeared to be in a nightclub of some sort. I couldn't tell if it was taken in New York or Sydney, not that it mattered. This must have been why I couldn't get a hold of him.

How had I been so wrong about him?

Ryder knew how I felt about Lana, and there he was with her. I wanted to be sick, scream, and at the same time, slash his tires if he had any. While I'd been missing him since we'd left Rio, now I was heartbroken.

"Why don't we take the rest of the day off? The hotel has agreed to our terms, and I've got them booked for the entire week in December, so we should have plenty of time to get all the shots we want."

Raine looked at me with sad, puppy dog eyes. "Are you sure? We still have so much work to do."

"I'm more than sure. You're tired and could use some sleep, and I need to wrap my head around the picture you showed me."

"I'm really sorry, Lexie. I didn't know what to do. I knew you'd want to know and hadn't talked to him in a few days, but I also didn't want to upset you."

It was better Raine did it than someone else who was trying to hurt me. "No, you did the right thing. I needed to know the truth. While I knew Lana wanted to get in his pants, I never thought Ryder would fall for her."

"Maybe you should talk to him and get his side of the story. Like you said—"

"Do you think that picture is lying?" I cut her off, not wanting to hear what else Raine had to say. "What about not being able to get into contact with him? Why isn't he answering my calls or text messages?"

"I have no answers, but I've seen the way he looks at you, and I don't think he'd do this to you."

I dropped my head and tightened my hands into fists. "I know you thought this was going to be some epic love story, but it was just lust and convenience. Did you really think someone as young as Ryder would go months and months without sex while we were apart? I understand being young and having needs. I was young once too, but the fact that it was Lana…" I gritted my teeth at her name to prevent myself from crying. I knew that if I started to cry, I wouldn't be able to stop, and I wanted to wait until I was alone and could wallow in my anger and heartbreak.

Raine stared back at me with tears in her eyes. I knew at any moment they'd break free, and once she started, I was going to follow right along with her.

Hopping up from my chair, I picked up a stack of head-shots and handed them to her. "If you want to be helpful, go home and get some sleep. Once you're caught up, start going through these and see if you think any of them will work for Mathers' campaign."

"Are you sure?"

"I'm more than sure. You won't do me any good when you're running on no sleep." Picking up my phone, I started for the stairs. "When are you going to find some-place else to live? I gave you a raise, so you don't need a roommate if you don't want one." Raine's eyes shifted to the side as she bit her lip. If she was using the extra money I gave her for something stupid, I would kick her ass. "What's going on? And don't even think about lying to me."

"I wouldn't lie to you." She pointed to her phone as if

that made a point. "The only places I've found I can afford on my own are crap and far away."

"Are you asking for another raise?" While I loved Raine as my assistant, I wasn't going to let my liking her sway my judgment. She hadn't worked here long enough to make any more than what I was paying her. If she worked anywhere else, she'd be making significantly less.

"Oh gosh no, I would never ask that of you, especially after you just gave me a raise. It's just going to take some time."

"Perfect, you've got time now. Get some sleep and then scour the internet for a new place to live. Forget the head-shots, your job is to find a new place to live so you can work effectively for me."

"I can do that," she nodded vigorously, so hard, I thought she might strain her neck and then need to go to the hospital.

Internally I rolled my eyes at myself. I hated what Ryder had done to me. I'd opened myself up to him, had started to care about him, and maybe if I was honest with myself, had started to fall for him. Now I wasn't acting like myself, and I needed to get over him so he didn't affect my work.

"You deserve more than those shitty roommates you've got. If I knew of a place you could live, I'd tell you." A thought popped into my head, and I started back toward her. "Did you check the building I lived in before? Maybe they haven't rented out my old apartment?"

Raine's eyes lit up like I'd just told her tomorrow was Christmas. "I hadn't thought of that, although I'm not sure I could afford it."

"It wasn't that bad. Trust me, it also wasn't that nice. I lived there for a long time. If you want, I could give the building supervisor a call and see if it's still open. If it is, I can give you a recommendation. That is if Ben hasn't soured him toward me. I know he was showing up almost daily for a while."

"Oh my gosh, Lexie, that would be so amazing of you. I would absolutely love to live there." She bounced in her seat, she was so happy. I hoped that my apartment was still vacant, and they'd accept her as a tenant. I'd give them my best recommendation and promise that she'd have a job with me for as long as she wanted.

"Let me call Henry and see if the apartment is still available before I get your hopes up too high."

With bright eyes, she nodded with her hands clasped in front of her chest. Damn, I hoped it was still available because I didn't want to take away that happiness from her.

Pulling up my contacts, I dialed Henry, who answered on the first ring. "Lexie," he answered, with happiness brimming from his voice. Hearing him, I instantly missed Henry. He was one of the nicest people I'd ever met.

"Henry, how are you?"

"I'm better now that I've heard your voice. It's been too long. I miss seeing your smiling face every day." And that was why I loved him.

"I miss you too. I know you're probably busy, but I wanted to see if anyone had rented my apartment."

"Are you wanting to move back?" The hopefulness in his voice nearly killed me. He was like a grandfather to me, and I'd abandoned him after I moved out. I should ask him out to lunch or dinner to catch up. It was the least I could do.

"Not quite. My assistant, Raine, do you remember her?" I didn't wait for his answer. "She's looking for an apartment, and I know it's a long shot, but I thought I'd see if mine was still available."

"Oh." In that one word, he sounded so sad. I didn't blame him because I missed seeing him daily too. "I'm sorry to inform you that it has been rented." Damn it. I knew it was a long shot, but I was hopeful that I could help Raine out. "But…there is another unit that's opened up. It's not a two-bedroom like the one you had. Would she be okay with a one-bedroom on the corner?"

"I'm pretty sure she'd be over the moon. She's sitting right here, so let me ask her."

"Take your time, honey," Henry answered.

Putting my phone to my chest, I turned to see Raine about ready to jump out of her skin with excitement. I bit back my smile. "He doesn't have my old apartment anymore, but he does have a one-bedroom corner apartment."

"I'll take anything." She jumped out of her seat and started forward, but stopped abruptly with a frown on her face. "Wait, how much does it cost? Because I might not be able to afford it."

Putting the phone back up to my ear, I prayed Henry had the correct answer. "Henry, what's the price of the apartment?"

"Oh, I hadn't thought of that. I'm not sure, but if she can afford yours, she'll be fine. I know it's less, but not by how much. Do you think she could stop by today to fill out an application? Even though she's your friend, it's required for all tenants."

"I already gave her the rest of the day off, so she'll be over shortly."

"Very good, Ms. Lexie. I do hope that if your friend moves in, I'll be seeing more of you."

"You can bet on it, Henry. Thank you so much for your help."

"Anytime, I look forward to meeting her. I hope you have a good rest of your afternoon."

"I will, and I'll see you soon." I hung up and put my phone in my back pocket. "He said you have to come by and fill out an application, but it sounds like it's only a formality. I do believe you've got yourself a new apartment."

"Can I just say you are the best boss ever?" Raine shrieked as she ran at me with her arms wide before giving me a big hug.

"I'm glad you think so now because you might not be thinking that tomorrow when I'm making you work late," I said from the top of her head. Even though I was short at five foot four, Raine was four-foot-something, and she hated it, but it was one of the things that made her so damn cute.

"Perfectly acceptable." She stepped back with a blinding smile on her face. "Are you sure you want me to leave?" Her words were a reminder of why I had given her the day off in the first place. Never had I been so sure I wanted to be alone. I wanted to cry and be moody and maybe scream a little or a lot, depending on how it made me feel.

"Of course, I'm sure. Go get yourself an awesome apartment, and I'll see you bright and early tomorrow morning."

"Again, thank you, Lexie. You don't know how much this means to me." She was still bouncing on her heels as she collected her stuff. Her face was lit with pure joy. "I'll be here tomorrow, ready to work. I promise."

Waving her off, I gave her a weak smile before I closed the door and set my alarm. I couldn't be too careful with Ben out there with a vengeance against me.

With each step I took toward the stairs, tears welled until I could no longer see. Everything was blurry as I let myself finally break down over Ryder. I knew he was too good to be true, and yet I had let myself fall for him. Trudging up the stairs, I let each tear burn whatever kindness I held for him in my heart. Never would I let another man deep inside of me again. They were all the same good for nothing liars, and I wanted nothing to do with the lot of them.

Stepping into my apartment, I was glad he'd never set foot in this space. I didn't want to see him everywhere I turned. I had moved here for a new start, and it would continue to be one. I spotted the t-shirt Ryder gave me so I could continue to breathe in his piney scent. The urge to burn it was overpowering, but I couldn't do it. No matter how hard I wanted to hate him, there was still a part of me that was a little in love with him.

Picking up his shirt from the end of my bed, I lifted it to my nose and took in a deep breath. Just like yesterday, his scent had faded so much so that I could barely get the smallest of piney whiffs. While I'd been sad yesterday when I couldn't get his scent, now I was devastated. I wasn't sure if it was a good thing or a bad thing that I could no longer smell him. Throwing his shirt into the back of my closet, I closed the door, not wanting to see the garment ever again.

Bile rose in my throat out of nowhere and forced me to run to the bathroom to let loose the yogurt and coffee I'd had that morning, heave after heave until there was nothing left in my aching stomach. I hated nothing more than throwing up, and I did everything within my power not to throw up, so it was a surprise this had hit me so hard. Flushing the vile contents, I folded my arms over the seat and rested my head against them. My head was pounding, and the hair around my face was sweaty and stuck to me as I took deep breaths to try and calm down. I felt like a revolting mess as I let tears stream down my face, run off my arm, and splash into the toilet.

I was happy I'd told Raine to take the rest of the day off. She would probably be hovering over me all day and trying to baby me while I wanted to wallow in my misery alone. As another wave of nausea hit me, I cursed Ryder Williams for fooling me. His good looks, charm, amazing cock, and good boy attitude were to blame for all of this.

How had I let him convince me he was a good guy?

CHAPTER 17

LEXIE

Leaving the bathroom on the first floor, I swiped my mouth with the back of my arm as my stomach continued to twist and turn. I headed toward the stairs to finish setting up on the roof before the models were ready. After being up all night, I'd overslept this morning and couldn't take any more time for myself. Raine had been moving the last of her stuff into her new apartment in my old building and was on her way with lunch for the team. As I walked by the hair and makeup room, Brad and Annalise gave me worried looks that I ignored.

For the last two weeks, everyone had been walking around on eggshells, afraid that at any moment I might go off. After learning about Ryder, I'd been on edge. The one time he called, I exploded like a two-year-old having the temper tantrum to rival all temper tantrums when his number flashed across my screen. It would have been different if he'd manned up and confessed that he was into Lana. Instead, he waited an entire week to contact me after

Lana posted the photo of them together, so I didn't want to hear a word he had to say.

Not now or ever.

The air was stifling; I was already ready to be out of the heat, and we hadn't even started the shoot yet. Pulling the fan out of the little shed I had built, I moved it into the canopy I had set up for the team and me to stand under as much as possible during the day. The cabana was filled with all the fake tropical food and drinks, and all the pillows were fluffed. Everything was perfect as I headed downstairs for lunch until the smell of the food hit my overly sensitive stomach. Instead of making it downstairs, I flew into my bedroom and barely made it to the toilet before I started dry heaving. With the heat and the smell of the curry someone had ordered, it all got to me.

I waited upstairs until I knew I had given them enough time to eat their lunch. Once I heard everyone go up the stairs, I made my way downstairs to my desk to grab my camera.

"Are you still sick?" When my only answer was a nod, Raine continued. "You need to go to the doctor." Her face was a picture of worry as she looked at me with her down-turned mouth. "It's been two weeks, and I've asked around. No one has the flu." She paused. "If you want, I can make you an appointment, I don't mind."

"You know I hate going to the doctor." Every time I stepped inside a doctor's office, I came out sicker than I was when I walked in. The last time I got strep and had to cancel all my appointments for a week. Otherwise, they never knew what was wrong with me and continued to charge an outlandish amount while asking me to make multiple appointments. Fuck that shit.

With her hands on her hips, Raine's face grew serious. "If you're not better by the end of the week, I'm making an appointment."

"Fine," I huffed, giving in.

"Great," she clapped. "Also, I picked up your new business cards with your new phone number," Raine handed the box to me from across my desk. "I took a peek to make sure they didn't mess up, and I love the new look. Should I email everyone in your contact list your new phone number tonight?" She bit her bottom lip and chewed on it.

"You don't have to stay late." I sat the box down on my desk. "You can do it tomorrow when you come in. Now, let's get to work before the natives get restless."

"We're going to melt out there. It's so hot."

"Too bad we don't have a mister. Can you tell me why we don't have one? It would make life so much easier."

"I can take a spray bottle and spray it in the fan when it gets too hot."

"Or we can take a dip in the pool," I cocked my head to the side. "I guess that wouldn't be very professional, would it?"

"Probably not, but I don't think anyone would fault us. You are planning to have Sebastian and Kamilah get in the water at some point, right?"

I grabbed my extra battery pack off the charger. "So, what are you saying, we should all jump in the pool together if we need to cool off?"

Raine shrugged as she picked up my clipboard with my notes for the shoot. It helped to be organized and to know ahead what you and the client wanted, especially when you weren't feeling well.

Two hours later, I was close to ruining the shoot. I felt

like at any moment I would projectile vomit all over Sebastian and Kamilah as I squatted down in front of them while sweat trickled down my back. If I had been able to shoot in the morning or evening, I would have, but the lighting wouldn't have been right, so we were all suffering.

The shoot was taking longer in part because I was swallowing back the bile that was sitting in the back of my throat, everyone was taking multiple water breaks and getting their makeup and hair retouched due to all the sweating.

"Lexie, are we almost done?" Kamilah whined. Her straight black hair was sticking to her back, and she looked utterly miserable in between each setup.

"As soon as I get this shot, we're done. I guess I should have held out on doing the water shots until now, huh?"

"If it was up to me, the entire shoot would have been in the water," Sebastian added.

We all nodded in agreement. We were afflicted by the unseasonable heat along with the humidity, making the time seem to drag on and on. Ninety-nine percent of the time, I found fun in any shoot I was doing, but not today, and my mood was reflected back at me.

"Get the misery out of your eyes and pretend you're in the mountains with snow all around you. Feel the cool breeze against your skin. Imagine goosebumps erupting on your skin. Now arch your back and bring your face closer to Sebastian's, Kamilah." She did as directed, and I could finally feel the shift. "Turn your head toward me, but keep looking out into the distance." I took the shot and knew it was flawless. "Sebastian, shift your hand on her hip." Moving his hand, his long digits gripped her inner thigh. His fingers were close to touching the purple underwear that I was trying to get customers to buy. I applauded Kamilah for keeping her composure. I wasn't sure I would have been comfortable having some stranger's hand that close to my most private parts for the last hour.

"Perfect. That's a wrap. Now go cool off," I ordered. I was already stepping back under the canopy and positioning myself in front of the fan as Kamilah and Sebastian jumped into the pool. The relief from the heat was instant. I sagged in my seat and closed my eyes as I felt the nausea slowly seep away. Taking in a deep breath, I let it calm my racing heart and slowly let it out. When I opened my eyes, Raine was standing in front of me with a concerned look.

"Are you okay? It seemed like you were struggling the whole day."

I wanted to tell her it wasn't nice to comment on such things, but I kept it locked down. "Everyone was struggling. It felt like the heat was melting us on this roof. Are you telling me it didn't bother you?" I knew it had. Raine's clothes were drenched with sweat, and the little tendrils of hair that had escaped her ponytail were plastered to the side of her face. She was a mess, and I didn't even want to know what I looked like. I'd sprayed mist on my face so many times throughout the last few hours and repeatedly put my hair up in a messy bun on the top of my head. I was sure my hair was sticking up all over the place.

Raine plopped down in the chair beside me and sprayed herself in the face. When some of the mist drifted over to me, feeling like heaven, I let out a happy sigh. With her hand resting on the back of the chair, she turned to look at me. "I thought my shoes were going to melt to the roof. Can you imagine how hot it would be if the ground was black?"

We wouldn't have been able to continue.

"How are you feeling?"

"Better now that I'm cooling off. I'm not sure why we're still up here and not inside with the air conditioning. I need to drink a gallon of water and take a nap after that."

"At least you look a little less green," she commented. "Now, you're slightly flushed."

What the hell was wrong with Raine today? I wanted to say she shouldn't say anything since she looked like shit too, but that wasn't nice, and I was trying to be better. For the last two weeks, I hadn't been pleasant to be around with Ryder's betrayal and lack of communication, dealing with Ben's incessant voicemails, and feeling like I wanted to throw up almost constantly, but I vowed to myself I wasn't going to let it get to me and affect my job.

Raine's cheeks pinked up. "I'm sorry I just realized how that sounded, but I'm worried about you and hate seeing you so sad."

"I know you are, and it's sweet. I can tell you're going to be a great mother one day with the way you've taken care of me. I don't like being like this either, and I'm trying not to let it get to me, but it's hard when I feel like I'm going to throw up at any given moment."

Raine cocked a knowing brow at me and mouthed 'doctor' at me.

Letting out a frustrated sigh, I stood. "When am I going to find the time to go to the doctor? I have too much work to do."

"You won't be able to work if there's something seriously wrong with you, or you end up dead."

A startled laugh escaped. "That's a little drastic, don't you think? I doubt I'm going to die, but to make you feel better, you can make me an appointment." Hopefully, the doctor could give me something to make me feel better, as well.

"Really?" When I nodded, she jumped up. "I'm going to do it now before you change your mind."

I'd go to the doctor, but they'd probably tell me that it would pass and all I needed to do was rest. I appreciated that Raine was worried about me and the situation with Ben. She'd offered to stay with me numerous times since she hated that I was here by myself all the time, but I was used to it. This was my life.

CHAPTER 18

RYDER

Sitting in a chair way too small for my size, I waited for my name to be called. My agent had insisted since I was in South Africa that I go to this casting call for a brand I'd never heard of. She assured me they were very big in the Latino culture, and it would be great for my career. I wasn't sure how a company in South Africa was big in the Latino world, but I'd take her word on it. I wanted to argue I was busy enough, but when she threatened me with no more gym time, I kept my mouth shut. She knew exactly where to hit me so it hurt. I couldn't be a successful model if I didn't work out, and we both knew it. It was a good thing I loved the post-workout high; otherwise, I'd never get out of bed.

With Lexie no longer taking my calls, I'd been working out during all my spare time. It was the only thing that got her out of my mind.

"Yo, what's up, dude?" Parker sat down beside me with a big grin. That guy was always happy.

"Chillin' while I wait for them to call my name. I didn't

expect to see you here. I thought you were in…where was it again? Paris?" It was hard to keep track of what country I was in, let alone someone else.

"I was, but once my job ended, Angie sent me here."

Fucking Angie. Not only did she want me here, but she was sending more competition for me as well. Only one guy was getting the job, and at this point, I didn't care if I got it or not. In a little over two months, I would be back in the US and headed to Washington to see my family for a whole month. I couldn't wait to see them and be lazy.

"You don't mind, do you?"

"Nah, man, I don't care. I'd be happy if you got the job. You deserve it."

Parker frowned. "So, do you. You work harder than anyone I know."

"Whoever gets the job will be busy traveling all over the world for the next six months, and I'm burned out. I need a break and a home-cooked meal."

"Why'd you come then if you don't want the job?"

"Angie," we both said in unison.

"Can I tell you something, and you won't tell anyone?" Parker was a good guy, but I wasn't sure if he was a secret keeper or not.

"Of course, we're friends so you can tell me anything." He pretended to zip his lips and threw away the key. I didn't even know people did that in real life. I'd only seen it on TV a handful of times.

"When my contract with Angie runs out at the end of the year, I don't think I'm going to sign with her again. I want to have more control over what jobs I pick. She has the mentality that I should take every job that's offered and while that's been great…"

"You need a break. I hear ya, man. I don't think I could handle the schedule you've kept this year. I fly out maybe once every month or two for a shoot, and that's all I can handle. You're constantly on the go."

"I am, and I know I've been lucky with Angie. She normally makes it so I can stay an extra day or two to sightsee before I move on to the next place, but damn, I'm tired. She threatened to cut my gym access if I didn't go on this casting call. Can you believe that?"

"What a fucking bitch. She's using your niceness to her advantage. I would love to be a fly on the wall when she finds out you won't be signing with her again."

Yeah, me too. Angie was going to blow her lid and would be relentless for me to sign with her again.

"Do you know who you're going to go with?"

I shook my head. "Not really. Lexie said she had some contacts for me, but..."

"But," Parker's eyes went wide, "what happened with that hottie photographer? You didn't fuck it up, did you? Because, seriously, when we were in Rio, I was so damn jealous of you. You're one lucky son of a bitch."

"I don't feel so lucky now. When I was in Sydney with Lana, my phone somehow got busted. I swear she did it on purpose."

"Your brand new iPhone? Dude, what the hell? And better yet, why were you with Lana?"

"Unfortunately, we were on a job together. If there was a way for me to make it so I never have to work with her, I would, but you know I can't."

"Not yet, but once you're the most famous male supermodel there is, you'll be able to," Parker cracked up beside me at his joke, making me laugh right along with him. If I ever did become a supermodel, I wouldn't become a diva like some models out there. "So, what happened?"

"She asked if she could borrow my phone because there was something wrong with hers and she needed to call her agent with some urgent matter. When she came back with my phone, it no longer worked. Instead of going off on her, I left the club for a little while to cool down."

"Wow, hold up there. Why were you in a club?"

"For the shoot. It was pretty awesome except for Lana being there."

"She ruins everything." His jaw ticked.

"It took a few days for me to get a new phone and phone number; when I called Lexie, she didn't answer or call me back. I didn't get a chance to call her again for a few days, and when I did finally get the time to call her, it said her phone was disconnected or was no longer in service. I don't know what I did to make her so pissed off at me. Before that, we were good and talking every few days and then nothing." I clenched my hands into fists at the thought.

Parker looked at me like I was crazy. "Why did you get a new phone number?"

"Because I'm stupid. I don't know. It made sense at the time with what the guy told me. Now it probably fucked me with Lexie."

"Are you sure it didn't have anything to do with the picture Lana posted on Instagram?"

My stomach sank.

"What picture?" I had a feeling what I was about to see wasn't going to be good.

"You're kidding me, right? Lana posted a picture of you

guys all up close and personal and made it seem like you two were together."

"Together?" I tried to gulp down the rock that had formed in my throat, but it wouldn't go down.

"Yeah, you don't follow her?"

"Why the hell would I follow Lana? I can't stand her and now…" And now I wanted to pull my hair out. Did Lexie seriously think I was with Lana now? I didn't think there was a person on the planet that she hated more and if she thought I'd fucked Lana or was with her…

She couldn't.

Parker pulled out his phone and scrolled with furrowed brows. "You only follow four people. What's wrong with you?"

"I only go on to post." And to try and stalk Lexie until she blocked me. "Angie didn't say I had to follow people, and who would I follow, anyway?"

"You're so lame, dude. Since you don't follow the_lovely_lana, here's what she posted." He handed his phone over to me.

I took it gingerly, like the surface was as hot as the sun, and stared down at a picture of Lana and me on a couch with her on my lap as she kissed my cheek. Her title read: Living my best life with this man. There were five emojis, all with heart eyes, that made me sick. I closed my eyes, trying to get rid of the image, but when I did, all I saw was Lexie with tears in her eyes from when we parted ways in Rio.

I should have known Lana was up to something when she turned sweet as pie halfway through the shoot and asked to borrow my phone. Why was I so stupid?

"Do you think Lexie saw this?"

"Why do you think she changed her phone number?"

Throwing his phone at him, I glared at Parker. "Lexie wouldn't change her number because of me." At least I didn't think so. I at least deserved the chance for her to hear me out. "When I first met her, her ex…" I broke off thinking of all the things she'd told me about Ben. He was unstable, and who knew what he'd done since I'd last talked to her. Did she change her number because of him? Had something more happened? Was she okay? He could have hurt her again, and I wouldn't even know it. My head spun with questions. Maybe once I was finished here, I'd find someplace with internet and google her.

Parker cleared his throat, and I tried to shake off my worry for the time being. "What happened with her ex? It can't be good if she changed her number because of him."

No shit, Sherlock.

I'd never mentioned it to Lexie, but every time I saw what her ex had done to her, I wanted to fly into a rage. I knew if I touched upon it, she would have felt self-conscious about the mark, and by the time we left Rio, it had been looking better. Now I wasn't sure what state she was in.

"I don't know if you noticed she had a long scratch on her neck."

"Of course, I saw it, but I wasn't going to say anything about it." Thank God for that. He finally used his brain.

"That was why she met me in Rio. It happened a couple of days before, and Lexie was scared. Her ex seems deranged, and now I don't know what's going on with her or the situation with him."

"So, what are you going to do about it? Are you going to give up on that little hottie photographer?"

I hated him calling her that, but Lexie was indeed a hottie, and I wasn't the only one who noticed.

"I don't want to, but what can I do? I don't have her number, and I'm out of the country until the end of November?"

"Go see her when you get back to The States. Explain what happened and beg for forgiveness. Get down on your knees if you have to, do whatever it takes. You don't want to let 'the one' get away."

"What makes you think Lexie's 'the one'?" I thought maybe it had all been in my head after she stopped communicating with me. She never seemed to want more, and I never asked. Maybe if I had…

I stopped that train of thought. I knew I couldn't go down the 'what if' train or my mind would be reeling with questions.

"What makes you think she isn't?" Parker fired back.

"When we left, Rio I thought she was, but now…"

"Now?"

"I still think she is, but what do you do when your person hates you?" Because Lexie had to hate me after seeing that damn picture. The next time I saw Lana, I was going to…hell, I didn't know what I was going to do. I was too pissed off to even think straight when it came to her, and it made me realize why Lexie felt the way she did about Lana.

Parker put his hand on my shoulder. "I think in a couple more months she'll be cooled down and ready to listen to what you have to say."

And if she wasn't?

As if he could read my mind, Parker gave me a sad smile. "Do what I said. I only saw you two together for a short time, but I believe you're meant to be together. The way you looked at each other when the other wasn't looking. Hell, even when you were looking at each other." He shook his head. "I knew then you had it bad."

I had it more than bad, and it had been eating away at me that Lexie wouldn't talk to me. At least now I knew why, and I could work with that. I'd find a way to get her to listen to me, the circumstances of how the picture was taken, and what happened to my phone.

"Ryder Williams." A woman in a bright white pantsuit called my name from a door down the hall.

I stood, and Parker clapped my back. "Go lose this job."

"I'll do my best, so you'll get it." Halfway down the hall, I turned back and looked over my shoulder. "Thanks for the advice. I appreciate it."

He gave me a chin nod. "Glad I could help."

As I walked to the door, I knew if I got the job, I could turn it down. I had to because I couldn't travel for another six months nonstop.

"Thank you for joining us today, Mr. Williams. I'm Rhonda." I held out a hand to shake, but she ignored it and turned without a word to start directing me. "First, we'll need you down to your underwear. You can get undressed behind there." She pointed to a curtained off area. "And when you're ready, walk toward us at the table where we'll give you further instructions."

Stepping behind the curtain, I blew out my frustrations. Even though I didn't want the job, I still needed to come off professional. And even though I needed a break, I did want more jobs in the future.

After an hour of doing seemingly everything but turning my eyelids inside out, the casting call was over.

Once I was back in my clothes, I stepped out from behind the curtain to find Rhonda waiting for me. She held a clipboard with a single piece of paper attached to it in her hands.

"Mr. Williams, after looking through your portfolio and what we saw today, we would like for you to be the face of Igolide. I was told you wouldn't be able to start working until December, so I've written in the dates of where we'd need you and when."

I wanted to explode. Angie knew I was taking the entire month of December off and for her to assume I'd take a job that would require me to travel for the next six months proved how much she didn't listen to me.

After only staring down at the paper, Rhonda smiled at me tightly before she took the clipboard back and wrote something down. "This is what we're willing to pay you, and of course, we'll also pay for all of your travel expenses."

I stared down at the number and wasn't sure if the figure I saw was in US dollars or the rand here in Cape Town. I had no idea the conversion, but it didn't matter, for the sake of my sanity, I had to turn down the job. There would be bigger and better jobs on the horizon. I knew it.

"This is an amazing offer, and I want to thank you for your time, but unfortunately, I won't be able to accept your job offer."

Her eyes widened as if she expected me to sign a contract on the spot, and just as quickly, Rhonda schooled her features. "I'm sorry to hear that. Are you sure there's nothing we can do to persuade you to change your mind? I'll have to ask my supervisor, but I'm sure there's a little wiggle room in the budget to offer you more."

"I can assure you it's not the money."

Rhonda nodded, but I knew she couldn't understand why I was turning down this amazing chance of a lifetime. "If we could rearrange the schedule for it to be more suitable for your needs, would that change your mind?"

"Perhaps, but I don't want to put you out."

"When would you be available?" she asked, hopeful.

"Mid-January?" Or never, I wanted to say.

"Let me see what we can do because Igolide wants to work with you. We think you're perfect for the direction we want to go for the next year."

I gave her a tight smile. "You have my contact information, right?"

"Yes, and you'll be hearing from us very soon."

Parker was in the chair where I had left him, asleep in what looked like an uncomfortable position. As I passed, I kicked at his shoe. It wouldn't look good if they came out to call his name, and he was passed out in the hall. While Igolide said they'd work with me, I still wasn't sure if I wanted the job. The next best person to get it would be Parker.

Parker jumped out of his seat and looked around until he spotted me by the elevator. With a chin nod, he sat back down and pulled out his phone.

Stepping onto the elevator, I knew I had my work cut out for me. As soon as Angie heard about me not accepting Igolide's proposal, she would be hitting up my phone, and I'd never hear the end of it. In the end, Angie wasn't the worst of my problems. Somehow, I had to find a way to get into contact with Lexie and convince her to listen to me.

CHAPTER 19

LEXIE

I chewed on my bottom lip as I sat on the crinkle paper lining the table in the doctor's office. I swung my legs as I tried to work off some of the nervous energy of being here. I'd already put hand sanitizer on three times and would probably do it another handful of times before I left. I was determined not to catch anything else while I was here.

A knock resounded on the door, and my heart rate picked up with it. There was nothing worse than sitting in a thin gown while you froze your ass off and talked to someone you saw maybe once a year.

"Lexie?" Dr. Bloom smiled softly at me. "I'm sorry to keep you waiting for so long. When I was in here earlier, you mentioned that you didn't know when your last period was, and you've been under a lot of stress. Since your periods have never been regular, I wanted to do a pregnancy test as a precaution."

Why was she dragging this out? I just wanted her to get to it.

"Our test confirmed you are pregnant. I know…"

Dr. Bloom's words faded as I tried to comprehend them. How was I pregnant? I obviously knew how, but the thought never crossed my mind that the reason I'd been throwing up was that I might be pregnant. Now I had to try and get a hold of Ryder to tell him the news. I didn't expect anything from him now that he was with Lana, but he deserved to know he was going to be a father.

Holy shit! I was going to be a mother.

And I was so not ready.

Dr. Bloom placed her hand on my knee and gave it a little squeeze. "Lexie, are you okay?"

I blinked and swallowed the lump in my throat. "I think so."

"Did you hear a word I said?"

"Um…not really. I'm sorry."

"That's okay, I know it's unexpected, and it's a lot to take in. Why don't we do an ultrasound so we can see how far along you are, and then we can discuss your options?"

Options?

"I know this is scary, so if at any time you have any questions, feel free to stop me and ask. I'll try to answer to the best of my ability, and if you do decide to continue this pregnancy, I can recommend a few doctors."

Was this how she talked to all patients who were pregnant? I understood her not wanting to assume how any woman would want to proceed and for those who wanted to choose an abortion to not feel intimidated, but I didn't like hearing it.

It was now or never. "Can I say something now?"

"Of course, please."

"No matter how far along in this pregnancy I am, I plan

to keep the baby. I know I'm in shock right now, but for me, there's no other option."

Dr. Bloom nodded, handing me a tissue. I hadn't even realized I was crying up until that point. "Would you like a few moments to collect yourself before we continue on?"

"No," I cleared the tears from my throat, "I promise I'm fine."

I sat in a daze as Dr. Bloom went over everything from the vitamins I needed to start taking to not being able to drink any caffeine while pregnant. That was going to be the hardest challenge of all. She gave me a sheet of OBGYN's she recommended and even a few pediatricians. I wasn't ready to find a doctor for my baby when I could barely grasp I had a life growing inside of me.

The rest of the day went by in a blur as I stopped by the pharmacy, picked up dinner, and somehow made it home. As I threw away my takeout containers, I didn't even remember eating; all I knew was that I had to call Ryder. He needed to know what I was planning.

Laying down on my bed, I pulled up Ryder's number and let my finger hover over his name. Never once did I think I would be nervous to talk to Ryder, but now I wanted to throw up at the thought, and I didn't think it was the morning sickness either. It had been a little over a month since I'd last spoken with him. I still couldn't get that picture of Lana and him together out of my head, and I hated that my memories of him were tainted now.

Placing my phone on my nightstand, I buried my head in my pillow and let out a stifled sob. I wasn't sure how I was going to be a single parent and work the hours I worked, but I was going to have to figure it out.

I wished my mom was alive for me to talk to. If she

hadn't died giving birth to me, my life would have been so much different. All my life, I knew my dad blamed me for the death of my mother. When I turned fifteen, I looked exactly like her causing my father to start drinking excessively. I tried everything I could to not resemble my mother. My hair was almost platinum blonde, so it didn't take much to start coloring it in fun colors. Back then, hardly anyone had their hair purple, green, or neon colors. My makeup and clothing were sexy goth, making me stand out from the crowd. From there, I lied about my age and started getting tattoos and piercings to further change my appearance. At school, I was the outcast because of my looks, but I didn't care. It took my dad's attention off me, and that was all that mattered.

When my dad's drinking drove him to trash the house and bang on my door for half the night, yelling for me to let him in, I knew I had to leave. At sixteen, without any place to go, I packed up what little I had and moved out of the only home I'd ever known. Sixteen years later and I hadn't heard a word from my father. As far as I know, he never even looked for me after I left.

All my life, I've been a loner, and now it was coming back to haunt me. Attempting to change that, I rolled over and grabbed my phone. Without thinking too much about it, I dialed Ryder's number only to hear it had been disconnected.

What were the odds he'd also changed his number?

Tears spilled down my cheeks. I wanted nothing more than to talk to Ryder. I didn't care if he was with Lana; I only wanted to hear his voice and for him to tell me everything was going to be okay.

Slamming my phone on the bed, I curled into a ball and let the tears fall. Tomorrow I would come up with a plan, but tonight I would cry until I couldn't cry anymore.

CHAPTER 20
LEXIE

1 Month Later

Raine's mouth opened and closed a few times before she staggered back and fell into a chair. "You're what?"

"I'm pregnant with Ryder Williams' baby. I'm about eleven or twelve weeks along going by what my regular doctor thought I was when I found out. I have a doctor's appointment tomorrow with an obstetrician." I wasn't excited for someone new to poke and prod me, but from what I'd read, I was going to have to get over it. There were going to be a lot of people up in my business until I had this baby.

"How did this happen?"

I'd asked myself the same thing. "We got carried away and didn't use protection. Sometimes he'd pull out and sometimes he'd—

"TMI," Raine shouted. "I don't need the specifics. I just thought—"

This time it was my turn to interrupt her. "What, that I was a responsible adult? Well, you're wrong when it comes to Ryder." I let my head fall back against my chair and stared up at the ceiling. It was still surreal that I was pregnant, but I knew I had to tell Raine when I nearly threw up at the smell of the breakfast burrito she brought in this morning. I couldn't hide it any longer, and I wanted someone to know.

Taking a sip of her coffee, she asked. "How did he take the news?"

"I can't have coffee anymore, so you're going to have to drink yours in the car or at home because smelling it right now, I want to rip your cup out of your hand and suck down the entire thing." I was lucky she rarely brought it in, or I would have had to say something sooner. The mornings were hard, without any caffeine.

"Oh, okay, I can do that." She blinked at me as if she expected me to say something else, but I had no idea what. Finally, she huffed, crossing her arms over her pink t-shirt. "What did Ryder say?"

"Absolutely nothing because…wait for it…he changed his number."

"No," she drew out the word, her mouth forming a tiny 'O.' "What are the odds?"

"I don't know, a million to point one."

"Really?"

"No, how the hell would I know what the odds are? First, he sleeps with…with fucking Lana," I gritted my teeth on her name, "and takes days to finally call me, and then he pulls this shit. I still can't believe I was fooled by his nice guy act."

"I really don't think it was an act." I shot Raine a death glare from my spot on the couch. "But what do I know? I was only around him a short period of time." She tilted her head to the side. "Do you have a plan?"

"The first thing I did was go to Instagram and unblock him. I sent a message, but he hasn't answered back. After a month, I need a new tactic. I looked through his profile and saw it had been quite a while since he last posted." I was sure his agent wasn't happy about that. I bit the inside of my cheek. "When we first got the Mathers project, I wanted Ryder as the male model, but I know he isn't planning on working in December, so we need to make it enticing. See if you can get his contact information. Even if it's just an email, I'll take it. I want you to do whatever you can to get him to sign. Offer whatever you have to up to a certain point. I can't wreck the campaign to get him."

Her eyes lit up. "I like this idea."

I was glad someone did because I was desperate for a way to contact Ryder.

In a flash, her mouth turned into a thin line. "I can't believe you've kept this from me for a whole month."

Me either, but it took me this long to work up the nerve after not being able to tell Ryder. I was tired of being alone in this.

"Do you want me to come to the doctor with you tomorrow?"

Did I? It would be kind of nice.

"I guess I can let you off work to go with me."

Her grin grew. "Now that you know you want Ryder as the model, who else are you going to get?"

"I haven't decided. No one has seemed right. The only thing I do know is it won't be Lana. If by some off-chance Mathers demanded her, I would terminate my contract with them."

"I don't blame you. If we weren't better people, we could spread rumors about her." She tapped her foot and screwed up her face in concentration.

"They wouldn't be rumors but truth. I can't let her affect my life any more than she already has. I can tell by the look in your eyes you think Ryder and I are going to ride off into the sunset, but you need to slow your horses. We don't know if he's with Lana or not."

"We don't know why any of this happened. I really don't think he's with her. I check her IG regularly to see if she posts anything about them, and there's been nothing." Her grin said she thought all was right in the world, and everything would end in a happy ever after.

Raine didn't know how wrong she was. I wasn't sure if I could get over Ryder ever being with Lana once, let alone if they were in a relationship. But I would give him a chance to tell me what happened—or at least I thought I would. I wasn't sure how I'd feel when or if I saw him again. With the way my hormones were, I'd be lucky to hold it together.

"I can see you're doubtful, and I understand why. I'm going to get on my task. This is important in more ways than one. Ryder Williams must join us in Vegas."

I liked her spirit. "You do that and keep me updated. I'm going to get online and look at more headshots. I need to find someone who can stand alongside Ryder, and it's not going to be an easy task."

"This is going to be the best photo shoot ever. It's going to blow everyone's mind." She clapped her hands. "I'm going to get rid of this coffee and get to work unless you have more you need to talk about."

I was glad she had confidence in it. I'd been worried I couldn't pull it all together when I couldn't pick any models, but now I was starting to get hopeful again.

"Get to work. I'm going to work from here, so you can use my desk." I was snuggled into a blanket on my comfy couch and didn't want to move.

I hadn't had much to smile about lately, but seeing Raine happy made my lips twitch. Pulling my laptop onto my lap, I started my millionth search for the perfect woman who now needed to stand next to Ryder at the Lux.

A couple of hours later, my eyelids started to flutter shut. I'd been staring at my screen nonstop since Raine had gotten up. I hadn't heard a peep from her, and I wasn't sure if that was a good thing. I had a feeling Ryder's agent wasn't going to be easy to work with, especially not if he had mentioned to her how I thought she should be focusing on the quality and not the quantity of his work.

Raine yelled from my office area, and I had a feeling it had been her who had woken me up. Leaving the warm cocoon of my blanket, I hurried to my feet when it sounded like she was stomping around and growling. Raine was always easygoing, so for her to sound like this was not a good sign. I found Raine with her hands splayed out on my desk, her head tipped down, and what little I could see of her face was beet red.

Sitting down across from her, I asked. "Should I ask?"

Raine shook her head slowly before she looked up at me with murderous eyes. "I called Ryder's agent, Angie, and at first, I thought I was making some headway with her. She said that Ryder wasn't taking any more work until the beginning of next year, but if the right opportunity came along, she was sure she could convince him to take the job." Her face grew redder as she stood stalk still before me, breathing heavily.

After she stood there for a full two minutes and said nothing, I prompted her. "What happened?"

"She asked who I was with," Raine sat down behind the desk and shook her head. "I was surprised she didn't ask at the beginning, but the second I said I was your assistant, her tune changed. I know you said to offer anything, but she was asking for more than you're getting paid for the entire job."

"As much as I want to tell Ryder the news, I'm not going bankrupt to pay him to be there. Did she give you his email by any chance?" I knew deep down that Raine wouldn't be this upset if we had a way to contact Ryder.

"No, she kept shutting me down. Do you know if he has a website?"

"If he does, it would be one she put up. It wouldn't have his actual contact information, but hers." What was I going to do if I couldn't get Ryder for the job?

"He needs a new agent." Raine let out a frustrated sigh.

"I couldn't agree more. I told him I'd give him the names of ones I've worked with that will keep his best interest at heart. I do have to give Angie credit, though. She's got him out there and made him very sought after, but she has got to know how wearing it is to be constantly traveling." I felt bad for Ryder, even if he had betrayed me. He had no place to call his own, and I couldn't imagine having to find a friend's couch to sleep on when he wasn't in a hotel.

Raine let out a strange, happy sound. It was a mix

between a sigh and a giggle, causing me to cock my head in question. "What was that sound about?"

"You and the look on your face."

"Please tell me what my face was saying."

She pursed her lips and shook her head. "I'm not sure you want to know."

I so wasn't in the mood for her games. "If I didn't want to know, I wouldn't have asked."

"Fine." She flipped her ponytail over her shoulder. "You love him, and there's a very good chance you'll give him another chance." She blurted it out and then clamped her mouth shut. Her eyes were wide as she stared back at me.

"I already told you I'd give him the chance to explain, but that doesn't mean I'll take him back." When her eyes lit up, I held my hand up. "Not that we were ever together. All we were doing is fucking when we were in proximity to each other."

Raine grimaced at my words. "It was more than that, and you know it. While I wasn't there in Rio, I saw some of your pictures and how you looked when you got home. You were happy."

"I was happy. I never denied that I liked spending time with Ryder because I did, but I always knew something like this would happen. He's so young and just starting out. Ryder has a lot of growing to do."

"That may be true, but that doesn't mean he couldn't do it with you."

"It does because I'm not traveling all over the world to spend little bits of time with him only to find him in bed with someone else."

"Don't let that picture jade you. I don't think Ryder

would be a cheater, but you have to trust him. Otherwise, your distrust would ruin your relationship."

"There is no relationship. Please don't get your or my hopes up when I don't know if I'll ever see him again."

Dropping her elbows to the desk, Raine rested her head on top of her hands. "Now you're the one being dramatic. You'll see him again, that I can promise you. Today is day one in trying to acquire Ryder Williams. I'll figure out something, even if I have to set up a fake company email so I can lie to that bitch."

That wasn't a bad idea. If we offered enough money and used a different name, Angie would never know. "I think you're onto something. Angie may never even contact Ryder if she knows it's me who's trying to hire him, but if it's someone else, we might have a shot."

Raine's head perked up, and her bright smile came out, making me feel hopeful again. "What are you thinking?"

"We come up with a new name, and I'll quickly put together a website with some pictures that haven't been used. Once we come up with a name, I'll set up a new email address for us." This could work. I jumped up and rounded my desk, hugging Raine as she sat in shock. "You're brilliant."

"I do what I can," she mumbled into my shoulder.

"Great, let's get to work."

VEGAS

LETTING OUT A DEEP BREATH, I MADE MY WAY DOWNSTAIRS TO the meeting room. I wasn't used to having a meeting before a shoot, but this seemed to be a big campaign, so I'd do what I had to do. Angie had begged me and then informed me she'd already said I'd do the job after they doubled how much they'd pay me. It would be my most lucrative job by far and would set me up for slowing down next year. Angie still had no idea I had no intention to re-sign the contract with her, and after her booking this job without even asking me, there was no way I would change my mind. The only problem was I had very little work for the next year in the books, and it was a little worrying. I could always take the job with Igolide since they didn't seem to want to take no for an answer. Angie had been pestering me about signing with them and to renew her contract. Neither was happening now that I was doing this job.

I found the conference room with Mathers - Skön written on a piece of paper, taped to the door. For some reason, I was nervous about this job. I wasn't sure if I should knock or walk right in and ended up standing there until I felt someone walk up behind me.

A man cleared his throat. "Are you going in?"

Turning around, I found another model standing behind me. "Oh, I wasn't sure what to do. Normally I just show up, and they start taking pictures. I've never had to go to a meeting beforehand."

"Ah, that would be my doing. Sorry, this is an important account, and we want everything perfect. We thought if the models knew what we wanted, it would be beneficial all around."

Wait, this guy wasn't a model? He had to be. He was probably in his mid-twenties, the same height as me, with dark hair, the lightest green eyes I'd ever seen, and amazing bone structure. I was around enough models to know what to look for, and he was it. If Angie or any modeling agency saw him, they'd try to sign him on the spot. How'd he slip by them?

"Are you the photographer?"

He smiled and held his hand out for me to shake. "I'm Tyson Jacobs. I work for Mathers."

"Ryder Williams, one of the models."

He gave me a tight smile. "I know who you are, Mr. Williams."

Shaking his hand, I tried to wrap my head around this job. I'd never heard of any of the companies, yet they were desperate to use me. I tried looking up Blue Stars Photography, but only found a website with very little information on it. They seemed relatively new, so it didn't make sense they'd be used on such a big and important job. Maybe the photographer knew someone from Mathers. I had no idea.

Leaning around me, Tyson put his hand on the door-knob. "What do you say we go inside and get this meeting started?"

I let Tyson go inside ahead of me and followed in behind him. There were only a few people in the room, but what caught my attention was the woman on the other side of the room with blue hair cascading down her back. There was no else in the world it could have been.

It was my Lexie.

Hope filled me, and a deep burn spread through every inch of my soul. I had no idea what she was doing here, and I didn't care. With all that was in me, I tried to hold back from running to her. I'd been patiently waiting for this moment for months, and I couldn't screw it up now that I had her in my sights.

As I walked toward her, all eyes were on me. It was as if they knew our history, and they were waiting to see the fallout when she finally saw me. Standing only a few inches away from her, I could smell her scent. She always smelled of coconut and saltwater, even when we were hundreds of miles away from the ocean.

Reaching out to finally touch Lexie, her name slipped from my lips. It was a mix between a prayer and an apology. She moved as if in slow motion. Turning ever so slowly, I took in each inch of her. I loved everything about her, from her petite frame to the beautiful tattoos she adorned her body with, to her deep blue eyes that stood out against her hair. She was more beautiful than any woman

I'd ever seen, and this time I wasn't going to let her slip away from me.

My gaze snagged on the slight protrusion of her belly that was covered up with a tight white t-shirt. I blinked, and in the next instant, Lexie was looking up at me with tears brimming in her eyes.

Was Lexie pregnant?

How? Who had she hooked up with since I last saw her?

I didn't understand. None of this made sense.

And it didn't seem possible.

"And that's our cue to leave," I heard someone say behind me.

Lexie shook her head and stepped around me. I turned, unable to take my eyes off her. "I think it would be better if Ryder and I leave to have our talk." She pulled out her phone and then just as quickly put it back into the back pocket of her short jean shorts. "Why don't we meet back in here after lunch? Say, one o'clock? That should give us enough time."

Our meeting was scheduled for ten, and I'd left my room to get here early, so I knew it was only a little after ten if that. What did she have to say that would take three hours?

"Are you sure it's enough time? We could call off today and maybe start tomorrow an hour earlier than had planned," a cute brunette said from beside the man I'd met outside. With the shock of seeing Lexie and the news I couldn't quite wrap my head around, I couldn't remember his name.

"That should give you enough time." He nodded as if all this made perfect sense to him.

Enough time for what? My head to explode?

I wanted to ask questions, but my mouth wouldn't work as my mind spun with my new reality. Tears streamed down Lexie's beautiful face. Her eyes were full of anger and questions. Grabbing onto my arm, she pulled me out of the room and down the hallway to the elevator. We were silent the entire way. I watched her hit the button for the twenty-fourth floor and then move to the other side of the elevator, where she stood looking at the doors. She didn't even want to look at me. If that was the case, why did she go to all this trouble to bring me here?

I realized at that moment, it could have all been a trick. Was Angie in on this as well? Was Lexie so angry at me for what she thought happened with Lana that she brought me here to rub it in my face she was pregnant with another man's child?

When the doors opened, I followed her out and down another hall to what I assumed was her room. Was her boyfriend in there waiting for me? I didn't think Lexie had it in her, but did I really know her?

Slipping her keycard in the door, she stepped inside and waited for me to enter before she went to the bar and poured a drink. She held it out to me, and I gratefully took it. I had a feeling I was going to need it. She pulled out a water bottle for herself and drank half of it. I had a feeling she wished she was drinking what I had instead of water.

Her eyes traveled my body and stopped on my clenched hand at my side. Slowly she walked over to one of the couches and sank down onto it. Pulling her knees to her chest, Lexie motioned for the chair across from her.

Downing my drink, I sat the glass down on the bar before I moved to sit across from her. "Are we alone?"

Her brows pulled together before she nodded. While

she was no longer crying, wetness still brimmed in her dark blue eyes. Her voice was soft and full of sadness when she finally spoke. "The whole point of coming up here was for us to be alone so we could talk without a room full of people hanging on our every word."

"I wasn't sure if someone was going to step out of one of the rooms and announce he was your boyfriend and baby daddy." Leaning back in the chair, I closed my eyes as I said my next words. "This isn't how expected the next time I saw you going. I thought you'd be fuming and demanding answers."

She cleared her throat. "I do want answers as I'm sure you do as well. I...this isn't how I saw this going either. I didn't think you'd look at me the way you did, and I'd be so...devastated." Her voice broke on the last word.

What did she have to be wrecked about? I just found out the woman I loved was carrying another man's baby. If she wasn't with someone and that was a big if, I wasn't sure it would matter or if we could move past this.

Taking in a shaky breath, I opened my eyes and asked her. "Who's the father?"

Wrapping her arms around her legs, Lexie rested her chin on her knees. "Is that why you're looking so..." she pulled her bottom lip between her teeth before letting it go, "heartbroken?"

A dark laugh built up in my chest and filled the room. I didn't want to give her any more ammunition than she already had. "Just answer the question."

Straightening, Lexie's eyes hardened as she took me in. "No matter what you think, I'm not a slut. I know we jumped into bed after only knowing each other a handful of hours, but that's not who I am."

"Who are you, Lexie? Because I tried calling you when I could, I tried to get a hold of you on social media, and I was shut down at every turn. It seems to me that you were done with me and didn't have the balls to tell me."

A tear slipped down her cheek, and even though I was mad as hell at her, I wanted nothing more than to pull her in my arms and make everything better. Instead, I sat on my hands to keep from reaching out to her.

"I declined one phone call. One." She jutted her chin out at me. "After I saw that…that picture. When I tried to call you back, you had changed your number or some shit."

"So, you had to change yours?" I shot back. My hands clenched into fists under my legs.

"Yes, I had to change mine, but not because of you. I changed it because Ben was…he was making my life a living hell, and I couldn't take it anymore. The only way I saw to keep him from his constant threatening voicemails was to change my number."

I hated hearing that Ben was the reason. I had been worried he might have been the cause. What were the odds we'd both have to change our numbers and not be able to contact each other?

Resting her head on her knees once again, she continued. "Once I couldn't reach you, and I found out I was pregnant, I knew I had to come up with a plan to see you again, or at the very least, get your new contact information. Only your agent is a huge bitch who seems to hate me and refused to give us your information."

Angie did hate Lexie. One time I'd accidentally let it slip that it was Lexie who had given me the advice to be smarter on the jobs I took and that I was going to slow down next year. After listening to her tirade, I knew I couldn't mention Lexie's name to her again without an epic meltdown.

"How did you get me here then?"

"We came up with a fake company name, and I built a little website to make it look legit. Even with all that, Angie wouldn't give us your contact info."

I gritted my teeth and barely got the words out. "That's an awful lot of trouble to go to just to let someone know you've found someone else, and you don't want to hear from me any longer."

Lexie's head popped up, and her eyes were wide with shock. "Have you been listening to a word that's come out of my mouth? There was only one time I didn't want to talk to you, and it was after Raine showed me the picture Lana posted. You know how I feel about her."

Yes, I most definitely did know how Lexie felt about Lana, and after the shit Lana pulled, I understood why she felt that way. I never knew a person could be so devious.

Relaxing my hands, I let out a cleansing breath. "I cannot control who gets booked on the jobs I'm hired for."

Cocking her head, she narrowed her eyes at me. "Actually, you can. You can have a rider that states you won't work with her. If you had an agent that gave a damn about you, they would help you come up with one."

I hadn't thought of that.

"I don't want it put out there I'm difficult to work with. You told me I needed to be professional."

Lexie laughed without humor. "Anyone who's worked with Lana would commend you on putting your foot down." Her lips thinned out into a firm line as she shook her head. "I don't know how she still gets jobs."

"Great, once I find a new agent, I'll make sure to have

that I won't work with Lana as a clause." It would be a relief.

Lexie blinked rapidly in my direction. "So, you're not with Lana?"

"I've never touched her, let alone fucked her," I growled out.

Squaring her shoulders, she asked. "Why did she post that picture then?"

"Probably to cause exactly what happened between us." Running my hand through my hair, I shot up out of the chair and sat next to Lexie. I couldn't stay away from her any longer. I needed to feel the heat of her body next to mine, and for her to understand, I would never be with Lana for as long as I lived. "I didn't know she posted that picture for almost a month. I was on a casting call and ran into Parker. When he asked how we were doing, and I told him I hadn't talked to you. That's when he showed me the picture Lana had posted. All of a sudden, everything made sense. Well," I moved my head from side to side, "I wouldn't say it made sense, but I understood why you wouldn't want to talk to me. It killed me when I couldn't get a hold of you. All I did was eat, sleep, work, and work-out, and not in that order."

The majority of my time was spent working or working out.

Lexie shuffled on the couch until her back was against the arm, and she was facing me with her forehead wrinkled in confusion. "Why did you change your number?"

"Fucking Lana, that's why. She broke my phone on my last night in Sydney, and I couldn't get a replacement for it for a few days. By then, I was in a foreign country where I could barely understand what the guy was saying. The next thing I knew, I had a different phone number. I tried calling you right after I got my phone, but when I did, it said your number had been disconnected or was no longer in service. I didn't know how to contact you, but I promised myself once I got back, I was going to come to see you. Then Angie told me I had this job." I hung my head, realizing that I'd almost told her I didn't care what she had to do but to get me out of doing it. If I had done that, I wouldn't be sitting here with Lexie. "Now that I know she staged and posted that picture, I think she shattered my phone on purpose."

"That's a lot to take in." Lexie puffed out her cheeks and let it out in a noisy breath. She didn't believe me. "I was so mad at you when I saw that picture. The betrayal that ran through my veins, I can't express it. It made me think everything was a lie."

So, she went and got knocked up by the first guy she saw?

"When I found out I was pregnant and couldn't contact you, I was broken." Her chin dipped, and her shoulders started to shake before a hiccupped cry escaped.

Unable to take the distance and now her crying right in front of my eyes, I picked Lexie up and placed her on my lap. She curled into a ball and rested her head against my chest as she continued to cry. I hugged her closer to my chest and rocked us back and forth for what felt like an eternity until she finally calmed down. I breathed in her scent as I kissed the top of her head.

God, please don't let her be with anyone else. I can love this baby just like I love its mother, but please don't take her away from me.

"I missed being in your arms like this." She nuzzled into my chest a little more than sighed. "I miss your scent.

When the t-shirt you gave to me stopped smelling like you, I cried myself to sleep that night." She giggled into my shirt. "Looking back on it now, it was probably the hormones."

Sitting up to look me in the eyes, Lexie cupped my face in her hands. Her blue eyes were still watery and puffy from all the crying she'd done, but she was still beautiful. I wanted to kiss her, knowing her lips would be extra soft. It didn't help that it had been too long since my mouth had been on her skin. "I haven't even asked. How do you feel about all this? I know it's a lot to take in."

I wasn't sure how to explain what I was feeling, but I wanted to be honest with her.

"To be honest, I'm still trying to wrap my head around everything that's happened today. Never in my wildest dreams did I think you'd be in that room when I walked inside. Was this planned?"

"Was what planned?" She tilted her head to the side. "No," she shook her head. "I told Sadie and Ty that I'd hired you because you're the father of my baby, and I hadn't been able to contact you. They were livid that I used the trust they'd given me for my own needs, but once I showed them some of your pictures, they were on board with me wanting you as the male model. Now they're rooting for us."

After hearing the words 'you're the father,' I didn't comprehend the rest of what Lexie had said. I had to have heard what I wanted to hear.

Lexie's feather-light touch over my face dragged me out of my fog. "Ryder, are you okay? Are you mad I set this all up? I didn't know what else to do. I would have hated—"

Interrupting her, I asked her the most important question I'd ever ask her in my life. "Did you say I'm the father?"

Getting up on her knees, Lexie straddled my legs. Her blue eyes scanned my face. "Unless it was an immaculate conception, the baby is yours. I understand that you're young and just starting out in your career, so you may not want to be a part of his or her life." She bit down so hard on her bottom lip I thought she might draw blood before she continued. "I wanted you to know as soon as possible so you can be involved as little or a much as you like."

As little or as much as I'd like?

"I know this wasn't planned, but I'm at a good place in my life and want this baby." Her hands rested on the tiny bump that had formed since I last saw her. I knew then that she'd be a good mother, but I had to wonder if I could be a good father.

She wanted the child growing inside of her, but I had another important question. "Do you want me?"

Her face contorted in confusion. "What do you mean? Of course, I want my baby to know its father, but there are many ways to achieve that."

My hackles rose. Did she think so little of me, or was she just trying to give me a way out? "I'm not going miss being in my child's life. Yes, I didn't plan on this, but you weren't alone in making our baby."

"To answer your question, we were reckless, but I don't regret it." Her face softened. "I don't regret you."

I prayed that I hadn't fucked everything up in the months we'd been apart. "Are you saying you're done with me?"

"That's not what I'm saying, but I don't know how to

make this work." Her shoulders slumped as she slid off my lap and back onto the couch.

I immediately felt the loss of her body and wanted nothing more than to pull her back on top of me, but we needed to talk and figure this out. No wonder the guy downstairs gave us the whole day to talk.

"I don't know either, but if I get the choice of having you or not, I want you. When we left Rio, I swear you took a big piece of my heart with you. I've missed you so damn much, I literally ached." I rubbed the spot over my heart that had stopped burning the moment Lexie said she wasn't done with me.

"Ryder," she said my name so softly and so full of love that I nearly combusted, "I missed you too, but I don't want to trap you into something that you say you want right this moment and once we part again, you feel differently."

"We've known each other for almost a year, and in all that time, I've fought to not ask for more from you. But now I'm done fighting myself. I want you to be mine. I don't want you to be with anyone else, now or ever."

"What about you? Are you going to only be with me?"

She had no idea how far gone I was for her.

"I haven't been with anyone else but you, and I don't want to be."

"I feel the same, but…"

"No, buts," I shook my head at her. "Why are you fighting this?"

"Because I don't think I could take it if you walked away from me, but now I have to think about more than just myself."

I let out a frustrated breath. Why was she being so difficult and not listening to me?

"I can promise I'm not going to walk away. I know you think I'm young, and while I am, I know what I want. I've watched my father believe he was going to lose the love of his life while my mom had cancer. I've traveled the world this last year. Both experiences made me grow up and appreciate life, and to go for what I want. And you, Lexie Keene, are what I want. I want a life with you and our baby. Please don't deny me."

Lexie tried to blink back tears and failed. I watched as they streamed down her face, unsure if they were happy tears or if she was about to break my heart again. "I don't want to refuse you."

"Then don't. Marry me."

He couldn't mean the words that had just fallen out of his mouth.

"You don't have to give me an answer today, but think about it." Sadness clouded his eyes, and it broke my heart to see.

As I stared back at him, I was sure I looked like a gaping fish. My mind swirled with his words. Marry him? We'd never even been a couple. But hadn't we though? We used to talk almost every day, and I hadn't been with anyone else since he showed up in my life. I wanted Ryder almost more than anything, but I couldn't stand the thought that in a few years, he'd resent the fact that he'd gotten me pregnant and then gotten married in a rush.

Gripping the back of his neck, Ryder let out a shaky breath. "I thought I was a good guy."

"You are a good guy. The best man I've ever known." I tried to assure him. "Don't doubt that because of my hesitation."

"I can't help it when I see all those thoughts running across your face."

"I don't want to sound like a broken record, but I feel like you need more time to let this news settle in and to figure out your feelings."

Ryder growled, his fingers twisting the long strands of his hair. "I know what I feel for you. What I've felt for you for a long time." He moved across the cushions until he was almost on top of me. Wrapping his large hand around mine, he pulled it to his chest. "The only thing I've doubted were your feelings for me. I understood why you wanted to keep us casual with my traveling, and although you didn't say it, I'm sure you thought I'd eventually move on to someone else."

Those were my exact thoughts.

"Am I so easy to read?"

One shoulder lifted. "We've gotten to know each other pretty well over this last year. Mostly by phone, but when we were in Rio, I thought there was more. The way tears filled your eyes as we said goodbye…" he swallowed roughly, "I thought they meant more."

"They did mean more, but—"

"No, more buts. Stop fighting your feelings. Not now while I'm sitting right here in front of you, spilling my heart out to you. It is not the time. I know I can't predict the future, but I'm not going to break your heart, Lexie. If I did, I would be breaking my own. Please open up to me. Tell me I'm not alone."

"You're not alone." The words tumbled out of my mouth in little more than a whisper. I moved to wrap my arm around his waist and rested my head against the furious beat of his heart in his chest. When his arms snuggly wrapped around me, I closed my eyes and opened up to him. "I've never felt this way about anyone in my life, and it scares me. Look what happened with my last boyfriend. He turned crazy and probably wants to hurt me." My breath caught at finally spilling what I'd been dreading about Ben.

Ryder's arms tightened to the point of crushing the breath out of me. "I won't let him hurt you." When I made a strangled noise, he loosened his hold on me.

I wasn't sure how he could promise that when he was always halfway around the world from me, but I didn't argue. Instead, I continued to crack open my heart and let everything out. "I won't deny I've wanted more, but what's the point when I only see you every five or six months and then for you to break my heart? Even unintentionally, you did break my heart when I saw that picture of you with Lana. Who's to say that won't happen in the future?"

"Because I won't let it. I won't put myself in the position for it to ever happen. Every move I make, I'll think about how it would affect you." His index finger trailed down my cheek until it rested under my chin. Slowly he lifted my face until we were eye to eye. "Even though I haven't had the life experience you've had, I've never felt this way, and the chance of me ever feeling this way about another human again is next to impossible. I don't want anyone else but you. Tell me you feel the same."

Ryder rested his forehead against mine and closed his eyes. I desperately wanted him to open them. I loved everything about his eyes. From the open and honest way they conveyed how he was feeling, to their beautiful color. I could see deep down into his soul if I looked close enough.

It had been too long since I'd last seen them, and I missed gazing into them.

God, how was he so good at expressing his feelings when he was so young? I was an emotionally stunted mess who could barely articulate what had been building up in my chest since I knew I'd see him again. If I was honest with myself, those feelings had been building since before Rio.

"I feel it." I paused, unsure of how to express what I wanted to say. Knowing he'd fight me on it, but how could he know what he wanted at this stage in his life without really knowing me? We'd only spent a little less than two weeks together in the year we'd known each other.

Opening his eyes, he kissed the corner of my mouth. "Stop fighting what you want."

"I don't want to fight it anymore." My lips brushed against his as his hand ran down my back and pushed me closer to him. "Let's see where the week takes us."

His handsome face scrunched up. "What do you mean?"

"Let's be a couple, access our feelings, and at the end circle back to your question."

He squared his shoulders as he stared down at me. "You'll answer me at the end of the week?"

"Yes," I answered breathlessly. I wanted to pull him down to me, to feel his lips on mine until I felt him stiffen.

"When we were in Hawaii and Rio, we were a couple." His breath hitched. "Even when we were apart."

"I won't deny that, but before we weren't contemplating spending the rest of our lives together. We weren't going to be bound to one another for the rest of our lives by a child." It didn't feel like he was taking this seriously. I didn't want to get married for the sake of being married. I didn't even know where he'd be when the baby was born.

"Do you want to know what I felt when we were in Rio?" Even though I was afraid to know, I nodded. "That I was falling in love with you and that I wanted to marry you."

He was lying. He had to have been. Feeling bold, I asked. "Why didn't you say anything?"

"Say anything?" He bristled. "I was afraid I couldn't even ask you to be exclusive or even my girlfriend, let alone declare my love for you."

Every word that spilled from his lips was perfect. Ryder said everything I wanted to hear and more, so why couldn't I trust him?

Rising to my knees, I leaned forward, my eyes locked on his. When I was only a hair's breadth away from his lips, I spoke. "I'm sorry I made you feel that way. That was never my intention. I was only trying to look out for both of us."

Gripping my hips, Ryder pulled me onto his lap. "Stop being scared of your feelings for me. Look into my eyes, and you'll see my love for you, reflecting back at you."

I saw more than his love for me in his eyes. I saw how much he wanted me to trust him for the rest of time, and how much he craved me. "How are you not scared?"

He smiled, and those damn dimples of his popped out. Just as quickly as they appeared, I melted against him. My hands cupped his cheeks, and my thumbs rested over those undeniable indentations. I wanted to tell Ryder how much I loved him, and as if he could read my mind, he started to kiss up my neck, his voice was muffled as he spoke against my quickly overheating skin. "Would you run away if I told you I love you?"

"No," I answered breathlessly. Angling my neck to give him further access, I tangled my fingers in the hair at the top of his head. I loved his messy, crazy hair, and so did everyone else. It was part of his signature look. "If you told me, I'd never let you go."

Ryder stood with me in his arms with my legs wrapped around his trim waist and briskly walked into the bedroom before throwing me on the bed.

Looking up at him, I saw his blue eyes darken with lust. Ryder quickly kicked off his jeans and shoes, his length was already hard and weeping as it bobbed from his movements. Gripping his shirt behind his neck, he pulled it up and over his head. I was in awe as each inch of golden skin was unveiled. He'd bulked up some since I last saw him making his body more defined and tantalizing. The man before me was perfection inside and out, and he wanted me.

Forever.

Ryder wasted no time removing my clothes. I'd been too distracted by watching him strip and the body that was under all those clothes to think about getting naked myself, let alone move. His eyes were dark, and his face was set as he prowled toward me. He was a man on a mission, and that mission was me. Gripping my thighs, he swiveled on the bed until he was underneath me.

"You have no idea all the things I want to do to you," he growled out. I felt the vibration through my pussy as he glided me up his chest and didn't stop until he I was straddling his face. "I want you to ride my face until you can't scream anymore, and then I'm going to fuck you so hard, you'll barely be able to walk tomorrow. It will feel like we were never apart."

Wetness dripped down my legs as he spoke. I loved how much he wanted to possess me and didn't hold back. Rocking back and forth, his tongue found my clit and swirled. It felt like pure heaven. When he added two fingers into my core, they sent me into overdrive. It had been too long since he'd had his mouth between my legs.

"Fucking hell, the noises you're making are driving me wild. Come for me on my tongue, my sexy Lexie. I want to lick up every last drop of your pleasure." The things he said to me and the vibrations of his words pushed me over the edge. My walls clamped down on his fingers as they continued their rhythmic pumping, and I nearly took flight as his skilled mouth sucked hard on my sensitive bud.

"Ryder," I moaned his name as I fell against the headboard.

"There's nothing better than hearing my name on your lips while I pleasure you." He kissed the inside of my thigh and then carefully laid me down beside him. Leaning up on his elbow, Ryder smiled lazily down on me. His chin was still wet from my juices as he dipped down and placed a soft kiss to my mouth.

"Come here." He demanded lightly as he moved back onto his back and took me with him. He positioned me again, only this time, I was placed with my head on his chest as he slowly ran one hand up and down my back, almost putting me in a trance. My eyes started to flutter shut until his hand dipped down between my legs. One finger pushed inside once and then twice before it moved to a place no man had ever been before. My body tensed and started to slide away.

"Relax," he tried to soothe me. "I know you're scared, but I promise if you don't like it, I'll stop. I only want to make you feel good." His index finger breached my puckered hole, and my body went on full alert.

Stilling my body, I looked up at him and asked. "What about you? Don't you want to feel good?"

"I do, and part of the experience is pleasing your lover, your other half. Relax." He pushed his finger in a little bit more before pulling out slightly. "Do you not get off on hearing the noises that come from me and watching the way my body moves with each lap of your tongue or rise of your hips?"

"I do," I moaned and wiggled my hips.

"That's my girl. I know what will make this all better." He slipped his finger out, and even though I didn't think I'd like it, I kind of missed feeling his digit inside of me. Ryder slid out from under me and moved in behind me. Tagging me by my waist, Ryder pulled me up until I was on my hands and knees, moving me like I was a rag doll. His hot length dragged against my thigh, leaving a trail of pre-cum before he rubbed it up and down my slit until it was coated in my juices. Placing it at my entrance, he pushed inside with one brutal thrust. He wasn't kidding about fucking me hard. My excitement built up as he slammed into me from behind. His balls struck my swollen nub with every thrust while his guttural moan drowned out the slapping of our skin.

One hand pushed down between my shoulder blades while the other continued to glide down until it met the base of my spine. Softly, his fingers ran along one cheek of my ass before they moved to the other. His hips picked up speed until they were driving into me at a savage pace. His thumb pushed against me, and this time, I relaxed as I felt fuller than I'd ever been before in my life.

"Oh my God, Ryder," I groaned into the mattress.

"I told you it would feel good. You're already clenching around me, my sexy girl." He matched my groan as he pumped faster, making me spiral into the abyss.

As Ryder transcended me into another world with the rapture he was delivering on my sex-starved body, he stilled and collapsed on top of me. His chest heaved as he breathed against the nape of my neck. Pulling himself out, I immediately felt the loss and was already starving to feel him fill me again. I wasn't sure how we were going to get any work done when all I wanted was to have Ryder deep inside of me.

He flopped down on the bed with a wide grin on his face, his dimples popping out. Kissing his shoulder, I moved my ministrations up until I reached his adorable indentations. Placing a kiss on each, I smiled down at him. "Even though I was mad at you, I missed you, dimples."

His smile disappeared. "If I would have known, I...I don't know what I could have done differently, but I would have done anything to prevent you from thinking I would have...I can't even say it. The thought of touching her makes me sick. If she were a man, I'd kicked her ass the next time I saw her."

Of course, the good guy wouldn't want to hit a woman, but that didn't mean I couldn't. I'd probably claw her eyes out.

"Hey," Ryder's gravelly voice brought me out of my musing, "stop thinking about her. She may have fucked with a short portion of our lives, but no longer."

He was right. I wouldn't let her take Ryder away from me again. How was it that Ryder had a much better grip on reality than I did?

"You're wise beyond your years."

"I'm glad you think so," he swallowed roughly, looking down. "Does my age bother you?" he asked hesitantly.

"Most of the time, I don't think about it. If you were immature, then maybe, but most of the time, you seem to think more logically and bring me down from my crazy thoughts. I mean, it's in the back of my head when I think about the fact that your career is taking off, and in all truth, I am afraid you'll eventually want to be with someone else."

"It doesn't matter how old someone is; that's the risk you take in any relationship."

"I know. It's just an excuse to help me with my fears."

His eyes flared wide. "Do I really scare you that much?"

"More than you could possibly know, but I'm not going to let my fears get in the way of living my life."

If I let my fears control me, I wouldn't be where I was.

CHAPTER 23

RYDER

Exiting the elevator with our hands clasped together, I asked. "How should we do this?"

Turning to look toward me, Lexie scrunched her nose up. "What do you mean, just like any other photo shoot, except everyone knows we're probably together."

I didn't want people to wonder if we were together or not. If it was up to me, she'd already have my ring on her finger, but I'd yet to convince Lexie to find a little white chapel and get married.

"What do you mean, probably?"

Lexie stopped outside the room we'd met in yesterday, her hand rested on my chest as she looked up at me. "Who's to say I'd take you back if you had hooked up with Lana, hell she might have been your girlfriend. I shuttered at the thought of Lana ever being my girlfriend. "What if you'd be pissed about me being pregnant?"

"That was never a possibility." Although I was still trying to wrap my head around everything I'd learned since I'd arrived in Vegas.

"It will be fine. They were all rooting for us. Now, all we have to do is get through this shoot."

I had another idea of what we needed to do before we left Vegas, but I wasn't going to push my agenda on her. I understood why Lexie was hesitant, but that didn't mean I liked it. And it meant I had to prove to her that she was the only woman in the world for me.

Lexie opened the door to a full room. No one seemed to notice us as we stepped inside, but the moment we sat down, all eyes were on us. My leg started to bounce, and Lexie's hand gripped my thigh underneath the table to calm me. No one asked if everything was okay between us. Instead, they took one look and immediately started to smile.

Raine handed out packets to each of us, and a shift took over Lexie as she went over what she planned for each day. She even had some sketches for what she was hoping to capture as she photographed me and Alyssa, a model I'd never worked with before. She was beautiful with long blonde hair with caramel highlights and eyes to match her hair. I wasn't sure if they were contacts or not, but either way, she was striking.

I knew we were already behind after not working yesterday, but no one seemed to mind. I stood by a craft table, adding a little sugar to my coffee when Alyssa came to stand beside me. She gave me a hesitant smile as she poured herself a cup. I wasn't sure if she was uneasy because of what transpired yesterday or because she liked me. Training my eyes to the ceiling, I prayed Alyssa didn't like me. If she did, it could get uncomfortable, and the last thing I needed was for Lexie to start thinking I was better off with someone else my own age.

"Have you worked with everyone before?" She took a sip of her coffee and hid behind her cup.

I swept the room to see who was in it. All of Lexie's team seemed to be here. I'd only worked with them once and ran into them in Hawaii, but I had a knack for remembering people. Besides Sadie and Tyson, there were a few others I had no idea what they would be doing.

"Not everyone. Only Lexie and her people."

Looking out of the side of her eye, Alyssa eyed Lexie and Raine before she whispered, "She seems intense."

That wasn't the word I would use to describe Lexie. She was driven and talented and knew exactly what she wanted. She knew how to get it out of the models she worked with. Alyssa hadn't seen any of that yet, so I was curious how she'd come up with that assumption.

I shrugged the shoulder that wasn't holding the coffee. "Only when working but in the best way possible. This shoot will probably launch your career."

Her eyes gleamed with that knowledge. "That would be great." She clapped her hands together softly. "I was surprised she was so adamant about wanting me on the project."

Lexie wanting Alyssa on the shoot was a little strange.

"Excuse me, I need to ask a question about one of the scenes they're hoping for," I lied. Kind of. The scene I wanted to know about was why Lexie wanted Alyssa so badly.

Lexie's back was turned toward me, but Raine and Sadie were looking right at me as I strode toward them.

"Trouble in paradise, already?" Sadie asked quietly but not so that I didn't hear her.

I watched as Lexie let out a sultry laugh and shook her head. "It was a good talk, and we cleared everything up."

Wrapping my arm around her waist, I let my hand rest on her hip. "Except for the fact that she hasn't answered whether or not she'll marry me."

All eyes turned wide as Raine and Sadie gaped at me, and I could feel Lexie's body tense before she pulled away and stood staring at me with fire in her eyes.

"That is not to be discussed while we're working," she hissed. "If that's why you came over here, you can leave."

Fuck, I'd pissed her off and royally too.

Holding my hands up in surrender, I pleaded with her to forgive me. "It's not. I'm sorry. I can't help it if I want to marry you." I eyed Raine and Sadie as they stood there watching us and knew now was not the time to get into this. "I wanted to ask about Alyssa."

Lexie's posture relaxed a fraction. "Please don't tell me she's being a bitch. I've only heard good things about her."

"But you haven't worked with her." It was a statement. Not a question.

"Never, but I thought you complemented each other, and her eyes are gorgeous."

They really were.

Sadie stepped forward. "Is she giving you any problems?"

"Nothing like that. She seems kind of quiet but nice. Maybe a little nervous."

"She should be nervous because if she doesn't deliver…" Sadie's cheeks heated up.

Lexie placed her hand on Sadie's arm. "She will. I guarantee it. Why don't I prove it? We should probably head down to the lobby and get started. I'm hoping to do the pool shots tomorrow, and I can't do that if everyone's working on no sleep."

Sadie clapped her hands loudly, getting everyone's attention. "Let's head down to the lobby, and get to work."

Lexie smiled at her with stars in her eyes. I think she had a girl crush on Sadie. "Oh, you're perfect. I can't wait for you to put everyone in line this week."

"I'm happy to be of assistance."

Tyson came over and stood next to Sadie. "Is there anything you need me to grab?"

Lexie cocked her head as she took him in and I can't lie, I was jealous of the way she looked at him. "Have you ever modeled, Ty?"

"Can't say that I have. Why?" His cheeks and ears turned pink.

I stifled a chuckle as he blushed.

Lexie scoffed. "Don't tell me no one has ever said you could be a model."

"Only my wife." He draped his arm over Sadie's shoulders, and she looked up to him with only love in her eyes.

"Because it's true." She turned back to us. "He pretends he doesn't know how good looking he is and that he never looks in a mirror."

Lexie bobbed her head like that was normal. "Would you be opposed to maybe being in a few shots? I'm still trying to work it out in my head, but I think you'd add something to the campaign."

Tyson took a step back, away from all of us, his eyes wide in alarm. "Oh, I don't know. That wouldn't be very professional if I posed for a campaign we've been hired to do."

Lexie shrugged. "It happens. Let's head down to the

lobby and I'll tell you about what happened this one time in Rio."

'Interesting,' Ty mouthed.

"I'd definitely like to hear that story," Sadie chimed in.

Silently, I trailed behind them as Lexie told them what happened with Rob, and how she ended up being in one of the shots they used for the campaign. She even pulled a few of the pictures up on her phone to show them. Sadie hung on her every word while Tyson looked a little green. He probably thought he'd end up in the campaign, but I knew Lexie wouldn't try to use him if he was against it. Going by his looks, he would make a good model, but I understood why he wouldn't want to do it. It would be difficult to go back to work after everyone saw him in that light. I wondered how the dynamic at work was with them working together and Sadie being his boss.

We filed into an area off the lobby where a few people had come down to set up with lights and to help redirect traffic from the area. The good thing about only shooting with a camera was it didn't matter how noisy it was around when the shot was taken. If we'd been filming, it would have been a whole other matter altogether. Still, it was hard for me to concentrate sometimes when there was too much going on, and Lexie, in all likelihood, had the same problem.

"Places everyone," Lexie clapped and then started pointing to where she wanted each of us. Alyssa clung to my side as we waited for Lexie to measure the lighting and be happy with it. I didn't understand the process, but over the months, I'd looked up her photos, and she knew what she was doing, so I'd wait until she was content to get her shots.

With a nod, she stepped back and lifted her camera to her eye. "Let's make some magic."

◌

"We should break to eat," Sadie announced. She looked at her watch and shook her head. "I'm not sure what meal you're eating since we're working abnormal hours but go eat. I can't have anyone fainting, and we've still got plenty to do before we stop for the day."

We'd been going since around midnight, and it felt like it had been hours since we started. I felt bad for Lexie as she let out a large yawn. Earlier, she had explained she couldn't drink coffee while pregnant, and how much she didn't like giving it up. I didn't want to consume any caffeine out of solidarity, but I couldn't function without it after the long day I'd had.

Not that I'd complain. The way I felt now compared to how I felt when I walked into the meeting room earlier was like night and day. I felt like the sun had finally decided to shine on my face for the first time since I'd last seen her. For months I'd been in the dark, but now she illuminated my life with her sheer presence.

Raine, Sadie, Ty, and Lexie stood huddled together around a makeshift podium with a laptop on top as they examined each photo she'd taken the last few hours.

Separating, Sadie placed a hand on Lexie's shoulder as they both nodded. "The shots look great and just what we wanted. We've got a gem here with our Lexie. She knows how to get what she wants and relatively quickly." There were a few chuckles at her comment. "We're going to move on to the next location, so please eat and get some rest.

We'll be reconvening at…" Her questioning gaze looked to Lexie for the answer.

"Models meet at hair and makeup at four a.m., we'll be shooting at sunrise on the rooftop. The rest of you, please make sure everything is in place before that time. The most important thing I can stress is, do not be late. I know we're here in Sin City but now is not playtime. We'll get to that later."

Everyone stood straighter, and their eyes lit up when she spoke even though they were dead tired. I loved how much everyone admired her. I missed working with her and wished everyone I worked with was as easygoing and competent as she was.

"Are you going to eat?" Alyssa asked from beside me. I felt bad. I was sure from her point of view, it looked as if everyone knew each other, and she was the outsider. I didn't want her to feel left out, but I also wasn't too sure how Lexie would be with others around us. I wanted her by my side as much as possible, and if Alyssa or anyone else's presence hindered that, I wouldn't be too happy.

"Most definitely," my stomach let out a loud rumble declaring my hunger, "I'm just not sure where. Let me go see what's going on," I left her by one of the pillars and made my way over to Lexie. She and Raine were happily chatting away as I came up to them. "How are things, ladies?"

"Good," Raine blushed and looked down at her shoes.

"Good, I was wondering if there were any plans for… what time is it, anyway? I hate not having a watch on." I tapped my wrist.

"Oh, it's a little after seven in the morning, so I guess that means it's time for breakfast," Raine answered quietly.

Lexie's finger hooked my pinky and shook it. "I think the hotel has a breakfast buffet. What do you say we hit it, and then everyone can get some sleep? Or do you need like some super disgusting healthy breakfast?"

"Right now, I'll eat anything, we should have eaten before we started."

A sly smile spread across her face. "We were busy doing better things."

"Oh, God." Raine's cheeks turned redder as she stepped away.

"You shouldn't be skipping meals." It couldn't be good for her or the baby for her to not eat for so long. My head swam at the thought of Lexie carrying my child. Before, I had dreamed about one day becoming a parent, but I didn't know it would happen so soon in my life. I wasn't going to complain, though. There was no other woman on the planet I wanted to have children with than the woman standing next to me.

"I know, and I usually don't, but you are a mighty fine distraction. I promise to fill myself to the brim and then go sleep off my food coma."

Leaning down until my lips caressed her ear, I asked. "Am I staying in your room, or should I keep mine?"

"I hate you even have to ask that question. I want you with me, and if we're trying to see what life is like together while we're here, I think you should be in my bed, but it's up to you."

"Our bed," I growled, frustrated. "I already know what it's like staying in a hotel room with you for a week. You're not going to do anything that's not going to make me not want to marry you."

"I don't know. I might fart all night in my sleep

now that I'm pregnant," she giggled. I wasn't sure how she could make a damn giggle sound so sultry, but she did.

"Your stinky ass wouldn't bother me if I was by your side."

"Damn." She shook her head and whispered for only me to hear, "You're too sweet."

"You love it."

Her soft lips brushed across the column of my neck. "I do. I really do, and I bet if you lifted your head right now, those dimples that I love so much would be showing themselves."

"You do make me smile."

Tyson cleared his throat. "Raine said there was a breakfast buffet in the hotel. Are you both going?"

"Yes," I answered for both of us. "Alyssa was asking me if everyone was going or not, and I wasn't sure what the plan was."

"We can all go. I don't care. Do you?" Lexie asked Tyson.

"The only thing I care about is eating and getting some sleep. I had no idea a photo shoot could be so tiring."

"It can be," Lexie answered as if it was no big deal, and maybe to her, it wasn't, but for most, they weren't used to working such strange hours of the day. "Let's go eat. Why don't you go tell Alyssa to join us?"

I had barely taken two steps in Alyssa's direction when she scurried over to me. "We're going to a buffet that's in the hotel if you want to join us."

"Oh." She looked down at the floor with the corners of her mouth turned down. "Do you think they'll have a healthy option?"

"It's Vegas, so probably." The others had started to leave, so I followed them with Alyssa following at my side.

"Have you ever been before?"

"Vegas?"

She nodded.

"It's my first time. How about you?"

"I've been a few times for shoots."

Ty was standing at the entrance with Sadie when we got to the restaurant. She held a credit card in her hand and waved us closer. "Go on in, Mathers is picking up the tab. "

Alyssa perked up as she spotted all the food. There were rows of every possible breakfast dish you could imagine and some you couldn't. Picking up a plate, I filled mine with bacon, a ham and spinach omelet, one slice of French toast, and a banana. It wasn't my usual breakfast, but I needed to eat, and I was going to splurge this morning. Today was a good day, and I was celebrating.

I found Lexie sitting at a booth next to Raine, and Tyson and Sadie on the other side of them. I wasn't sure how they'd managed to get their food before me, but they had. I sat down next to Lexie at the end of the bench, and a moment later, Alyssa slid in beside Sadie.

Everyone looked at her with curiosity, but didn't say anything and went back to eating. I didn't want her to feel like an outsider, but this was uncomfortable. For the next few minutes, no one said anything as we all ate. With each bite, I could see everyone's eyes slowly start to droop a little bit more. We'd be lucky to not fall asleep at the table at the rate we were going.

"So, what is everyone going to do once they've got some sleep in their systems?" Tyson asked.

"I might hang out at the pool or go shopping," Alyssa

spoke up. Her plate mostly consisted of fruit with a lone hard-boiled egg in the mix.

"I'm going to see if I can get a ticket to a show," Raine announced.

"What's playing? I might be interested," Lexie said, perking up some.

"Us too," Sadie nodded excitedly. "We haven't been here since we got married, and let's just say we didn't see any of the local attractions."

"Did you honeymoon here?" Alyssa asked a little more boldly. She was starting to break out of her shell, and I liked that we'd made her comfortable enough to do that.

"No, we got married here." Tyson looked down at his wife. I could see his pupils dilate all the way from across the table. I had a pretty good feeling he was remembering their time in Vegas.

"Really? Was it planned?" Alyssa leaned on her hand as she looked toward the couple.

"If you count a couple of days planning, then yes," Sadie laughed. "It was spur-of-the-moment, and once we were here, we went to the first chapel we saw." One side of her mouth turned down. "Maybe not the best decision, but it got the job done."

"But you'd recommend getting married in Vegas?" I asked Tyson.

He looked back and forth between Lexie and me. "Um...if you're ready to get married, then yeah. We couldn't wait a single minute longer and jumped on a plane."

"That sounds so romantic," Raine sighed dreamily.

It did, and it didn't. While I wanted to marry Lexie

today if she'd let me, maybe she wanted a big wedding or something more special.

Setting down my fork, I turned to her. "Do you want a big wedding?"

She finished chewing before she answered. "Not really. In all actuality, I've never put much thought into it."

"Why?" Alyssa asked a little too loudly. "Didn't you used to dream about your wedding when you were a child?"

Lexie frowned before she picked her fork back up and started eating again. Each time, she stabbed her food a little bit harder. Maybe she never wanted to get married, and that's why she was upset. Wrapping my arm around her shoulders, I pulled her into my side and kissed her temple. Instantly, she relaxed into me and started to eat with her usual grace.

Ducking, so my mouth was near her ear, I spoke quietly enough for only her to hear. "I'm sorry if her question bothered you."

She sat up straighter and spoke so everyone could hear what she had to say. "It's okay. I just never thought being married was in the cards for me, especially seeing how much it wrecked my dad after my mom died."

"Being married can heal those wounds if you find the right person." Sadie looked at us with kind eyes.

"And I think you have," Tyson added. "Why don't you put the poor sap out of his misery and marry him?"

"How do you know?" Lexie and I both asked at the same time.

"It's written all over his face. He's dying to marry you. Trust me, I've been there and know the look all too well."

Alyssa looked uncomfortably at us from across the table

like she needed to use the restroom. I wanted to laugh, but I also didn't want to distract Lexie.

"We're trying this week out." I hated the words as soon as they left my mouth.

"What kind of bullshit is that?" Tyson barked out with a laugh. His wife's soft face instantly went hard as she glared at him.

Leaning over the table, my eyes narrowed at him. "Hey, don't speak to her like that. I don't want to force her into doing anything she doesn't want to do, and if she doesn't want to marry me, then I'll find a way to live with that."

I gulped down the words that had just come out of my mouth. I wasn't sure how I'd manage, but I would. I'd take Lexie anyway I could get her, even if that meant she wouldn't be my wife now or ever.

Lexie cleared her throat. "If you'll excuse us." She turned in her place to look at me, her eyes watery. Her voice was whisper quiet as she spoke. "Please come with me."

Standing up, I wasn't sure what was happening. Was Lexie going to yell at me for what I'd said at the table? Taking my hand in hers, she led the way out of the restaurant and down the hall until we were clear from any onlookers. When we finally stopped, and she looked up at me, there were tears cascading down her cheeks. She pushed me up against the wall, her small hands cupping my cheeks. "I want you to know, I do want to marry you, but I'm not sure right now is the right time."

Now was the perfect time.

With my hands firmly planted on her hips, I tried to explain myself calmly. "I know it may seem old-fashioned, but I want us to be married before our baby is born. There's nothing that's going to change the way I feel about you. But if you're not ready, I'll marry you today, tomorrow, next week or a month, or even a year from now. You say the word, and I'll be there."

A soft smile tipped her lips as her blue eyes glittered up at me. "Why is it when you say endearing things like that all my worries disappear?"

"Because that's how it should be. When I'm with you, the rest of the world fades away, and all I see is you. I want to do the same for you. For you to be able to share your worries and troubles, and we work them out together."

Pushing up on the tips of her toes, Lexie pressed her lips to mine. It was desperate and healing all at the same time, and when she opened her mouth over mine, I knew she'd be mine until the end of time.

Breaking apart, she rubbed her nose along mine. "You're a very convincing man, Ryder Williams."

Blinking rapidly as wetness built in my eyes, I placed my hands over hers. "Does that mean what I think it does?"

"Why don't you ask me and find out?"

Letting go of her, I dropped down to one knee faster than the speed of light. I wasn't going to give her a chance to change her mind. Holding both her hands in mine, I brought them to my mouth with our eyes locked on each other and kissed the back of each hand. "My beautiful and talented woman, and the mother of my unborn child. The one person in this world I can't live without, will you please do me the honor of becoming my wife, my partner in life?"

Nodding vehemently, tears raced down her face. "I'd love nothing more than to spend the rest of my life with you."

Pulling her down to sit on my knee, I peppered kisses all

over her gorgeous smiling face. "Thank you, I promise I won't make you regret your decision."

Clapping from the direction of the restaurant interrupted our moment, and when we turned to look, we found everyone in our crew who'd been at breakfast standing just outside the entrance with smiles on their face.

Holding onto her hips as I stood, I placed her on her feet. "What do you say we go celebrate?"

"I like the way you think."

CHAPTER 24
LEXIE

Shooting off an email to the wedding planner, I leaned back in the booth and watched as our crew trickled in. It had become somewhat of a tradition for us to hit up the buffet after our late-night shows. I grabbed what I wanted to eat and tried to get some work done before I was surrounded by everyone and couldn't think for myself.

"Are you finished?" Raine slid into the booth on the other side and made her way down until she was across from me.

Resting my head against the wall, I let out an exhausted sigh. "I doubt it. I'll probably wake up with an email from her and a hundred other things she needs for me to do before tomorrow."

Reaching across the table, Raine rested her hand on mine. "Hey, if you need any help, you know I'm here for you."

"Why did I think I could put a wedding together in a matter of days?"

"Uh…because you thought it would be a few simple things." She giggled.

I had thought we'd head to a little white chapel one day during the time we had off since we'd agreed to get married while we were here. I had no family, and everyone important to me was here. I tried to reason with Ryder that his mom would be disappointed she missed it, but he was adamant she'd understand. When the hotel heard Ryder and I were getting married this week, they offered up their wedding services free of charge. Now I wish I had turned them down because I was up to my eyeballs in wedding stuff I didn't care about. I tried to put on a happy face as Ryder placed his plate next to mine and slid in beside me.

His arm wrapped around my shoulders as he pulled me to him while he placed a kiss on the side of my head. It was sweet, and he was happy, so I wouldn't complain. "You look tired. When did you fall asleep?" He picked up his phone to look at the time. "Yesterday? I'm so messed up on time right now."

"We all are, but we have to shoot during the least busy times at the hotel, and that's practically never. At least it's warm, so your pool shots weren't when it was freezing outside." I let out a big yawn. All I wanted to do was close my eyes and fall asleep, but there was too much to do.

"Maybe we should pack up our breakfast and take it upstairs."

"I'm fine." I rested my head on his shoulder. "I need to eat, and I might as well do it here."

"I'll try to eat fast." He shoved a bite of his omelet in his mouth and chewed. Ryder had no problem eating fast. He could have an entire plate full of food and finish faster than I could with a quarter of the food.

"Do you think we'll run late tonight?"

Tonight, we had booked the rooftop for two hours to get some shots at sunset. They'd only let me close down one section in all the time we were shooting, and this was it. I couldn't control the sun, and there were bound to be plenty of people wanting to hang out on the rooftop bar at sunset.

"If we don't get the shot, we don't get it, so it should be an early night." And luckily, our last thing to shoot.

."Good, I want you to get some rest. I know we're all dragging, but you've got a tiny human growing inside of you, and that's much more important than work."

I patted his thigh. I didn't think Ryder would hate me for getting pregnant, but I never thought he'd be this accepting and supportive either.

"I promise to sleep. I'll even silence my phone, so the wedding planner doesn't wake me up with her thousand messages."

"If she calls, I'll take care of it."

I wasn't sure how he'd help when he didn't know half the details, but at that point, I didn't care if everything was messed up. Did the colors, flowers, and food really matter in the scheme of things? All I cared about was the man sitting next to me.

"Do you have kids?" Alyssa asked Sadie. She'd taken to eating and hanging out with us, and each day she seemed to be becoming a little bit bolder. Which was a good thing; she needed to be bold in this business.

I felt the shift in Ty and Sadie immediately. He looked down at his plate and started to move his food around, and Sadie's lips turned down as she took in her husband. There definitely was a story there, but I wasn't going to pry. They'd been wonderful about me hijacking their project to get Ryder here. Now they knew he was the best man for the job, but it still wasn't my best move. I wouldn't have done it if I knew of any way better to get him back in my life to tell him the news.

"No, but we do have an amazing dog that we spoil." Sadie tried to sound upbeat but failed.

Alyssa wasn't picking up on the clues that this was an unwanted topic. "Why not? You two would make beautiful babies." She sighed dreamily as if she was conjuring up the images of them at that moment.

Lifting his head, Ty grimaced. "When I was in college, I had testicular cancer, and now I can't have children."

Alyssa's caramel eyes widened before she looked around the table to see us all staring at her. I wasn't sure what anyone else's face looked like, but mine was one of sadness. It was obviously a sore topic, and she had ripped the band-aid right off. "I'm so sorry. I was just trying to make small talk. I never meant to offend or hurt anyone's feelings. Please forgive me." She looked close to crying, and I didn't blame her. I wanted to cry for Ty and Sadie and their situation.

Sadie reached around her husband to pat Alyssa's arm. "Nothing to forgive. How could you have known? We're happy where we are in our life right now, but one day if we decide we want a child, we might adopt. Until then, we're happy."

"I think I'm ready for some sleep. Anyone else ready to head up?" The look on Ty's face said he appreciated the break in the tension.

Ryder stretched his arms above his head and let out a dramatic yawn. I watched as his t-shirt rode up to reveal a tiny slice of his abs, but I was too tired to be turned on. I knew then I needed sleep and badly.

"I'm more than ready. Make sure you know your time to meet with hair, makeup, and wardrobe. I expect to see everyone up on the roof at three o'clock. No later," I announced as I slipped out of the booth before we said our goodbyes to everyone.

We were halfway to the elevator when Ryder leaned down and spoke against the shell of my ear. "I like it when you're bossy."

"Good, because I'm one bossy bitch."

He laughed and pulled me closer to his side.

Stepping onto the elevator, we saw Alyssa walking with Brad and Annalise, but were too far away for us to hold the doors for them.

"Why did you want her on the project?" He nodded outside the elevator.

Looking up, I saw his brows were pulled tight. "Alyssa?"

"You wanted her, and yet you'd never worked with her before."

"I did because once I saw her, I knew you two would look perfect together, and I wanted to help your career as much as I could. Trust me, I called anyone I knew who'd worked with her in the past to make sure she was qualified. Did you think I'd hire Lana?"

"Only if there was a possibility of a serial killer on the set." He chuckled but quieted down quickly. "Besides her being quiet and opening her mouth when she shouldn't, Alyssa's easy to work with." Pulling my back to his front and his hands cradling my tiny bump, we looked at ourselves in the mirrored walls of the elevator. We were unconventional, but we looked good together. "She's not as nice as working with you."

Placing my hands over his, our eyes connected in the mirror. "It was one time, and it won't happen again."

"Never, say never." Leaning down, he trailed kisses up the column of my neck. "Look where we are now. Who would have thought when we met, we'd be getting married?"

Certainly not me. I thought it was an incredible one-night stand with the hottest model who'd ever walked into my studio, and who I might one day work with again. If I was lucky, we'd hook up again.

"I never thought I'd get married at all and most definitely not in Vegas unless I was drunk." People would undoubtedly think Ryder had been drunk when they found out he'd married me in Sin City. "Did you ever picture yourself married?"

Resting his cheek on the top of my head, he tightened his grip around my waist. "Eventually, when I found the right woman, yes, but not this early in my life," he let out a contented sigh. "Then, I spotted you. I'm not going to lie to you and say I thought we'd get married the day we met because that would be a lie. It was pure lust. You are unlike anyone I've ever met. Everything about you turns me on from your blue hair, beautiful tattoos, all the way down to your cute little toes." One hand skated up my ribcage, and with his thumb and forefinger, Ryder expertly found my nipple ring through my clothing. He pulled roughly sending zings of pleasure straight down to my core. I looked up to see we still had ten more floors before we could get off the elevator. I wanted to hit the emergency button, so I could strip him bare and swallow his cock deep into my throat. "You didn't think I forgot about these, did you? They're hot as hell and make me want to do something crazy like pierce my dick.

Yes, please!

His chuckle was deep and low as he pulled me out of the elevator and down the hall to our room. "I see you like the sound of that idea. Why don't you let me play with yours tonight and let me show you how much they turn me on?"

"I'll never say no to that."

Ryder slipped the card into the door as my hands went around his waist from behind. My fingers deftly undid first his button and then the zipper before reaching inside his pants to pull him out. I loved that he didn't wear underwear. It was just one of the things about him that turned me on.

"I thought you were tired."

My hands slid up his rock-hard abs. "Not anymore. I want to feel you inside of me, and then I can fall asleep. I'm desperate to feel the weight of your body on mine. To feel your hands trace along my heated skin, and for you to fill me with your cock."

"Fuck," he moaned. "You have no idea how sexy you are, do you? I was going to try and be good and let you get some sleep, and then you had to go and say that." Leaning down, he bit through the fabric of my t-shirt and bra to pull at my nipple. Lifting his head, he smirked down at me before he whipped my shirt over my head and had my bra off in one-second flat. Bending down, he helped me out of my shorts and panties with care before he popped back up. His hands were already pulled at his waistband when he ordered in a voice deeper than I'd ever heard it before. "Get on the bed."

Backing up to the bed, I laid down and watched as Ryder stalked toward me, his long legs ate up the space between us. Moving onto the bed, he straddled my chest with one hand going to the headboard. Raising up onto his knees, he inched closer, and I watched in wonder. I had an idea where this was going and wondered if he could read my mind. Did he know how much I wanted to taste him?

With his free hand, Ryder gripped his length and rimmed my lips with his pre-cum. "Open your pretty little mouth for me and suck my cock. I want to feel it in your throat."

Obeying his command, I opened my mouth as he fed each glorious inch passed my parted lips until his mushroomed head hit the back of my throat. I wasn't great at deep throating, but damn if Ryder didn't bring out the inner slut in me and make me want to try until I was a champion.

"Swallow me, my sexy girl." Relaxing my throat, I swallowed and gagged, making me have to breathe deeply through my nose. Ryder held back and watched me as I tried again. This time when I was successful, he slid the rest of the way in and growled out. "Are you ready for me to fuck your pretty mouth?"

My only reaction was for my hands to grab his ass and push him forward. That was all the signal Ryder needed. He didn't hold back as he thrust deep and pulled back only to do it over and over again. His deep moans caused my clit to throb. I moved one hand between my legs and circled my bundle of nerves.

"Oh, God, I don't know what I want to watch more. You touching yourself or your lips around my dick."

My answer was to swirl my tongue around the thick vein underneath as he pulled out almost to the tip.

"Fuck," he moaned. His face looked almost pained as I sucked on the tip. "I...I want to be inside of you when I come. I want to be the one to bring you pleasure now and always." He pulled out and sat back on his haunches. "Come, let me fill you with my cock."

I couldn't deny that I'd much rather feel Ryder inside of me.

With my hands on his shoulders, I slowly lowered myself down on his length. Ryder's hands rested on my hips as he watched inch by inch of his magnificent cock disappear. Closing my eyes, I relished how he filled and stretched me. When I was fully seated, I opened my eyes to see his normally blue-green orbs were dark with need.

His thumb grazed along my bottom lip. "I love seeing your lips swollen from sucking my cock. There's nothing hotter."

Slowly I started to move, rocking back and forth and then up and down. One hand grasped onto the back of Ryder's neck, and the other tangled in the long hair at the top of his head.

Ryder started to move with me. His arms lifted me and pulled me down as he surged up. Each time I moaned and clutched him a little harder as he brought me closer and closer to the edge. It wouldn't take long with how worked up I was and how he always seemed to know exactly the right thing to do to bring me the most pleasure.

His thumb found my clit and circled hard and fast. Heat flooded my body as a rush of electricity raced down my spine and up my legs, converging at the epicenter between my legs. My back bowed as I threw my head back and screamed out his name.

This man was magic. He was a god in bed and the keeper of my soul.

I stayed suspended in the air as he continued to drive to his own release. With one last thrust, he called out my name with a long groan. We stayed like that until our breathing slowed, and our hearts weren't threatening to beat out of our chests. Slowly Ryder lifted me off him and gently laid me down on the bed.

Disappearing into the bathroom, he came out with a warm wet washcloth that he used to tenderly clean me up with. Once he was done, he dropped it on the floor and settled in beside me. He pulled the covers over us as I moved into him. I didn't want to be away from him for a single second that wasn't necessary.

"Are you feeling better now?" Ryder wrapped his body around me, one leg nestled between mine, and his arms held me close.

"Much." I snuggled deeper into his hold.

"Good, let's get some sleep."

I closed my eyes and instantly started to drift off into dreamland when I felt Ryder kiss the top of my head and whisper. "I can't wait to make you mine tomorrow."

WASHINGTON

"Mom, Dad, meet my wife, Lexie." Not how I was planning on introducing her, but when they eyed the rings on our fingers the moment we stepped inside, my brain went on the fritz, and I said the first thing that came to me. At least I didn't blurt out she was pregnant.

My dad stepped back, crossing his arms over his chest while my mom's eyes got round with delight. She clasped her hands together and held them in front of her heart. "Is this the young lady you were telling me about? The one you like and who's so talented."

If she wasn't, that would have put a damper on their meeting.

"The one and only," I confirmed. Pulling Lexie closer, I wrapped my arm around her shoulders and kissed her temple.

"It's so nice to meet you, Mr. and Mrs. Williams. Ryder has said such lovely things about you."

"Oh, you call me mom, dear. I won't have you call me anything else, do you hear me?"

"Yes…Mom," she answered back uncomfortably. I wish I could have seen her face, but I also hoped she'd one day love my mom. Lexie deserved a mother figure, and I knew mine had always wanted another child and would want to adopt Lexie into the family as soon as she got to know her.

"Now, you both need to give me a hug." My mom went for Lexie first.

Lexie gave her a tentative squeeze before she stood back by my side. I stepped forward and picked up my mom, giving her a big bear hug. It had been too long since I'd last seen her. She had gained some more of her weight back, which was good, and her hair had grown out into a short bob. I loved seeing her happy and healthy.

"It's so good to see you, Mom."

"It's good to see you, too, my baby boy. I wish I had known you were bringing a guest, or I guess I should say a wife home with you. I would have—"

"And that's why I didn't tell you. There's no need to overwork yourself." She always kept the house spick and span and now wasn't any different. If I thought for one moment she would be embarrassed, I would have given her a heads up.

She swatted my back before pulling away. "Why don't we all go sit in the living room, and you can tell me why we weren't invited to the wedding."

"We really should bring our bags in before it gets dark." We'd come from rather warm temperatures in Vegas to the cold of Washington, and it would only be worse once the sun went down.

"Fine, go get your things and clean up, but then we're going to sit down and have a long talk over dinner."

I stifled a laugh. She made it sound like she was going to give me the birds and the bees talk. It was a little too late for that. I couldn't wait to see the look on her face once she found out she was going to be a grandmother.

The second we stepped outside, Lexie turned toward me with wide eyes. "Your dad hates me."

When her chin started to tremble, I pulled her into me. I hated to see her cry, but I was getting accustomed to her tears. Lexie cried at the drop of a hat these days. "No, he doesn't. He doesn't even know you."

"Tell me the truth; is it because of my hair and tattoos?"

"He's not like that. I promise he'll warm up to you." At least I hoped he would. My dad had never reacted that way to my girlfriends in the past. And although Lexie was twelve years my senior, she looked like she was twenty-four, so I knew that wasn't what was eating at my dad.

Pushing back enough to look up at me, Lexie tried to blink back the wetness in her eyes. One lone tear traveled down her cheek. "So, you do admit he does have something against me."

Wiping her tear away, I leaned down until our foreheads met. "I admit he wasn't acting his usual self, and for that I'm sorry. I don't want you to be uncomfortable while we're here."

Lexie squeezed her eyes shut. "Maybe I should go back to LA and…" she huffed, "I don't even know. We haven't talked about what we're going to do yet."

What was she talking about?

Taking a deep calming breath, I tried to be patient. Why hadn't she mentioned anything on our long drive up here? "I thought we were in this together. I was planning to talk to my parents and explain to them why I would be going back to LA with you instead of being here for Christmas."

"We never talked about it." Stepping out of my arms, she wrapped her arms around herself. "Why are we so bad at this?" Her voiced hitched.

"Because all we've been doing is working, having sex, and sleeping for the last week. I need you to be able to talk to me and tell me what you want, so please tell me what you need. Do you want us to leave now and go back to LA?"

She looked up at me with sad eyes. "Not us, but maybe me. I know how much you've missed your family and how much they mean to you. I'd never ask you to not spend time with them."

She didn't get it. "Where you go, I go. What do you say we take our stuff inside and break our other news to my parents?"

"Why not?" She threw her hands in the air.

"Hey," I said as I backed her up against the car, "my mom already loves you, and I know my dad will too."

The corners of her lips tipped up. "You told her about me."

"Of course, I did. I don't keep anything from her, and you are no exception. She told me to follow my heart and not to give up when you changed your number. And I never did. I didn't know how long it would take to get you back, but I wasn't going to stop until you were mine." I kissed the corner of her mouth. "Never did I think I'd walk into that room, and you'd be standing there, or our little surprise." I kissed the other corner of her mouth as I rested my hand over her stomach. "Promise me you'll talk to me, and I'll do the same. I know it's only been a week, but we're a team now."

Tears built in her eyes and glinted in the fading sunlight. The sun had dipped behind the mountain, and the temperature had started to drop while we were out here. "I like being on a team with you."

"Don't cry. This is a good thing."

"I know it's a good thing." She rested her hands on my biceps. "I never thought I'd have any of this. I'm happy. This," she pointed to her eyes, "it's these damn hormones. I can't control when I cry, and it's stupid."

Leaning down, I kissed her nose. "It's part of being pregnant, and I promise I won't hold it against you. Now relax." Taking her hands, I held them between us and kissed her knuckles.

"Is this what it's always going to be like with us?"

"Me kissing you?" I pressed my hips into her and brushed my lips against hers. "Every chance I get."

"Not the kissing. I'll never tire of your kisses or you for that matter. What I was talking about is you talking me down, making everything okay. Normally, no one can calm me down, but a few simple words from you, and I'm putty."

Damn, that made me feel invincible. Little did Lexie know, she did the same for me, and I knew it was because we were meant for each other.

Bringing our hands up, she used them to hold my face between her hands. "Thank you for coming back into my life." Pressing up on her toes, our mouths locked. Her tongue met mine in a dance that was our own, slow and passionate. When we broke apart, I was left panting. Little puffs of breath skated across my skin as Lexie spoke the most beautiful words. "I love you."

It was strange that we'd only said the words a few times, and every time I heard them, my heart rate sped up.

The front door squeaked open. "Ryder, honey, is everything okay? Do you need some help bringing your things in?"

"No, Mom, we're fine. We'll be inside in just a minute."

Lexie pressed her forehead into my chest. "Oh god, I'm making the worst first impression ever."

"I promise you're not. Now let me grab our stuff." It would take me at least two, maybe three trips to bring everything in. I'd learned my wife didn't know how to pack lightly. She had two large suitcases and a large bag of toiletries to stay here for a week.

Lexie started to grab one of the suitcases until I pulled it out of her hand. She stood with a pinched look on her face and her hands on her hips. "What are you doing? I'm not an invalid."

"I know you're not, but my momma raised me right, and she would kick my ass if I let you carry your suitcases in." Especially if she knew how heavy they were.

"So, this is you being chivalrous and not because I'm pregnant?"

"Remember, I'm a good guy?" I kissed her cheek and pulled all our luggage out of the car.

Lexie swung her purse over her shoulder and smiled at me. "Of course, I remember."

"And Lexie?"

"Yeah?" She turned back to me.

"I love you too, and our baby."

A bright smile spread across her face. "If I hadn't been sick for weeks on end, I wouldn't believe we made a baby, but we did." Her hands rested over her stomach as she looked over her shoulder at my parents' house. "I hope they take the news okay."

"They will, and they're going to love you both. I promise."

I managed to get everything upstairs with only two trips, and when I brought the last of our stuff inside, I found Lexie taking my childhood bedroom in with a twinkle in her eye. It wasn't much. The walls were light blue with car posters scattered throughout. I didn't have any trophies since we never had the money for me to be in any sports, and there were no posters of women in bikinis since I didn't want to disrespect my mother. The same navy bedding still covered my bed. It was probably boring to the outside eye.

"We should probably head downstairs. We can unpack later if you want."

Lexie bit her bottom lip before she nodded as I held out my hand for her to take. With our fingers intertwined, we started to descend the stairs and make our way to my parents.

"Your room is cute. I'm not sure what I thought it would look like, but—"

"Probably half-naked women covering every inch of my walls." Leaning down, I nipped at her chin.

"Something like that." She grinned.

"I can't wait to bring you back up here and get you naked once my parents go to sleep."

"No," she backed away until her back hit the wall in the

hall, "there will be none of that while we're here. They already hate me enough."

Internally I rolled my eyes. I wished I could convince her that my parents didn't hate her.

"Don't be so hasty, or we'll be leaving first thing in the morning."

"Oh please," she lightly swatted my arm. "You can go without for a week. You did before."

"There's been no one else but you since we met." Lacing our fingers together, I pulled her down the stairs. "Now stop stalling, and let's go make a good impression."

Lexie squeezed my hand but said nothing as we made our way downstairs and into the living room where my parents were sitting on the couch side by side, waiting. My mom's face was lit up with happiness while my dad's knee bounced in agitation.

"I'm sorry we took so long. Ryder was showing me his room and—"

"That's perfectly fine, dear."

"We understand since it's your first time here," my dad said, and both he and Lexie frowned.

What the hell was his problem?

Lexie and I both sat on the love seat. My wife trying to sit as far away from me as possible, but it was a tiny piece of furniture that put us close together, no matter how hard she tried. Putting my arm around her shoulders, I pulled her close to my side and flashed her a smile. "Relax. He can smell your fear."

"Not funny, dimples."

"When did you two meet?" My father directed his question at Lexie.

"Now, Jim, you know the answer to that. I told you all

about her after Ryder called home and told me all about her."

"Well, maybe I want to hear it from her."

That was strange. Seriously, what had gotten into my dad?

Standing, I moved in front of Lexie. "I know you have questions, but I thought you'd be happy for me. This is no way to greet your daughter-in-law, and if you're going to continue, we'll pack our stuff back in the car and head back to LA."

Tears filled my mom's eyes before she turned to my father and glared at him. I felt like I'd walked into a parallel universe. My dad didn't act like this, and my parents never fought.

Until today.

"You will stop," my mom gritted out. "Lexie is a beautiful girl who our son loves. Didn't you see how happy she makes him until you opened your mouth?"

"I never meant to cause any problems." Lexie's voice sounded shaky, and I knew her eyes were already wet with tears.

"Sit down, son, and talk to us. I promise I won't say any more to upset…anyone."

Turning around, I saw Lexie wiping away a tear from her cheek. "I'm fine. Please, sit down."

I did as I was told, only this time I nearly pulled Lexie onto my lap.

"Lexie and I met on a shoot, and we hit it off, but we didn't see each other for another few months. We were both working and ran into each other in Hawaii. After that, we stayed in contact. The best pictures in my portfolio are the ones Lexie has taken. She's crazy talented, and she's helped me so much already in my career."

My dad's forehead scrunched up. "So, you married her to further your career? That's not like you."

"And this is not like you. I love Lexie, and she loves me. That's why we got married."

Lexie's hand started to tremble as she sat forward. "I love your son very much, and everything he's said is true, but there's more." She let out a shaky breath, and a serene smile crossed her face. "I'm pregnant, and while normally I wouldn't think I need to clarify, I'm going to. Ryder is the father."

"You're going to be grandparents," I interjected.

"Really?" My mom's eyes shined with happiness. "You're full of surprises today."

Lexie looked over at me with only love in her eyes. She had for some time, but each time still knocked me on my ass when she looked at me like that. "He's good at that, isn't he? When he proposed, I was more than a little shocked."

I only hoped she wouldn't mention how she was hesitant for us to get married. With the way my dad was acting, I wasn't sure how he'd take the news.

"Was it romantic?" my mom asked wistfully.

I wished we had a better story to tell her than me asking her after I found out she was pregnant, and her pulling me out of breakfast for me to get down on one knee. It definitely could have been more romantic. Maybe next year, I'd ask her to marry me all over again and have a trip planned for us.

"He asked me every day for three days until I said yes. I

couldn't ask for a better proposal than all the ways Ryder told me he loved me."

"He's always been a sweet boy." My mom gave us a watery smile.

"He's the best, and I'm sorry you weren't there for the wedding. Maybe later we can have a reception or something."

My mom jumped in her seat. I loved seeing her so happy and accepting of Lexie. "Oh, if you need help with anything, I'd be happy to help."

"We'll definitely need help with a baby on the way and how busy our work schedules are." I'd love to get my mom down to LA after the baby was born. I needed to ask Lexie when we were alone when the due date was. It wouldn't look good if I asked in front of my parents even though my mom did know that we weren't talking for a while there.

The oven buzzer went off in the kitchen, making Lexie jump. I hadn't realized how wound up she was until then. I thought maybe my mom had put her at ease at least a little bit.

Jumping up, my mom rushed to the kitchen. "Dinner's ready," she called over her shoulder. "I hope you like lasagna."

"Who doesn't?" Lexie answered as she followed after my mother. "Do you need any help?"

Going to help set the table, I followed behind and watched as Lexie's hips swayed. I was going to have to convince her to have sex while we were here, or I was going to be walking around with a permanent hard on the entire time.

"No, dear. You're a guest in our house. Besides, you're carrying my grandbaby, so you sit back and relax."

"I've got it." I kissed my mom on the cheek as I passed by to get the plates down.

Placing a plate down in from of Lexie, I kissed the top of her head. Lifting her head to look up at me, she spoke quietly so only I could hear. "Is this what I can expect from you?"

"This, and so much more. I'm going to spoil the shit out of you." After my mom uncovered it, I took the pan from her. "You're going to love my mom's lasagna. It's the best I've ever eaten."

"He's being kind. I'm pretty sure he's only ever eaten mine."

I shook my head as I sat the pan down. My mouth was salivating at the smell. "I've had others, and I choose to only eat yours now."

My dad sat down and cut himself a big piece and flopped it on his plate. Before anyone else could get their food, he was already shoveling his food into his mouth. Lexie didn't seem to notice how rude he was being, but my mom sure did. With him acting so strange, I had to wonder if everything was okay between him and my mom. I knew her being sick had been hard on them both, but I thought things were looking up. Was he acting like this because there had been bad news at my mom's last appointment? I'd have to get her alone to ask her if she was still feeling okay or if this was all an act.

After both my mom and Lexie had a piece on their plates, I dug in. I had restrained myself long enough. It had been too long since I'd had a good home-cooked meal. I'd either have to work out extra while we were here or remind my mom I couldn't eat like this every day, but for now, I'd enjoy it.

Lexie let out a low moan that shot straight to my dick. If she kept that up, I'd never be able to leave the table.

"I have to agree with your son. This is one of the best lasagnas I've ever had."

"Thank you, dear. I'm glad you like it. It's a recipe that's been handed down generation after generation. I'll share it with you before you leave so you can make it for Ryder. I'm sure he'd love it if he could eat it more than once a year."

I would, but I couldn't afford to eat like this regularly. My mom seemed to forget that when I was home.

"I'd like that. I love to cook, but it's lonely cooking for one, so most of the time, I order out or have my assistant bring me something to eat."

"You've got your own assistant?"

"Mom, I told you Lexie has her own company. She's famous for her photography. You should see the amount she negotiated for the job I did in Vegas." I wouldn't mention how much she made on the few pictures she sold of us together in Rio.

"So you'll be living in LA now?" my dad asked with an annoyed tone.

"That was always the plan. I've been saving up so I could afford an apartment that isn't in a bad neighborhood. I want to base my modeling in LA and not around the world."

"My place isn't big. Only a studio apartment since I didn't think I needed more room, but now I'm going to have someone come in and add another bedroom or two and a bathroom."

"I thought you said it was small?" My dad's brows rose like he'd caught her in a lie.

"Well," Lexie started hesitantly, "I only did a small

portion of the second floor since it was only me, but there's room for more. I was impatient and didn't want to wait any longer before I moved in." Her gaze turned to me. "Maybe if you want, we could even put in a gym so you can work out at home."

I chewed my bite of food slowly. I didn't feel I had the right to tell her what she could and couldn't do with her money. Our dynamic had changed so much in the last week, and we were still trying to find our places. It was strange to think that I was planning on staying here for the next month and then was going to hit the road again, but now I had a wife and a baby on the way. I had no idea what I was going to do, but I knew I couldn't keep traveling the way I had.

"That would be great, but expensive. Plus, I know you never planned for that to be your forever home."

"It's not, but who knows when a place will open up at the beach and have everything I need, so I'll make this place be what we need, and if you want a gym, it's a possibility, that's all I'm saying."

"We can figure it out later."

For the rest of dinner, my mom gushed over Lexie. They became fast friends, and I knew my mom already considered her a daughter. Nothing had changed with my dad. He was still acting out of the ordinary, and I wanted to find out why. I wasn't sure if I should corner him or my mom to find out what was happening. Deep down in the pit of my stomach, I felt something was off, and when I woke up early the next morning to go for a run and found my dad sleeping on the couch, I knew my intuition had been right.

Slipping out the front door, I ran longer than my normal thirty minutes. I couldn't get the picture of my dad on the couch out of my head—or the way he'd acted the day before. My arms and legs kept pumping, pushing me faster. When I arrived back at the house, it had been a little over an hour. My legs felt like noodles as I leaned forward with my hands on my knees and tried to catch my breath. I spotted movement inside and saw it was my dad folding up the blanket he'd slept on. I hoped everyone else was asleep because we were about to have a serious talk.

Quickly I stretched as I kept my eye on my dad moving around inside. No one else seemed to be up as I walked in. He was at the counter, pouring himself a cup of coffee and jumped when he heard the front door close, causing him to spill his coffee on his hand.

"Shit," he hissed. Moving over to the sink, he held his hand under the water.

I went to the fridge, pulled out a bottle of water, and drank half of it down in one slug. Leaning my hip against the counter, I waited. Every minute that went by, I got madder as he kept his back to me with his hand under the water. I knew he didn't burn himself that bad and was only trying to avoid me.

"Enough." I finally gritted out. "Turn around and face me like a man."

Letting out a defeated sigh, his shoulders slumped, and he turned to look at me. "Son, it's not—"

"Don't lie to me. All day yesterday, you acted like an entirely different man than the one who raised me. I tell you I'm in love with the woman of my dreams and we're married, and you treated her like shit."

His posture straightened. "You didn't use those words."

"Would it have mattered? No, I don't think it would have." I let out a disappointed huff. "Well, she is the love of my life. I love her more than anything, and I won't let you continue to treat her like shit." I looked over at the couch and then back at him. "Why were you on the couch?"

"We should probably sit down." He picked up his coffee and sat down at the kitchen table. His eyes were haunted as he looked at me over the brim of his cup. Shakily, I made my way over and sat down on the opposite side of him. "You don't want any coffee?"

"I'm trying not to drink any while Lexie's pregnant. She loves coffee and can't have any, so I'm supporting her the only way I know how."

"That's…" he gulped, "admirable of you. I can see how much you love her." He gave a small nod. "Your mom and I were going to talk to you after dinner last night, but then you revealed a new wife and baby, and we thought we should wait until today."

"Wait for what?" I finished off my bottle of water and crushed the plastic in my hand.

Sad eyes that matched my own looked back at me. "Your mother and I are getting a divorce. I moved out a few weeks ago and—"

Jumping up, my hands went to my hair and pulled at the strands. "Why didn't she say anything when I talked to her?"

"Because she knew you'd blow off whatever job you were on and come running home."

"Damn right, I would have."

"And it wouldn't have made a difference. She asked me to move out, and I had to respect her wishes." His hands wrapped around his coffee cup as he looked down at it with a pinched face.

"What did you do to make her ask that of you?" My

mother wouldn't have asked unless he'd done something unforgivable.

"That's between your mother and me." His voice was hard, like it wasn't his fault he was in this situation.

My body slumped in the chair. "Where are you living?"

"A couple of towns over in—"

There were only two things I could think of that would make my mom demand he leave and for him to live so far away. "Did you cheat on her?"

He let out a disappointed noise, and when his eyes met mine, they were full of tears. "It wasn't planned, but that's no excuse. I lost my way for a short time, and I betrayed your mother. Along the way, I found a woman who—"

Shooting up from my seat, I towered over him as my eyes narrowed into slits. All I could see was red. There was no way for me to hold back my contempt for him. "I don't want to hear about her. How could you do that to the woman you loved while she was fighting for her life?"

Thunderous steps pounded down the stairs as I glared at my father. Never in my wildest dreams would I have thought he'd cheat, let alone when my mom was battling cancer.

"What's going on?" My mother's quiet voice broke our stare down. She moved between us, and the moment she saw my face, hers crumpled.

"Oh, Ryder, I didn't want you to find out like this."

Pulling her into my arms, I hugged her shaking body. "I knew something was wrong yesterday, but when I saw him sleeping on the couch this morning, I knew."

"Now that he knows, I'll be one my way. I know you're mad at me, son, and it may take you a while to forgive me, but when you do, I'll be here."

My voice was hard as stone as I gritted out the words. "When that time comes, will you be accepting of my wife?"

Lexie came up behind me and lifted her hand to rest between my shoulder blades, and with that simple action, she took a little of my anger away. My body melted into hers. I wasn't sure when she came into the room, but until she touched me, I didn't know how much I needed her by my side.

"I...I hate to break this to you, but she might be after what little fame you have."

"Ryder's fame as you call it isn't little." Lexie stepped around me and moved between us. "Not only is he gorgeous, but he's extremely talented and has a heart of gold. Everyone that works with him can see that, and they gravitate toward him. He's going to be big, but I can assure you, I'm not here to ride his coattails."

I wanted to laugh at the notion. If anyone was using someone in this relationship, it would be me. I was sure when news got out about our nuptials there would be plenty of people who would think that I had married Lexie to further my career. But I knew that if they saw us together, their opinion would change. There was no denying how much we loved each other or our chemistry.

"I'm not sure how to explain it to you for you to understand, Dad." His name came out like a curse. "Lexie isn't using me. I have nothing that she wants. In fact, after we were married, and I thought about it, I was surprised she didn't ask me to sign a prenup."

"What?" she questioned like it was the most absurd thing she'd ever heard. When she turned, the girl who had just been defending me was glaring at me with her jaw tight.

"While I don't know how much money you have, I do know it warrants a prenup. It only makes me love you more that it never crossed your mind to demand one and that in a world where couples barely last, you have faith in us."

Her eyes softened and filled with tears. "Oh, hell, not now," she murmured. My mom slipped to my side, knowing I needed to comfort my girl. Holding my arms out, Lexie stepped into me and buried her face in my chest. "I'm sorry. This isn't about me. I wanted to help you, and now I'm a mess."

I kissed the top of her head before I looked over to where my father stood. He had a look of regret on his face. I wasn't sure if it was from what he'd said about Lexie or if it was ruining what he had with his wife. "You're what's important. Why don't we go upstairs so I can get cleaned up, and you can get some rest?"

Lexie turned her head in my mom's direction. "He thinks I can't do anything now that I'm pregnant. It's both infuriating and incredibly sweet. From one minute to the next, I'm never sure which one will win out."

My mom patted her arm as she looked up at me with complete and utter love in her eyes. It was the same look she gave me every time I did something that made her proud. "He's only doing it because he cares. I didn't raise him to think women were inferior."

"No, ma'am." I knew they were both better than me in almost every way.

My dad cleared his throat from beside the front door. He'd already slipped his coat on unnoticed. "You've got my number when you're ready to talk." With a chin lift, he opened the front door and didn't look back.

I turned with Lexie in my arms as we watched my mom

lock the front door and then started to clean up the already clean kitchen. Leaning down, I spoke against her ear. "Why don't you head upstairs, and I'll be up there in a few minutes? I want to make sure my mom's okay."

She leaned back, her hands first going to my shoulders and then to wrap around my neck. Her thumbs rubbed back and forth in a soothing motion that made the morning a little less shitty. "Are you okay? I know how much you love your mom."

Out of the corner of my eye, I saw my mom falter for a moment before she started pulling items out of the refrigerator to make breakfast with a smile on her face. Maybe she'd be better off without my dad. Maybe they'd been unhappy for a long time, and I'd been too wrapped up in myself to realize. "If she's okay, I'm okay. What about you?"

Lexie scoffed. "I'm not letting what your dad said get to me. I know our truth, and that's all that matters."

"Are you sure?"

"Positive, if you're good, I'm good."

CHAPTER 26
LEXIE

Renovations had already started to expand on the second floor, and everything up there was a disaster, so I had to set up our Christmas tree downstairs. We were about to start using the bedroom we once used for photo shoots as our own for a short period of time.

I hadn't expected Ryder to wake up when I got out of bed. If he hadn't, this would have gone a lot smoother.

"Come back to bed," Ryder yelled from upstairs. I placed the last gift under the tree and then pulled out the lingerie I'd bought for today. When I saw it in the store, I knew I had to buy it. It was designed to wrap around me like a bow, so I could be my sexy as fuck husband's present.

"Coming," I called back as I finagled my way into the strange garment. I was lucky I'd tried it on and watched a video. Otherwise, he'd get tired of waiting, come down-stairs, and ruin my surprise.

Grabbing the tray with chocolate-covered strawberries and flutes filled with orange juice, I made my way upstairs. I'd left the door ajar so Ryder wouldn't see me as I approached. Pushing the door open with my hip, I walked in to find my husband sprawled out on the bed with the sheets thrown to the floor, completely naked and ready for me—stroking his length until he saw me. All movement stopped as he took me in. I loved the way his gaze raked down my body and made me feel sexy even with my baby bump.

"Holy fuck, Lexie," he groaned sexily.

Setting down the tray on the bedside table, I gave him a little twirl. Ryder's mouth hung open when I stopped in front of him and held my arms out to my side. "Merry Christmas, dimples."

"Merry fucking Christmas, my very sexy Lexie. Come up here and let me unwrap you." He quirked his finger at me and gave me the come-hither motion.

"Do you like it?" I asked as I tried to crawl up the bed as sexily as I could. Going by the way his blue eyes darkened, I had a feeling he liked what he saw.

"I more than like it. Can I wake up every day to this?" More so than usual, his voice was full of gravel. I loved how gritty it got when he was turned on.

"I think we could work something out." I straddled his legs, my swollen breasts grazed up his abs to his chest. "Would you like to unwrap me now?"

Grabbing me by the hips, Ryder flipped me over onto my back. I let out a squeal from the unexpected move. Hovering over me, his lustful gaze followed his hands as they traveled my body reverently.

Leaning down, he kissed the corner of my mouth before peering up at me. "I love you, you know."

"I know. I love you, too." Every time I told him those three words, it felt amazing. I didn't know how far gone I was until I thought he was with Lana and never wanted to speak to me again.

Ryder flashed me his dimples, and I melted on the spot. I wondered if they'd always have that effect on me. They were dangerous, and I'd do almost anything to see them. Cupping his cheeks in my palms, I kissed first the left and then his right dimple.

Pulling him down until almost all his weight was on me, I luxuriated in the feel of his body on mine. I loved the weight and the feel of his hard muscles against my soft body. "Make love to me."

"I'd love nothing more." Pushing himself up, Ryder slowly undid the bow leaving me bare underneath him. He had no problem figuring out how to get me naked, and I knew he never would. In an ideal world, we'd spend all our time like this. "You are so beautiful. If I had half the talent you do, I'd photograph you and try to capture even a fraction of your beauty. Instead, I'll try to show you what a knockout you are."

Wetness built behind my eyes, and before I could stop them, tears slipped down my cheeks. Ryder was used to my crying. It happened all the time, and he knew because of the cheesy grin I was sure to have on my face, these were tears of happiness.

Both hands cupped my breasts and lightly kneaded them. When his hot mouth closed around one nipple, my back arched off the bed. One hand fell away for his arm to fold around my back and hold me arched up into him.

The feel of his hard length against my leg had me desperate to have him inside of me. My hands skimmed his taut back and down his scrumptious ass. I gave each cheek a little squeeze before I moved on to what I really wanted.

When my fingers brushed against his silky member, it twitched. Ryder sucked my other nipple into his mouth, and wetness soaked my legs. I didn't want any more foreplay. I wanted to get to the main event. As his teeth grazed my aching peak, my fingers wrapped around his straining erection. He let go with a pop and moaned. I knew he was aching for me as much I was for him. I only stroked him once before I placed him at my entrance. I couldn't wait any longer. I was desperate for him. To feel his body move against mine, the way he stretched me as he entered me, how with each stroke he claimed me over and over again.

His hips pushed forward, and he was home. I wrapped my arms and legs around him, wanting to be as close to him as possible. Resting on his forearms, Ryder's eyes locked with mine as he slowly pulled out and then surged forward. Slowly out and then as if he couldn't stay away, he'd slam back into me. I loved the way our bodies were plastered against the other. The way we stuck together.

Steadily I was building, but I needed more. As if he could read my mind, Ryder dipped down and licked along the seam of my mouth before his tongue pushed forward. True to his word, the kiss showed me how beautiful Ryder thought I was. It was sensual, hot, and wet as our tongues danced together. Tasting, and telling each other how much we loved and cherished being with each other.

"I'm so close," I panted against his lush lips.

Dipping down, Ryder started to kiss and nip along the column of my neck as he picked up his pace. Gone was the slow. His hips thrust in a bruising rhythm, edging us closer and closer to the breaking point. My nails dug into his back. With one brush of his thumb on my clit, euphoria shot out of every pore of my body.

"Fucking hell, Lexie, you feel so good. Milk my cock with that sweet pussy of yours." He groaned, burying his head in the crook of my neck as he stilled inside of me.

My hands rubbed up and down his muscular back. Feeling each muscle contract and relax as I touched him had me turned on again. If I thought sex was good before I was pregnant, it was out of this world now. I couldn't get enough of the man on top of me, and luckily, he felt the same way about me.

Letting his body go slack against mine for only a second, Ryder slid off to the side and took me with him. His long body enveloped mine in a loving embrace as I held him back the same way. We lay silent as we tried to catch our breaths. My body shuddered with residual tingles.

"That was the best Christmas present I've ever received." His large hand skimmed down my back and cupped one butt cheek.

"I had a feeling you'd like it."

"If you can't tell I more than liked it, I did something wrong." He rubbed his nose along mine.

Ryder had thoroughly worn me out, so much so I could barely keep my eyes open. "You did everything right. So right, I need a nap." I nuzzled into his warm chest and let out a yawn. "Will you take one with me?"

Normally, I was on the go since I had something to work on, but I loved being able to laze in bed with my man. Sometimes we'd talk for hours, we watched movies, or he showed me how skillful he was with all the parts of his body for hours on end. It didn't matter what we did, I loved having him here with me.

"Sounds like the perfect plan. Maybe later we can take a drive and go to the beach. Watch the sunset."

How did he always know how to make every situation better?

"Perfect." Just like him.

A couple of hours later, I woke up with half my body on top of Ryder. He had one hand resting on my back, and the other was holding a book as he read. After placing a kiss on the camera tattoo he'd gotten on his bicep, I stretched out beside him with every curve of my body against his.

Ryder put down the book he was reading as soon as I got settled.

"Did you sleep long?"

He gave a half shoulder shrug. "My mom sent me a text, which woke me up, and I couldn't fall back to sleep after that."

And he stayed by my side the entire time. Damn, he really was the best.

Leaning up on my elbow, my fingertip traced along the ridges of Ryder's body. "I wish your mom would have reconsidered coming here for the holidays. I hate that she's all alone."

"Me too, but she knew that our place isn't exactly hospitable right now, and I think she wanted us to enjoy our first Christmas together with just the two of us."

"I love your mom." Seeing her and Ryder together made me long for the mother I'd never had, but Catherine had taken me under her wing and treated me like a daughter. Better than my dad had ever treated me when he was in my life.

"Come here." His voice was like a caress to my soul. I

moved into him until I was wrapped snuggly in his arms with one of his legs between mine. It was unnatural for us to lay any other way when we were together. "She loves you too, you know."

I swallowed down the emotion. I wasn't used to having people care for me the way they did. "I've never had that kind of acceptance before. Not until I met you and now your mom. It feels good to be loved." The emotions that built up in me were too much. I'd been deprived of them all my life, and maybe that was why I'd always been with men who treated me badly. I never thought I was worthy.

Cupping the side of my face, Ryder's thumb caressed my cheek before he leaned up and kissed me breathless. Rolling on top of me, our mouths broke apart with a sigh as he entered me. Ryder's lips brushed against mine with every word he vowed. "I'm going to make up for all those years you felt alone. Not a day will go by that you will doubt my love for you."

And for the rest of the day, he proved to me how much we were meant to be together.

CHAPTER 27

LEXIE

4 Months Later

"I miss you, and tell that little belly it's yours," my husband said sadly through the phone.

"We miss you too. I'm counting down the days until you get home." I tried to hold the tears back until we got off the phone.

"Only two more days and then I'll have you in my arms again."

Some days, I couldn't get over how incredibly sweet he was and that he was mine forever.

"You're staying off your feet, aren't you?" he asked, knowing I'd had a photo shoot earlier in the day.

"Yes," I sighed. "I did my shoot earlier on the rolling stool. It was quite entertaining when Raine had to push me around."

Ryder's low chuckle trickled down the line. "I wish I

could have seen that, but I seriously can't wait for us both to have some time off." I couldn't wait to have him all to myself for a few months. "By the way, you were right about Lars. He's great."

"I'm glad you like him. I think he's the best photographer in New York, and he knows how to get what he wants."

"The same as someone else I know, and for the record, I'd much rather work with you."

"I love working with you too, but don't let Lars hear you say that." Too bad that wasn't possible. I'd settle for my husband to stay in the states instead of working all over the world.

"I hate to say it…"

"But you've got to go." I hated how little time we had to talk, but I loved that he called me any chance he got.

"Yeah, sorry, I just wanted to hear your voice."

I couldn't stop the cheesy grin from spreading across my face. I loved that my man had no problem expressing how he felt. "Hey, never say sorry for wanting to talk to me."

"Why is this trip so much harder than the others?" I hated how sad he sounded and wanted to reach through the phone and hug him.

"Because I'm as big as a whale with ankles so swollen they resemble softballs." It was true, though. This trip was unbearable, but I understood why Ryder felt the need to work. We were in total nesting mode, and he wanted to do his part.

"I hate that I had to leave you, but please don't have our baby before I get back."

"I'll see what I can do. I love you, dimples." Once the baby was here, I wasn't about to let my sexy husband out of my sight. If he had to go out of town for work, we'd go with him. Luckily, he had taken my advice and found a new agent that took his wants and needs into account. She'd found Ryder a few choice jobs that had put him on the radar even more.

"I love you, sexy Lexie."

I wasn't sure how he still found me sexy when I couldn't even see my own feet, but remarkably he did. With my pregnancy hormones, I found him even more undeniable than ever.

He made a kissing sound before he sighed. "I'll call you tonight. Bye, baby."

Before I could say goodbye, the line was dead. I wanted to cry, but I didn't have time for that. I needed to go through all the photos I'd taken earlier before Ryder got home. I wanted to spend as much time with him as I could before our daughter was born, and our time was limited. Soon we'd be sleep deprived with poopy diapers all over the place. At least the apartment was finished. I wasn't sure if I could handle it if the place was torn apart any longer. We ended up having to live downstairs for two months, so I wasn't breathing in all the dust and fumes.

"Hey," Raine came to stand in front of me on the couch. "What do you say we go get a late lunch and then you can work? It will make you feel better."

Looking down at my swollen belly, I had no desire to move. I groaned while wiggling one swollen foot in the air. "Why don't you go pick us up something? Maybe tacos?"

"Are you sure you don't want to get out?"

"I'm more than sure. It's a feat to get out of the car right now." I placed my hands on my stomach. "Maybe I'll get some work done in the meantime."

"How many more days until your hubby comes home?" She smiled down at me.

"Two very long days." It would probably seem like a week.

Her hands went to her hips. "And then you're going on maternity leave, right?"

Leaning back, I put my feet up on the ottoman. "I don't think I have the energy to do more jobs, and I'm not willing to kill your back by having you pushing me around."

She laughed her tinkly laugh. "That was not in the job description."

"I know. You're going above and beyond. I want you to remember that if you have any questions, you can call me. I'll let offers dictate when we get back to work."

"But nothing too soon. You deserve a break and time to spend with Ryder and then your baby."

"I can't believe this is my life now. Never in my wildest dreams did I think I'd have a good guy with a baby on the way."

"Don't be ridiculous. Did you think you'd always have shitty guys?"

I shrugged because I thought I'd probably end up alone, and I was fine with that. I'd rather be alone than with a man who treated me like shit or cheated on me.

"You're being crazy with your pregnancy brain. Maybe food will help. I'm going to go get those tacos that you love, and then we'll get down to work and finish season five of Friends."

"Sounds good." Raine had never watched Friends, and when I found out, we started watching it while working. It had slowed down our productivity some, but it was worth it to witness her falling in love with the characters as much as I had when it was on the air.

"Do you need anything before I go?"

I shook my head. I should probably drink some more water, but I didn't want to have to get up and pee ten times while she was gone.

"Cool. I'll be back in thirty. Call me if you need anything."

Pulling my laptop onto my legs, I loaded the photos from that day's photo shoot. I needed to get the proofs ready for my client and had about two hundred pictures to pick through and touch up.

The baby kicked, causing my laptop to move a little, and an intense craving for ice cream came over me. "Hey Raine," I called out, hoping to catch her before she left.

"Yeah?" she yelled. It sounded like she was by the front door.

"Can you pick me up some pistachio ice cream while you're out?"

I heard her laugh before she answered. "Sure, text me if you need anything else."

"Thank you," I called back. She really was the best. I didn't know what I'd do without her.

Slipping my headphones on, I turned on Halsey to listen to while I worked through the pictures. First, I needed to pick my favorites and which ones I thought the client would want. I was on the third picture when movement caught my eye. Either I was slow, or Raine was fast. It felt like no time at all had passed since she'd left, and I knew she had to hit a certain store to pick me up my ice cream. Luckily, it was on the way from where she was picking up lunch.

"I can't believe you're back already."

When she didn't answer, I assumed she was putting away the ice cream so it wouldn't melt, but as seconds ticked by, I started to think maybe I'd just imagined seeing something. Raine would have answered me.

I fumbled around my body, trying to find my phone. It was always somewhere close, but now with my big belly, I could never find it, and that annoyed the shit out of me. Giving up, I hit the phone locator on my watch, only for it to beep behind me. I had no idea how it got there, but that always seemed to be the case. I decided to send Raine a quick text.

Lexie: How's it going?
Raine: At the grocery store now.

THIS PREGNANCY CAUSED A LOT OF THINGS, BUT hallucinations weren't one of them. Maybe I had been working myself too hard to get everything done before Ryder got home. Still, something didn't feel right. Taking my headphones off so I could be more aware, I went back to my picture. The model had been difficult to work with, but she ended up producing some of the best pictures I'd taken this year. Besides Ryder's, of course. He was film gold.

I heard movement in one of the studios, and I knew my mind wasn't playing tricks on me. It wasn't loud, but I was alone or supposed to be alone. Pulling up my security app, I saw that the alarm wasn't set, and the front door was unlocked. I had probably distracted Raine when she was leaving, causing her to forget.

It was probably some homeless person who slipped inside looking for food, but I wasn't taking any chances. Hitting the silent alarm, I started to pull up the video of the front door. It would take a few seconds before it would show me all the events that had triggered it.

"Do you know how long I've waited to do this?" A cold voice said from behind me.

My heart lodged in my throat as I panicked, trying to get up. My laptop crashed to the floor as I all but fell trying to get upright.

Ben stood behind the couch with an evil sneer on his face. His clothes were torn and dirty, hair greasy, and his face was smudged with dirt. He looked like a man who lived on the streets. With his face contorted in anger, I was truly scared for my life. What had I ever seen in this man? Over the last few months, I'd wondered how he seemed to become unhinged. Had I missed something during our time together?

"So he knocked you up," he nodded to himself. "Now I understand why he's been sticking around."

"What are you talking about?" I wasn't sure how long it would take the police to arrive, but I wanted to keep him talking in the hopes they'd get here before he hurt my baby or me.

"The guy who's been living here for the last few months." He jerked his arm out toward me, making me jump back. "That's why he's been here, but he's gone now."

"Gone?"

Had he done something to Ryder? No, it wasn't possible. He was in New York, and I'd talked to him only an hour before.

"I saw him leave with his things."

"How long have you been watching me?"

A low growl emanated from him. "All this time. Every time that you left with your annoying assistant until the timing was perfect."

"The perfect for what?"

"I've been patient. Oh, so patient as I waited for someone to slip up. When you added all your extra security, I thought my shot at getting to you was gone. I almost gave up, and now I'm glad I didn't."

My body started to shake at his words. He'd been watching for months waiting for the perfect opportunity to do what?

"Whatever you're looking for isn't here. The cops came and searched—"

"I know!" he screamed madly. "I saw the whole thing. Do you realize how much shit you've put me through?"

"Me? This is all on you. Why did you plant drugs in my things?"

"I was hiding them. I never thought you'd move out of the apartment." He shook his head in jerky movements. "You did this to me," he growled.

"Did what?" I asked, taking a step back only for the back of my knees to hit a table.

"This is all your fault, and now you have to pay the way I paid." He took a menacing step around the couch, and my heart nearly stopped. I wasn't sure how I was going to get out of this one.

Where the hell were the police?

"Ben, please don't do this. I'm pregnant and about to

have my baby any day now. You would never hurt an inno-cent child." I tried to reason with him.

"It astonishes me how little you know me."

Me too. I couldn't believe I'd ever been mixed up with him, and now he was here and willing to hurt me.

"That should be my child. Not that pretty boy's."

"We were never right for each other," I said in a soft, soothing manner.

"In the beginning, we were perfect." The anger subsided a tiny bit.

"In the beginning we were, but then the newness wore off, and you found—"

"I lost myself. Couldn't you see?" he barked.

I hadn't, and I wasn't sure how to respond, so I kept quiet and took a sidestep, for every step I took away from Ben, he took one toward me. I wasn't enjoying this cat-and-mouse game he was so keen on playing.

"All of this could have been avoided if you had just given me what was mine." He pulled at his hair. I was surprised he didn't pull out any hair with how hard he pulled. "You have no idea how much trouble I'm in or the people I'm dealing with."

"I'm sorry, I don't, Ben." I wanted to tell him he was stupid for getting mixed up with drugs and whatever else, but it didn't seem like a smart decision. I needed to keep him calm and hopefully talk him out of whatever he came here for.

"I've been hiding from the cops and the men who have been after me for so long, I don't have anywhere to go." He scratched his arm with his long dirty nails to the point I was sure he was going to draw blood.

Whatever he'd been doing, he'd done a good job at

evading everyone who was after him. Hopefully, after today, I wouldn't have to worry about him any longer. It had been so long since he'd been a problem; I thought he'd moved on, not continued to stalk me, and wait for a chance to get me alone.

Sirens sounded in the distance, and as they grew closer, my hopes of being saved soared. Ben didn't seem to notice them, which was a good thing. Probably because it wasn't an uncommon occurrence, and he had no idea that I'd hit the panic button. After the sirens passed, and there was no knock on my door, I wanted to break down and cry. I wasn't sure how much longer I could keep Ben talking. Taking in a cleansing breath, I tried to keep calm and rational. The police wouldn't come with their sirens blaring on a silent alarm. They would know someone had triggered the alarm.

Taking another two steps back, I held onto the chair that was now between us. It felt like a shield even though I knew it couldn't protect me. Ben didn't seem to like the space between us. He quickly moved until we were toe to toe, and his rancid breath blew in my face. One whiff and bile rose up. Now that I wasn't in control of my body, I wasn't sure if I could keep it down or not.

A dry heave wracked my body as someone pounded loudly at the door. Ben looked from me to the front and back again. "What did you do?" he seethed.

"I hit the silent alarm."

"Just when we were starting to have fun," he mumbled to himself. "I'm not sure how I'm going to get out of this one." I wasn't either, and I certainly didn't want to have to keep looking over my shoulder until he was finally behind bars or dead.

"This is the LAPD. We're coming in."

Ben and I turned to look toward the voice. One second, I was waiting for a swarm of police officers to come in, and the next, I felt a blinding pain on the side of my face. I turned to look at Ben as I started to fall. I don't know why I thought he'd help me when he'd just punched me, but I did. Instead, he watched with dead eyes as I fell on my hip with a resounding thud. My face and hip hurt, and I had no idea what Ben would do next. When a blinding pain unlike anything I'd ever felt before tightened across my abdomen, I let out a sharp cry.

No, I couldn't go into labor now. She had to wait until her daddy was here. Ryder would be devastated if he missed her birth. Clutching my stomach, I closed my eyes and prayed for the pain to go away. I heard lots of scuffling and grunts around me, but I had other things to worry about. I felt wetness seep into the fabric of my underwear, and I knew she wasn't going to wait.

Slowly I started to uncurl myself from the floor and tried to get up as I held my face with one hand and my stomach in the other. "Lexie," I heard Raine's hysterical voice in the background. She continued to call my name, but all I could see were three police officers who had Ben on the ground and were trying to cuff him. He was putting up a damn good fight.

"Raine," I called out to her as another shot of pain sliced through my stomach.

"I'm here, but they won't let me through."

"I need an ambulance and for someone to find my phone so I can call my husband!" I yelled back.

All three police officers' heads turned toward me at the same time, and Ben started to fight back harder. "Husband?

When the hell did that happen? You can't be married. You can't!"

Using the arm of the chair, I pulled myself to my feet and started to frantically search for my phone while trying to tune out Ben's yelling. When I spied it under the couch, I lost it. I didn't want to think about getting down on my hands and knees to grab it. Tears streamed down my face as I turned toward my ex. "What have you done? If anything happens to my baby, I will hunt you down and kill you. Mark my words."

"Lexie," Raine ran toward me. I wasn't sure how she'd made it past the police officers, and I didn't care. I'd never been happier to see my friend. She rushed over to me and pulled me into a big hug. She may have been tiny, but she gave fierce hugs. "Are you okay?" Pulling back, she started to look me over. Her gaze stopped when it landed on my legs. Looking down, I gasped when I saw blood trickle down my calf.

"My phone's under the couch. Grab it for me, please," I begged. "I need to call Ryder. He has to get on the first flight. Can you—"

"I've got it." Raine held my phone in her shaky hands. "You call him while I hop on your computer to see when the next flight is."

"Thank you, Raine," I cried. "I don't know what I'd do without you."

Pulling up my favorites, I hit Ryder's number and wasn't surprised when he didn't answer. Of course, he wouldn't have his phone on him during a shoot, and he had no reason to think he'd need it. I didn't want to leave him a message saying I was in labor, so I hung up. Searching through my contacts, I looked for Lars. I wasn't sure what I'd do if he didn't have his phone on him. Hitting Lars' number, I let it ring and ring, and when it went to voicemail, my body slumped against the chair.

I wasn't giving up, though. I hit Lars' name over and over again with each time going to voicemail. Raine watched me from behind my desk with worried eyes. I was sure she was thinking what I was thinking. Ryder wasn't going to find out he needed to get here until it might be too late.

Hitting Lars' number again, I gasped as another contraction hit me. Where the hell was the ambulance and the EMTs? Maybe I should have Raine skip finding a flight and drive me to the nearest hospital.

"Lars Mikkelsen's phone," a squeaky voice answered.

"Hi, yes, this is Lexie Keene, and I need you to take the phone to Lars right now," I demanded.

"I'm sorry, but he's working right now, and he doesn't allow for any interruptions."

"If you tell him I'm on the phone, he'll answer. I promise you." I tried to keep my voice light and not like I wanted to put my hand through the phone and rip her throat out.

"If I get fired for this—"

"You won't," I interrupted her. "I'll make sure of it."

"You better," she snapped. Her voice had gone from nice and squeaky to harsh. I could hear Lars talking in the background as she moved closer. His accent was so distinctive, and any other time I would have loved to listen to it, but not today. "I'm sorry, Lars, but there's a Lexie Keene on the phone for you. She said you wouldn't mind taking it." Her voice sounded like a small child's as she said the last words.

"Of course, I'll take her call." There was some rustling

and then his booming voice. "Hallo, Lexie. What can I do for you? Your husband is—"

"Please don't alarm him, Lars."

"Okay," he drew out the word. "Is everything okay?" he asked quietly.

"No, it's not. I need you to be done with Ryder. My place was broken into, and I fell. The fall has sent me into labor, and I need Ryder on the next plane out here. My assistant is looking up flights for him now. Please say you'll let him leave."

"What kind of a man do you take me for? Of course, I will do this for you. I…"

"Is that my Lexie on the phone?"

"Do you want to talk to him, or should I send him on his way?" Lars asked quietly.

"Is that my wife?" Ryder demanded. His voice was closer now.

"It is, and she wants to talk to you. When you get off the phone, you can grab your things and leave. If you leave your key to your hotel room, I'll make sure you get the rest of your things."

"What the hell is going on?" I could hear the worry in his tone.

I had calmed down some, but after hearing his voice and how distressed he was, I started to sob.

"Lexie? Why is Lars telling me to leave?"

"Can you FaceTime me from your phone? I need to see you," I managed to get out, but I wasn't sure if he understood what I said.

"Whatever you want. Can you tell me one thing first, are you okay?"

No, I wasn't. "I think so," I sobbed.

"Give me a minute, okay?"

The line went dead, and I started to hiccup-cry. Raine rushed over and wrapped her arms around me. "It's okay. I found a flight and already sent Ryder the information."

"Thank you. Do you know what's going on here? Have they called for an ambulance? If not, I need you to drive me."

"I don't know," she chewed on her bottom lip. "I can check."

"Please do, I need to get checked out." When she continued to gnaw on her lip, I knew there was something else. Something that wasn't good. "What is it you aren't telling me?"

Her eyes darted around the room before they came back to me. "The thing is, Ryder's flight's not for two more hours, and the flight's a little over six and a half hours. I don't know if he'll make it in time."

Normally labor took hours. Many hours, but with the trauma to my body, I wasn't sure how long I had. That's why I needed to get to the hospital so I could get answers.

"Let's go. Ryder's supposed to call me, and I want to be on my way." Raine jumped up and held out a hand for me to take. "Can you run upstairs and grab my bag?"

"Of course, I should have thought of that." Raine darted off while I headed over to my desk to grab my purse and slip on a pair of flip-flops. I was already headed to the front door as she came down the stairs. "Got it. Aren't you supposed to talk to someone?"

"Probably, but I don't have time. They can come to the hospital if they want to talk to me or wait. Do you still have the number of the police officer that you worked with when they searched the place?"

Raine's cheeks pinked up. "I do. I'll give him a call once we get you settled at the hospital."

What was taking Ryder so long to call me back? If Lars held him a moment longer, I was going to have his balls once this was all said and done.

As Raine started to open the front door, a police officer stopped us. "I'm sorry ma'am, you can't leave; we still need to get your statement."

"And she needs to go to the hospital. She's in labor and bleeding." Raine pushed by him. I pointed to the trail of blood that had made its way down my leg. Luckily, it didn't seem to be a lot, but it wasn't good either way. "I'm planning to call Officer Murphy once we get to the hospital to let him know what's going on. He can take it, or you can get her statement at the hospital."

The officer and I blinked at Raine. She was normally the sweetest and quietest thing, but not today. She was fighting for my baby and me, and I loved her for it.

"At least let me get your name, so I can make sure you're followed up with."

Another contraction hit me, causing me to double over in pain.

"Her name is Lexie Keene, and her number is…" Raine proceeded to give the officer all my info as I tried to breathe through my contraction. We definitely needed to get to the hospital so I could get some drugs. There was no way in hell I was doing this naturally.

Once the contraction subsided, I stood up and loosened my grip on Raine's arm. "Are we free to go?" I asked. I didn't really care, I was leaving anyway, but it would be nice if I didn't have any resistance.

He nodded. "I've got all your information. Are you sure you don't want to wait for an ambulance?"

"I'm sure. I can't sit around here waiting anymore." I couldn't hide the worry in my voice.

"Can we get a police escort?" Raine chimed in.

"Sure, where's your car?"

Raine pointed to my car sitting out front. Luckily, it wasn't blocked in by the three police cars that were out front. She took my purse from me and started to dig to find my keys when Ryder finally called back. With my phone still clutched in my hand, I answered.

His handsome but extremely worried face took up my screen. His hair was thoroughly tousled, and his eyes were red-rimmed. "Your face," he stated as his own face fell.

"Hey, dimples, I'm sure I don't look too hot right now. Are you already in a cab?"

"Yeah, I got Raine's email, and I'm headed to the airport now. Sorry, it took me longer than I planned to call you back."

"It's okay. You're here now, and that's all that matters," I cried and hiccupped at the end.

"I wish I was there with you. Are you in your car? Is Raine driving?"

"She is. How?" How did he already know what was going on?

"Raine was very thorough in her email."

I wondered what she'd told him. "Have you been crying?" I wasn't sure how Ryder would feel if Raine knew, so I asked as quietly as I could even though I knew she could hear me.

"Yeah," he tried to smile but was unsuccessful. "I'm worried about my girls."

"I'm doing okay, I think. We're on the way to the hospital now. I want you here with me." I felt my chin start to quiver and bit my lip in an attempt not to lose it.

"Me too. I'm doing my best to get to you as quickly as possible. Will you or Raine keep me updated even while I'm in the sky?"

"Of course, we will." Another contraction hit, making me wince in pain.

"Lexie, talk to me. Are you in pain?"

"One second," I breathed out. After a few more seconds, the pain ebbed away, and I held the phone so that I could see Ryder again.

"What was that?"

"A contraction," I answered. "I was right. I don't want to do this without drugs. It already hurts like a bitch, and I haven't even gotten to the hard part yet."

Ryder's eyes glistened. "I'm so fucking sorry I'm not there for you. Will you ever forgive me?"

"Hey, look at me. There's nothing to forgive. There was no way to predict the events of today would happen."

"I feel like shit for not being there. I won't be able to forgive myself as easily as you did."

"Should I pull up here and take you in?" Raine asked as she pulled to the front entrance of the hospital.

"I don't know. We can ask inside. That wasn't part of anything they told us in our classes."

"I'll text you when I get to the airport and right before I board. If you need anything during the time between…" He wiped his hand under his eye.

"I'll call or text. Whatever happens, I promise we'll keep you updated. Thank you for letting me see your face. It helped calm me down…some."

"It's the least I could do." He closed his eyes and swallowed roughly. "I love you more than anything, Lexie."

Why did it sound like he was saying goodbye forever?

"I love you too. Now hurry up and get your ass back here."

"Will do," he waved. "Bye, baby."

"Bye," I choked out.

"Enough of the sappy." Raine held out her hand to help me get out of the car.

"Thank you for telling him what was going on. I'm not sure how I would have told him and made it coherent."

"You're welcome. Now, let's get you inside so you don't have your baby in your car. I am so not driving your car ever again if that happens."

"Deal, now help me out."

Glancing down at my phone, I already missed seeing Ryder's face, but I knew I needed to suck it up.

Opening my messages, I sent him one last text.

Lexie: I love you madly. More than I love hearing the waves crashing as I fall asleep or ice cream. <3 <3 <3

Ryder: I love you more. :-*

CHAPTER 28

RYDER

Before I rounded the corner, I knew I was much too late. Raine had kept me updated throughout the process, and Lexie was being taken in to have an emergency c-section as I was boarding my plane. The last seven hours had been hell, knowing that I wasn't there for my wife. Not only was I not there for the birth of my daughter, but I wasn't there to protect Lexie from her crazy ass ex.

Stopping outside the door, I ran my hand down my face and took in a deep breath. I didn't want to upset Lexie. Raine had messaged me saying she was awake and in a lot of pain and hell if I didn't want to add to that. As quietly as I could, I opened the door to her hospital room. I wasn't prepared for what I saw when I walked inside. My gorgeous Lexie was propped up in bed with pillows, her blue hair was pulled back into a smooth ponytail, her eyes were shut with a serene smile on her face, and she had our daughter at her breast.

There were already flowers and balloons in the room. Something I hadn't thought of, but even if I had, I wanted to get up here as quickly as possible. Nothing was going to keep me from seeing my girls once I finally made it to the hospital.

I watched silently as my daughter's lips suckled at her mother's breast. I was in awe that I had anything to do with making the precious being that was in front of me.

"She's perfect, isn't she?" Lexie's soft voice startled me. Without opening her eyes, she held her hand out for me to take. "Come closer and see our daughter."

Gently, I sat on the side of the bed with Lexie's hand still in mine and held it to my chest. I never wanted to let her go or out of my sight after today. With my other hand, I brushed my finger across my daughter's soft cheek.

"She's so soft, so perfect," I whispered. I wasn't sure if I said it so quietly because I didn't want to disturb her or because of the emotion clogging in my throat. "I'm sorry I wasn't here for you."

"Hey, we already talked about this. It wasn't anything we could control." Her other hand reached up and brushed the wetness from my cheek. "You're here now, and that's all that matters."

Leaning down, I pressed my lips to hers, showing her how much I loved her and how sorry I was. Then I moved to kiss the bruise on her cheek furthest from me. It was swollen and already a horrible dark purple. I only brushed my mouth across it, afraid to hurt her. It looked painful as hell, but I was sure she wasn't feeling any pain with the meds they'd given her. Her eyes were glassy and tired.

Resting my forehead against her temple, I wanted to stay connected to Lexie. I'd missed her like crazy while I was in New York, and I wanted to be able to look at our daughter. It was still unbelievable that we created such a perfect person. I couldn't wait for my mom's reaction when she saw her. I'd called her when I was waiting to board my plane and explained everything to her. If it wasn't for her, I would have been an even bigger mess as I waited. She said all the right things to get me to calm down, but the second the plane landed, all her words went right out the window, and chaos took over my every thought as I traveled from the airport to the hospital. My mom was waiting for the all-clear, and then she was going to come for a visit to see her first grandbaby. I told her to pass the news on to my dad since we still weren't talking.

"Did you name her?"

"You act like you were gone for months. Of course, I didn't name her. I was waiting for you." She looked at me like I was crazy, with her eyes squinted. "What was your favorite on our list?"

I'd been MIA for so much of Lexie's pregnancy, and then I wasn't even there for the birth, I felt undeserving to name our baby. I already felt like the worst father in the world. "You should name her."

My finger swept over my daughter's tiny hand, and when she grasped it, it nearly brought me to my knees.

"She knows who you are, and she already loves you," Lexie spoke quietly but assuredly as she brushed the hair from my forehead.

"I already love her too. How can she already mean so much to me when I've only known her for a few short minutes?"

"It's a natural part of being a parent."

"It's unbelievable. I promise I will never let you or our daughter down again." And we needed to give her a name. Stat.

"What can I say to make you believe you didn't let us down?"

Nothing.

"Okay, going by your silence, that's not an option right now. Do you want to hold and burp her?"

I wanted nothing more in that moment as Lexie slipped our baby into my arms. She was so light. I didn't even know how much she weighed since I hadn't been there. Putting her up to my shoulder, I kissed her soft little cheek and lightly patted her back.

"Let's name her Delilah." The name popped into my head, and it felt right.

"Delilah Williams has a good ring to it," she mused.

"How much does she weigh? How long? I need to know everything."

Lexie rested her head on my arm, one hand on my leg. "She was six pounds and eleven ounces at twenty-one inches long."

"She's going to be tall," I stated as I continued to pat her.

"Probably. Look who her daddy is. She was born at four twenty-eight and came out crying." She let out a shuttered breath. "I was so scared when I realized Ben was there. All I could do was keep him talking and hoped the cops would get there before he did something to jeopardize the baby. Time was running out, and when the cops arrived, he…he punched me in the face, and I went down. I went into labor almost immediately, and all I wanted was to find my phone and talk to you."

"I should have been there."

"If you had been there, I'm not sure what he would have done. He went crazy when he found out we were married.

It doesn't even make sense. We'd been broken up for over six months when I met you and at the end of our relationship..." She hugged my arm. "It wasn't good. I don't know why he was upset."

When Delilah burped, I got up and put her in the plastic bassinet that was in the room. She was out cold and didn't even stir. Maybe I could handle this parenting gig better than I thought.

I started to sit in the chair by the bed, but Lexie wasn't having any of that. She patted the bed beside her and lifted up the blanket. The bed was tiny, but I didn't care. After the day she'd had, I'd half hang off of it to be by her side.

Slipping off my shoes, I climbed in beside her and let her rest her head on my shoulder. She could barely move after the caesarian, but my wife was a trooper as she snuggled into me.

Wrapping my arm around her, I held her tight. I could have lost her or Delilah. The thought shot tremors through my body. I kissed the top of her head and rested my head against hers. "You asked why he was upset, and I think I know the answer. Even though your relationship wasn't good in the end, I do believe Ben loved you. Then he got mixed up in drugs and couldn't find his way out. You, Lexie Williams, are a hard woman to get over. I know I wasn't going to give up on you when you all but threw my ass to the curb."

"I'd never do that to you," she answered softly. I could tell from the tight slur in her words she was close to falling asleep. "How did I get so lucky?"

"I ask myself that every day." I breathed her in. I had missed everything about her while I was gone. "How do you smell like the beach while lying in a hospital bed?"

She breathed in deep. "The same way you smell like the forest after a long plane ride."

Silently I laughed. We were quite the pair. I knew Lexie loved how I smelled. She frequently wore my shirts the day after I wore them and was constantly bringing them up to her nose or was sniffing me. I wasn't any better. When I smelled her, it took me back to our time in Hawaii and how fate had brought us together.

"Are you okay, now?" she mumbled. Almost half asleep, she was still worried about me.

"I'm fine, baby. Get some sleep, and I'll be right here when you wake up."

Lexie nuzzled my neck as her hand found mine. Bringing them up to my mouth, I kissed her knuckles before I rested them over my heart.

I wasn't sure how long I'd been going over the day in my head, but I was almost asleep when I heard some shuffling by the door. Opening one eye, I squinted at the bright light coming from out in the hall. I blinked, and a nurse was standing at the foot of the bed. I thought for sure she was going to kick me out, but she only smiled. After she came over and checked on Lexie, she left as quietly as she came in.

"She only let you stay in bed with me because you're so damn hot," Lexie murmured.

"I don't care what the reason is as long as they don't take me away from you."

Kissing my neck, I felt her hot breath seep into my skin as she spoke. "Don't let them hear you say sweet things like that, or we'll never get any privacy."

"My words are only for you." I dropped a kiss into her

hair, wanting to feel her lips but didn't want to shuffle her.

"Love you, baby."

"Love you, Dimples."

Closing my eyes, I let out a contented breath.

Everything I ever needed was in that room with me.

EPILGOUE

Three Years Later

THE SETTING WAS PICTURE PERFECT. THE SUN WAS DRIPPING low at the horizon as I wrapped myself around my husband while he kept us afloat in our infinity pool that looked out onto the Pacific Ocean. We were having a much-needed date night since Ryder's mom was in town for Delilah's birthday. She had our daughter for the night, and we were taking advantage since she refused to stay at our house. I loved her for it and put her up in a nice hotel so she could pamper herself when she wasn't with us.

It's not that I didn't love my daughter because I did, but it was nice not to have to steal moments with the man I loved. We'd already gone out to dinner and walked along the beach hand in hand, and now we were doing what we loved. We were in the water, and Ryder's tip was at my entrance.

He paused, cupping my cheek. "Shouldn't we use a condom?"

I had a feeling Ryder knew what I wanted to tell him tonight, but he was forcing me to say it before I was ready. Tightening my arms around his neck, I caught his lips with mine. It was slow and deep, a kiss that told him how much I loved him. When I pulled back, our eyes locked, and I slowly sank down on his hard length.

A slow smirk spread across his sun-kissed face. "When were you going to tell me?"

"I was waiting for the perfect moment, and you ruined it, dimples." With one hand on the back of his head, I slowly started to move up and down with a little grind on my clit at the end. Resting my forehead on his, our gazes locked.

One hand slipped to my waist, helping me move, and the other cupped my breast. When Ryder was inside of me, I was all need. There was nothing else in the world but us, intoxicated with one another even after all this time together. It was frenzied, erotic, and exquisite pleasure that drove us each time. I lost myself in him, and he found me each time, bringing me back, and making me whole.

Heat danced down my body as I rode him harder, bringing us closer to detonating together. Leaning down, I swept my tongue across his parted lips. Crushing his mouth to mine, Ryder consumed my every thought, my body, my breath, only stopping when we needed to breathe.

Licking along my collarbone, his rough voice nearly did me in. "I need to feel your sweet pussy pulse around my cock." He ground his pelvis into my bundle of nerves.

Picking up his tempo, Ryder hit me in just the right spot until I shattered in orgasmic bliss. It wasn't long until he followed me over the edge and was left panting in the crook of my neck.

With his breath still heavy, Ryder's arms tightened around me as he brought us out of the pool and walked us into our bedroom, leaving the door open so I could hear the waves crashing outside.

Resting his head on my stomach, Ryder placed a kiss just below my bellybutton. "I promise you I'm not going to miss this one's birth." Ryder still felt guilty about not being at the hospital when Delilah was born, and I knew he'd move heaven and earth to be there this time.

Running my fingers through his sexily tousled hair, I smiled down at him. "I know you won't, but how did you know I was pregnant? I only took the test after your mom picked up Delilah."

He angled his head so he could look up at me with one brow quirked up. "I know every inch of this body, and when these started to swell," he gently cupped one breast, knowing they were sore and sensitive, "I knew. It wasn't like it was a surprise. How long did you think it would take after you stopped taking your birth control?"

My hottie of a husband made a good point.

"Are you happy?"

Coming up on his hands and knees, Ryder's head dipped down as he kissed his way up my body. Kissing my chin, my forehead, my eyes, and each cheek, his lips brushed across mine in a gentle sweep.

"The happiest. We're both at places in our lives where we can take a step back and enjoy what life has given us. I love you more with each passing day, and our daughter brings me happiness like I never imagined. The sun rises and sets each time Delilah smiles at me or tells me she loves me. It's unlike anything I could have ever asked for, and for us to bring someone else into our lives that I know I will love for the rest of my life is a treasure."

Cupping my cheeks, he kissed away the tears I hadn't realized had started to fall.

"Truer words have never been spoken. It's like you read my soul and spoke its contents out loud."

Flashing me his dimples, Ryder pulled me on top of him and held me tight to his long, hard body.

I couldn't imagine not having Ryder or Delilah in my life now. They were the best things to ever happen to me, and true to his word, Ryder made sure I never once regretted marrying him by showing me each and every day how much he loved me. His presence grounded me in a way no one ever had. He brought out the best in me and I in him.

After Delilah was born, we made a pact that we'd never work at the same time. Someone was always home with her, and if one of us had to travel for a job, we all traveled together. If we needed some time alone, Ryder's mom was always happy to spend time with her granddaughter, and Raine was totally gaga over little Dilly as she liked to call her.

Ryder's career had skyrocketed in the last couple of years. While he was wildly sought after, he was pickier now about what jobs he chose to take. After watching many of my photo shoots, he'd even started to take pictures of his own. He knew he couldn't be a model forever and wanted a career path when he was done.

Running his hand up and down my back, Ryder spoke

against the column of my neck. "I have a surprise for you. My mom isn't here for only the weekend."

Sitting up, I straddled his waist with a wide smile stretched across my face. Was Catherine going to move here? We'd only been asking her since we found out Ryder's dad, Mitch, had cheated on her and she kicked him to the curb.

"And it's not what you're thinking, I've tried to convince her to move here so she can see Delilah more, but no dice." Ryder frowned.

My own frown followed. If it wasn't that, then what was it? "Is she staying for a week?"

"Try two, but we won't be here." He grinned up at me with his hands resting on my hips. Without thought, his thumbs rubbed circles into my skin.

"Are we all going on a trip?"

His smile grew wider, and I grew wetter at seeing those dimples of his. "Concentrate," he chided me.

"Hey, you know the power you wield with those things," I rotated my hips, letting him feel how wet I was.

"I can't stop how much you make me smile." His eyes crinkled as his naughty expression grew.

Leaning down, I licked up his chest before I looked at him with a wicked smile. "You are not helping the situation. Now tell me what's happening before I maul you."

"That's not a punishment." He laughed with me, bouncing around on top of him and his already semi-erect shaft hardening more. "But I'll answer because I love you, and afterward, I'm sure to get a little butt action."

Cocking my head, I laughed. "It better be damn good, dimples."

"Tomorrow afternoon, because I know you'll want to

say goodbye to Delilah, we're boarding a plane to Bora Bora to celebrate your birthday. I've got your suitcase already packed, filled to the brim with bikinis." A cheeky smile brightened his sexy as hell face. "No condoms needed."

"I like the way you think."

"I knew you would." He flashed those damn dimples again. "We'll be gone for a week and a half just you and me, naked with a private bungalow out on the water. If you weren't pregnant before, you would have been before we returned."

Leaning back, I nestled his growing arousal between my cheeks. "Were you planning on knocking me up while there?"

Ryder flashed his teeth. "I was planning on knocking you up, so we'd have twins."

My eyes widened at the thought of twins. "Please tell me there are no twins in your family."

Pulling me down, he pressed his lips firmly to mine before he started to laugh and pulled me underneath him. "None, I promise." One hand ran up my side until his thumb caressed the underside of my breast. "That's enough talking. Now let me properly wish you a happy birthday, my sexy Lexie."

Do you want to know Ty and Sadie's story?
Read their story in Intern.
Get more of Ryder and Lexie in The Bosun.

Did you enjoy The Model? If so, please consider leaving a review on Goodreads, Amazon, or BookBub. Reviews mean the world to authors especially to authors who are starting out. You can help get your favorite books into the hands of new readers.
I'd appreciate your help in spreading the word and it will only take a moment to leave a quick review. It can be as short or as long as you like. Your review could be the deciding factor or whether or not someone else buys my book.

To stay up to date on all my exclusive bonus scenes, releases, and sales, subscribe to my newsletter.
http://bit.ly/HarlowLayneNL

ACKNOWLEDGMENTS

My family- your support means so much. Thank you for all of your encouragement and giving me the time to do what makes me happy.

To my **girls**: QB Tyler , Carmel Rhodes, Kelsey Cheyenne, Melissa Spence Erica Marselas, Danielle James, Rose Croft, Helen Wilder, Gemini Jensen, and Alexis Rae. I love each and every one of you. Thank you for all of your support.

Denise Reyes: I don't know what I'd do without you. Thank you for EVERYTHING you do!

Kelly Russ: You're my champion. Thank you for pushing me when I need it, and for rooting for and every character I write.

Thank you **Kristen Breanne** for making my story into a book.

To all my **author friends**, you know who you are. Thank you for accepting me and making me feel welcome in this amazing community.

To **Wildfire Marketing Solutions**, thank you for all your knowledge and for helping me make Secret Admirer a success!

Lovers thank you for always being there.

To each and every **reader**, **reviewer**, and **blog** - I would be nowhere without you. Thank you for taking a chance on an unknown author.

ABOUT HARLOW

Harlow Layne is a hopeless romantic who is known for her contemporary writing style of beautiful slow-burn, sweet, sexy and swoon-worthy alpha and fast pace, super steamy romance in her Love is Blind series.

When Harlow's not writing you'll find her online shopping on Amazon, Facebook, or Instagram, reading, or hanging out with her family and two dogs.

Indie Author. Romance Writer. Reader. Mom. Wife. Dog Lover. Addicted to all things Happily Ever After and Amazon.

ALSO BY HARLOW LAYNE

Fairlane Series - Small Town Romance

Hollywood Redemption - Single Parent, Suspense

Unsteady in Love - Second Chance, Military

Kiss Me - Holiday, Insta-Love

Fearless to Love - Insta- Love

Love is Blind Series- Reverse Age Gap Romance

Intern - Office Romance

The Model - Workplace Romance

The Bosun - Military, First Responder

The Doctor - Surprise pregnancy

The Rocker - Rockstar

Hidden Oasis Series

Walk the Line - First Responder, Suspense

Secret Admirer - Damsel in Distress, Opposites Attract, Suspense

Til Death Do Us Part - Accidental Marriage, Insta-love

My Ex Girlfriend's Brother - MM, age gap

MM Romances

You Make It Easy -Second Chance

My Ex Girlfriend's Brother - MM - November 8

Chance Encounter - Enemies-to-Lovers

<u>Collaborations</u>

Basic Chemistry - Student/Teacher

Forever - Student/Teacher, Curvy girl, enemies-to-lovers

<u>Worlds</u>

Cocky Suit - RomCom, Office, Interracial

Risk - Forbidden, Sports

Affinity - Part of the Fairlane Series - Accidental Marriage, Enemies-to-Lovers

Until Delilah - Single Parent, Romantic Suspense with The Model tie-in